Our Community
Our Stories

Nuestra comunidad
Nuestros cuentos

ANNAPOLIS HIGH SCHOOL
GLOBAL COMMUNITY
CITIZENSHIP
SPRING 2023

CONTENTS

INTRODUCTION - *INTRODUCCIÓN*

In the spring of 2023, the Annapolis High School Global Community Citizenship (GCC) classes delved into the units of study related to community and identity. Through these units, students developed a deeper understanding of experiences and motivations of themselves and their classmates. Through this, students connected with people from a wide variety of cultural and linguistic backgrounds, and experiences. The following pages share their fictional accounts of joining a new community, exploring their identities, connecting with people they thought were very different from themselves and the unifying nature of having a shared goal.

To honor the linguistic backgrounds and assets of all our students, this book is written in the languages that each student feels most comfortable using. Texts written in Spanish will have an accompanying English translation.

En la primavera de 2023, las clases de Ciudadanía Comunitaria Global (GCC) de Annapolis High School profundizaron en las unidades de estudio relacionadas con la comunidad y la identidad. A través de estas unidades, los estudiantes desarrollaron una comprensión más profunda de las experiencias y motivaciones de ellos mismos y sus compañeros de clase. A través de esto, los estudiantes se conectaron con personas de una amplia variedad de experiencias y antecedentes culturales y lingüísticos. Las siguientes páginas comparten sus relatos ficticios de unirse a una nueva comunidad, explorar sus identidades, conectarse con personas que pensaban que eran muy diferentes a ellos y la naturaleza unificadora de tener un objetivo compartido.

Para honrar los antecedentes lingüísticos y los activos de todos nuestros estudiantes, este libro está escrito en los idiomas que cada estudiante se siente más cómodo usando. Los textos escritos en español irán acompañados de una traducción al inglés.

Surviving the Zombie Apocalypse

A Story of Identity and Community

Written by Ms. Pittman's 4B GCC Class Spring 2023

About the Zombie Apocalypse Book Project

This project integrates two themes we studied in Global Community Citizenship: Identity and the Stages of Community Formation. We learned about different aspects of identity - language, race, gender, education, personality, family structure, core values, religion, and culture. We also learned and experienced the stages of community formation - forming (coming together, often with some skepticism), storming (experiencing some conflict), norming (beginning to understand and embrace differences), and performing (working together as a team). As an example of both identity and community formation, we read the novel Seedfolks, the story of diverse members of a neglected neighborhood in Cleveland coming together around the building of a community garden.

In this writing project, students in each class collaborated to come up with a context for a story about Identity and Community (involving a bit of storming in the process!). In this class, students decided to write about a small group of survivors in Annapolis, after a Zombie Apocalypse has destroyed the city. Each student designed their own role in the story, choosing one aspect of identity and one stage of community formation to build their narrative around. Students chose aspects of identity that were meaningful to their own lives, but the characters are fictionalized. We hope you enjoy reading the results of our efforts! We certainly had fun creating these stories!

Alex

By Alexander Dukeman

I never thought the world would end like this. I nervously chuckle as I'm watching the zombie apocalypse devour the city. I watched as people I knew either turned or died to one of those, those things. I've been hidden in a rural part of Maryland until it died down enough to where I could safely look around and find survivors to restart Annapolis and make a new home. My old one was destroyed when the military dropped the bombs to try to "stop the spread" like that helped it just made it worse by mutating some of the zombies.

While looking through the city I found many useful things that can help me, luckily I was taught by myself and others how to survive in the wild. "This could possibly be considered the wild, just with deadly zombies and raiders," I thought. Luckily I managed to find a hatchet in one of the raided stores along with rations and various supplies in the other stores. Sadly I could only carry so much on myself considering I only had an old book bag that I used to store various items. Suddenly I see a man getting mauled by a wild animal and run over to help him, he was badly injured and could possibly die. I could possibly help him, but I don't know if he will live.

I take him into a rundown house so I can attempt to save him. The house had a hole in the ceiling and walls along with a small burned-out yard and various splatters of blood. I use various pieces of cloth and a liquor bottle to stop and sterilize the bleeding but cloth can only do so much on him. Over time I use my hatchet and survival skills to repair the house and armor it slightly to stop zombies from getting in.

Throughout the first night, we sit by a barrel fire and tell stories of our past. He told me his name was Shon. I told him about my old job as a mechanical engineer along with how my Grandpops taught me basic survival skills that I used to survive for so long. He also taught me how to be the person that I am today, and how I'm so independent because of him but when the outbreak happened I rushed to his house but I was too late. Shon told me that he was a martial arts teacher, "apparently not that good of a teacher if you get mauled" I thought.

The next day, Shon asked me to teach him basic survival skills. As much as I didn't want to teach anyone because I'm not good at explaining stuff, I've tried to teach other people but I just didn't have the social skills cause I didn't try to gain them in school, I was too busy learning the survival skills because as shown here they were more important than calculus. Although we were in a situation where if I don't he could end up dead in the near future, so I agreed to him that I will teach him.

During the day I taught Shon to hunt and basic things like how to start fires and make small bases for shelter. Later on, we found a strange man that went by the name "Ethan the Healer" and he asked if he can stay with us because he had nowhere else to go after his clan was murdered, and in exchange, he would help Shon. I agreed because with "healer" in your name you gotta know a thing or two about helping injured people. I figured I could have him join us in our lessons so then he will also know how to survive.

But a new problem started to arise. We were 3 people, and had 1 person's worth of rations. That was not gonna go well and we were gonna need to find more food. We tried to make a small garden with some basic seeds from an abandoned True Value store. Strangely though, nothing ever managed to pop up and if anything did it immediately died. So until we could find more food or someone who knew how to garden, we were gonna have to ration. During the night, Ethan told us more about his past and how everyone he had known had died. Sad.

Ethan the Healer

By Ethan Condra

I was a healer ninja. I was trained really, really good. Until my whole clan was killed because another clan called the Tech-Kin Clan. And then the Zombie Apocalypse happened.

I was scared at first, until I met Alex. He accepted me for my skills and we became partners. Until we met Shon. Shon had been mauled by a wild animal. Luckily it wasn't a Zombie bite. We had to take him to a shelter and we found a good hideout. Then I told Alex about my backstory.

A month ago I was on a mission. I had to heal someone who had been severely injured in my clan. Until we got ambushed. I had to take them all one by one stealthily. After three hours I was returning home until I smelled blood. I ran as fast as I could hoping that my clan was still alive, but I saw all of them dead. I saw almost 10 higher level Shinobis. I was enraged. So I had to take them all down. Until none of them was left.

Three weeks later, I heard about the Zombie Apocalypse in Annapolis. And then I met Alex.

After I told Alex my backstory, I told him the real reason I became a healer. The reason why I became a healer is because my mom was ill and then my dad became ill. I wanted to find a cure for this illness so I wanted to train as a doctor. I learned from another doctor as an apprentice because all the medical schools were closed. Sadly my parents succumbed to the illness. We heard Shon moaning and groaning so me and Alex went out there to see what was wrong with him.

Shon Ankhei
By Cristian Juarez Cruz

Sigh. I'm back out in this accursed wasteland, forced to scavenge for any little bit of food I am able to. Well, at least I was able to find some animals and get my food from them. I guess I'm sort of lucky, I don't have other mouths to feed other than myself, I guess one of the many perks of being alone. No contest to what I want to do or where I wish to go, but it does get somewhat lonely out here.

Well, there's an abandoned town up ahead, I guess I'll head there. (*I reach the town, unwavering in its depravity and solitude*.) Ah, Annapolis As barren as ever. I remember when this town was bustling with people, all around people came to visit the naval academy here, and downtown was very popular. I wonder what it must look like now? Is anyone alive? Well, these are just baseless questions of mine. I wonder if there's anything I am able to forage for, I'm getting somewhat hungry. Oh well, I'll just look for some plants if there are any that I can use to make food.

I hope I don't encounter any of those treacherous creatures they call "Zombies". They seem too powerful, even for my level of fist-to-fist combat. I miss my dojo, although it was small, it was a great place of learning. Oh well, I'm done with my expedition into the city. I guess I'll go into the woods and make an encampment for the night, it's getting dark outside. (*I set up a campfire and rest my sleeping bag, but I went out to get some water from a nearby stream.*) Ah, how refreshing, the moon looks really nice. Such a bittersweet moment, how beautiful the world can look even if it's gone to hell. (*a growl begins to creep closer, from a wolf*) Hello?

13

(*the wolf growls even louder, and pounces on me*) Get off of me! (*I manage to scare the wolf away, however I'm left with a brutal bite and can't walk any more*) Ow! (*I crawl over to a tree, where I lay for a while, trying to close up my wound*) Damn, I guess that wolf really packed a punch. (*a few minutes pass, and a man approached me asking if I'm okay*) "Hey! Are you alright?" Says the man, in a concerned tone. I'm fine, aside from this really big bite mark from a wolf, I scared him off, but be careful. "Ah, I see. Don't worry, I'll get you to safety, I'll carry you on my shoulders." (*He picks me up*) "I'll take you into one of these homes." Alright, but be careful. "I will." (*we head into an abandoned home, having a hole in the ceiling and walls along with a burned out yard and various splatters of blood*) "This should do." Cozy little place, huh? "I've never been here." Oh, I see. So, you just found this place, just for the two of us? "Don't talk too much, I still need to sterilize your wounds." Okay, I'll tone my voice down a bit. (*A while passes, he cleans up my wound and I rest for a while*)

Good morning. "Good morning, as well" Do you have anything you can teach me? "Yes, I can teach you some basic survival skills." I'm glad that you'll be able to teach me about basic skills. "Do you have anything in particular that you could teach me?" I can teach you how to hunt. (*We teach each other about our respective skills, and we solidify the house for a bit.*) So, what's your name? I ask.

      "Alex." Well, Alex, I'm Shon. "Glad to meet you, Shon."

Candy

By Cindy Ruiz

Well, hello there. My name is Candy and I am 16 years old. When I was 13, I suffered from cancer and other health problems. It really ruined my life by having those. When the first time the doctor told me that I have cancer, I was so scared and cried. I didn't know if I was going to live or not...I had a lot of surgery and treatment to help make me stay alive. Diabetes was the worst thing I ever had in my life. When I eat something my sugar goes up. It's really hard for me to eat the things I used to eat. So many people backstabbed me a lot and betrayed me. I always thought to myself why does this keep happening to me. But I know that I don't need friends that are acting like brats and just using me. When I turned 15, I went to health class, almost like a nurse class. I wanted to learn how to save people's lives when it's an emergency and learn more about cancer and other things. I always thought to myself, I miss the old times because it was more fun then. Now I have to smell horrible zombie smells. Ew!

I was hiding in some old house to not die from the zombies and turn into one of them and I kept some food to eat when I got hungry. When I heard someone yelling for help, I was confused. I thought everyone had died. I thought I was the only one alive, but I guess not. I went to see who was yelling for help so that I could help them live. It was a man. He was injured so badly. I saw another man go to find help. He seemed like a doctor or a nurse. He helped him and grabbed him and went to an old shed to prevent the zombies from coming. I went to see them to help them. I went to the the old shed with them. I told him that I can help the injured man because I went to heath and nursing classes and clubs at school but anyways I helped the injured man from bleeding and the man that is a real doctor gave him a shot and me and the doctor help put the bandage on the injured man and laid him down that he can relax and live. I asked them "What's your name?" The injured man said his name was Shon and the doctor said his name was Ethan. I told them my name is Candy. I said to them that I had thought I was the only one alive in this world. They said they thought the same too. So we helped one another. But Shon and Ethan were worried because they didn't have enough food to eat for staying alive.

I have some food in the old house I was hiding in, but I thought to myself, "Should I trust those people?" because I have been backstabbed so many times. But I got the food I had and shared it with Shon and Ethan.

Jack Daniel

By Michael Dougall

Hey, my name is Jack Daniel and I am 15 years old. I was working in my store when the outbreak started. My shop was destroyed but I managed to escape. With a few items. Now I'm on my way to find survivors and anything I could find.

Alejandro
By Alejandro Gutierrez

Hello there, my name is Alejandro and I am a Hispanic male. I am also a previous burn victim. Usually when people first meet me they are scared or frightened, but there is no need to be scared of me, because I am actually very useful. But I can also create problems. A lot of people don't like me or might be scared and that might create a problem with people, because they may not want to work with me. People also think that just because of the way I look no one wants to do business with me, even though I have a lot of essential materials.

But after the Zombie Apocalypse, no one expected me to have essentials so they just ignored me, except for one person, my best friend, my dog, Bruno. He was my one and only friend. He didn't care what I looked like.

Lizzie Roberts

By Darby Carroll

The world has been in shambles since before I was born. I was raised in a run-down house that somehow survived the government bombing. I was taught to manipulate people, to steal, and to be stealthy in everyday situations since I was little.

I had never been vaccinated before for common infections, though I wasn't too susceptible to them anyways. My immune system is strong, the only main sickness that I fear being the zombie virus. The virus was what took my parents, my friends, the people who brought me up and taught me all I know. They would constantly preach to me about my main concerns- dehydration, starvation, and, of course, the virus. "You can't have one without the other", they would tell me, meaning that if I got too hungry or too thirsty I'd be weaker and I would be more likely to get sick.

I was 7 when my house got ransacked for the first time. The adults who had built a community had been wiped out with a mysterious illness only a couple of days before. I was all alone when a group of boisterous adolescents broke a window on the ground floor. I hid underneath an old bed while they pillaged all I had, stealing all of my rations and anything I could use to keep myself warm for upcoming winters. I faintly remember being curled up, holding my breath under a sweltering wooden bedframe. I knew that if I made even the slightest of sounds, I'd be killed or looted. I felt insanely lucky I was so small.

After the group left, more thieves would come, scouring over even the slightest remains or valuables in the house. After countless raids, I knew I was no longer safe in the former seclusion of my house. I would stop sleeping the second I heard a rustle or cracking noise, and I could barely function due to my paranoia.

At 10, filled with constant horror at the daily raids, I packed up the few things that weren't stolen. I went on the road, walking day and night to try to find food and shelter. I was constantly walking, but never settling, like muddy water that was consistently being stirred.

My birth month, from what I could remember, was late March - any fallen snow was mainly melted away, and there would be the occasional cluster of daffodils peeking through the thawed ground. I had counted up to ten of those before, some based on what the adults had told me, so I knew that my 11th "birthday" was spent walking and searching, like I had done for over two seasons (The chilly season, the freezing one, and March, the flower season. I knew that the freezing season was winter, because that was the season with the most deaths and the least amount of food).

Even in March, food was hard to find. It was ALWAYS hard to find. All I could think of was my insatiable hunger, and the way my throat felt parched against the bitter air. I needed food, and I needed it *now*.

Then I found the house.

It was such a miracle, and it was seemingly abandoned. I raided houses often to search for food when I couldn't forage anything else. Even then, it was rare to find something even remotely edible, and of course, it affected my performance rates, making me slower while walking and causing me to take breaks more frequently. I knew it was morally wrong to be stealing people's hard-earned rations, but it wasn't *really* stealing if no one was even there, right?

I think to the observing eye, I seemed like a dusty, infected, obnoxious kid zombie, even though I truly wasn't infected. I had scars and cuts deep in my flesh though none of them were zombie bites, simply physical reminders of past memories. My butterfly knife, hidden under my sock, rose and fell against my ankle as I walked. The closer I approached the house, the more I could see how dilapidated it was.

But as I peered through a dirtied and slightly cracked window on the side of the house, I could make out some sort of hidden food pile within. I had to stand on my tiptoes just to see, I guess 'cause I'm pretty short. Then I had to jam my shoulder against the door *seven* times before it burst open, and I couldn't control myself as I ran to the food. I had stabbed open three cans of soup and somehow devoured each of their contents before I heard a screech from behind me.

My first instinct was that it was a zombie, because it certainly *sounded* like a zombie, but I was surprised when I turned around and came face to face with a lanky blonde man. I stood there for a few seconds, knife in my left hand and soup can in my right, before quickly dropping the can and setting myself into a defensive position, pointing my knife at his face and glaring. The blonde guy put his hands up and took a couple of steps back.

"Screw you!" I said, tilting my head down at him. "This is MY food, so back off." I kick the can behind me. Soup dribbles out of the puncture point and onto the floor. Tomato, I think. He glares back at me… but then begins chuckling.

"What's so funny?" I said, and I try to stand as tall as I can. My eyes are still narrowed towards him.

"That's *our* food," He said. "This is *our* camp." He's laughing hard now, and I feel my face heat up. I keep my knife out.

"Don't come closer. I'll kill you," I said. I wouldn't kill him yet, though, especially since he doesn't even have any weapons on him and hasn't even threatened me yet.

"I won't." He said, and stayed in his place.

"Let me stay here." I say. "I can fight. And I can steal."

"I *know* you can steal," He eyes the cans on the floor. "You can stay, I guess. But don't think I'll be babysitting you."

"I'm eleven, freak." I said. "I can handle myself."

I fold up my knife, and I keep my eyes on him as I pass by.

Lanii

By Delana Sterling

I walk to a house in the woods, as I lurk around my new surroundings after being run out by zombies after the third outbreak in the south. To me, it seems like that's the only house where I am. What could happen if I make it mine? It was a nice small one story ranch. It had nice yellow vinyl, a farm with my favorite healing berries of the season. Of course, no one would know that, unless they're a herbalist like me. I notice there's a shattered hole in the door. Great, now I have to make a new door for my home. I walked into what I guess what was the sun room and I started to hear a ruckus. My gun was in my bookbag, but from what I heard, they're humans so there's no need for bullets. I walk in the living room and I see a tall, poor, devious looking man and a child with no place to call home. Between the looks of them, I believe whatever the child says, I know I usually wouldn't but my opinions are short.

"Hey, that is A CHILD! Are you kidnapping her?" I say in a very aggressive tone, but in my mind, I am frightened by the man and even more scared for the girl. I ran to the girl, took her knife, unfolded it and stood in front of her, facing toward the man, waving it as I'm saying, "If you do anything to her, I will kill you!" He ran off, I walked over to her, slowly in a gentle motion with my hands up as **I looked at her hands and neck for bruises, scratches, scars, wounds and unfortunately I found some. She wasn't infected, though, or was she?**- "HEY, I'M NOT A ZOMBIE! CAN'T YOU SEE I'M JUST A HUMAN?" the kid yells. I completely snap out of my safety and cautious mood. "Okay! I just had to make sure, there's not a lot of us around here anymore." I looked her in the eyes and say, "You are okay, right?" The child looks at me and say "Yes, I'm fine. I wouldn't be so nice if I wasn't." I looked at her in disgust, I've never seen a more miserable looking child, so shabby.

"You call that respect? Ha, you wouldn't last where I came from! Food down there is so low that they eat people like you!" I told her while I was pointing at her while leaning down frontward to match her height. The child grabbed my index finger, tightly squeezes it and says to me, "I'm trying not to do anything to you because you saved me, but don't push it. I was doing just fine before you came here." She let go while smiling at me. I was so tired of her impertinent remarks. She was so impolite. You could tell she had no home training. Maybe I should just take her in anyways, I thought. I know no one else is going take her in. She was okay in my book but that's only because I knew she wouldn't be in anyone else's. Plus, I couldn't just leave her out here. She's a child, I thought.

"Hey, little girl. I got a question for you. How old are you?" She rolled her eyes and put her hands on her hips and said to me "My name is Lizzie, thank you." She points at me, mocking my earlier posture. "I'm 11." I look down at her and cross my arms. "So, where are your parents? Did you run away? You seem like the type. Come on, tell me all about who raised you." I say, smiling, I backhand her shoulder, rolling my hand in a "You can tell me." motion, as I was so interested in her story about her parents. I looked at her for a few more seconds and I watched her legs wobble. Tears started to form in her eyes, a lot of tears actually. Her eyes were open but she wasn't speaking, it was as if she saw something far away in the distance.

24

She began to say "**You can't have one without the other, you can't have one without the other**" over and over again. I didn't know what to do, but I noticed it was a tough question and I instantly regretted my decision putting my nose where it shouldn't be. I went to hug her. I know hugging might be disgusting right now since it last rained in 3 days but at least it wasn't a week like the drought we had 5 months ago in July. As I'm hugging her, I feel her heart beating and her shaking uncontrollably until **she stops**. Her heart went back to normal but her eyes went back. "No!No!No!No!No!No!No!No!..No!No!" I begin to panic, but that's not helpful. I felt her legs give out - she was completely unconscious. I sat her down on the couch as I went into a clean bedroom, nice and stylish, very kid-themed. It could be her room, because it would not be mine. I went back into the living room and lock the door to the sunroom, at least I have that. I picked her up, very heavy, **and must've been well fed** to my knowledge. I put her into the bed, covered her up. The weather happened to be wishy-washy in Annapolis but still cold on most days.

And then I saw the others…

Fiona

By Violet Acosta

I am an only child. I have always wanted a brother or a sister just to hangout with when I'm bored. My parents don't want another child, they say that "I am enough" and that they are "finished" with having children. But it's okay. I guess I *am* enough. Everyday at school there is always that one popular and mean girl that always bullies you. But for me, that 'popular and mean' girl's name is Angela. Her name has the word *angel* in it. She is no angel. She makes fun of me but I always find a way to bully her back. That's what my dad told me. He told me "If someone hits you first, hit them back" type of thing. But with bullying instead of hitting. I'm not quite sure why I am so mean. I guess I'm just irritated with anyone who's around me.

When I got to school, I saw the ugly, blonde, popular, and mean girl Angela. She said that my clothes looked disgusting, then I told her that her face looks disgusting, just to get back at her. And I walked away. Next class was 2nd period English, the class was super boring, as always. All we did was read two chapters of a book and write a summary of each chapter. Once I was finished I was so tired and bored, I decided to put in my earpods to listen to music and take a nap in class. I put my head down on my desk and put my arms around my head. I then fell asleep. I put my head up and saw everyone left. I had been sleeping for two hours!! It was only noon so school wasn't over yet. I got up, rubbed my eyes and smeared my mascara, and put my bag on my shoulder. I then walked around the hallway and saw absolutely no one in sight. I looked in every classroom I walked past and still, no one in sight. I saw a classroom with windows and looked outside towards the front of the building and saw… Zombies!!!!! My eyes widened and I was horrified. I saw so many dead bodies of students and teachers. I saw a Zombie eating my English teacher too! I don't know how no one tried to wake me up. I can't believe I slept through all of that!

The first thing that came to my mind was my parents. I had to go home and see if they're okay. I was too scared to go outside since all the Zombies were roaming around. I thought about it for a good 10 minutes and decided to go. I grabbed some weapons in the principal's office that were confiscated by teachers. I got some knives, lighters, laser pointers, and the principal's keys. I opened the front door to see if the coast was clear. Then I grabbed a knife and the keys in my hand and began to run for my life towards the principal's car. I opened the door and locked it fast. I drove away nervous because I didn't want to crash. I drove home so fast and got in even faster. I walked into the living room to see my parents dead… I started to cry.

I went up to my room and locked the door. I sat on my bed crying for minutes. I wiped away my tears and went downstairs to lock all the windows and doors in my house so no Zombies could get in. I gathered two backpacks. One full of clothes, snacks, two water bottles, and toiletries. And the other is full of weapons like knives, lighters, a small gun with extra bullets, and more snacks that I could fit. My dad had the gun locked in a safe place but I got to it. I made sure to put in three bullets. I needed to get out of my house before more Zombies came in. I planned to drive to a different state to make sure I was completely safe. I quietly but quickly ran out to the car. I began driving along a bloody, fleshy road to get where I needed to go.

All of a sudden, the car broke down. I was soooo furious. I decided to abandon the car and go into the forest that was next to the road to seek shelter. It was about a 20 minute walk when I saw an abandoned house. I decided to go inside to see if it was safe to stay in. As I peeked around the corner, I saw a small group of people. And no, they weren't zombies. They were all very different.

I was curious and walked towards them and said hello. They all welcomed me and said hello back. We started a nice conversation and each person spoke about where they all came from and what they want to bring into the new group. We didn't have much in common but we began showing each other what we can all do. I told everyone that I am really good at defending myself and others when I'm at school. I also brought some weapons that everyone can share.

In the corner of my eye, I saw a little girl walking away from what seemed like an argument between her and a random blonde dude. I came up to her to say hello, but she yelled, "Get away from me, weirdo!" I was shocked to hear that from a little girl. I said, "Okay, I will, but can I at least know your name?" She said quietly but angrily, "My name is Lizzie. Lizzie Roberts." "Nice to meet you Lizzie, how old are you?" I said. She said she was 11. She's quite young to be all by herself in an apocalypse. I asked her if she lives here in this house, she said that she just got here from running away from zombies. I then walked away to look for a bathroom to clean up all the dirt and scratches on my body from roaming around in the forest for so long. As I was putting bandages on my wounds, I heard a lot of yelling outside of the bathroom. I leave the bathroom and see that little girl Lizzie arguing with everyone.

Sam

By Samuel Brennan

I arrived at a new base with a couple other survivors, though the tensions were high. Everyone at the camp fought over the food that was left and nobody trusted one another. They seemed to have a hard time finding new food in the city and nobody knew how to hunt or grow their own crop. These people would tear themselves apart if they kept on this track and continued to be hateful people. I wish to teach them about my religion and how to be grateful for what we have and to work together to find peace in our new situation.

After I arrived and saw what was going on I asked if anyone practiced religion, yet nobody did. I asked if they would like to join me in prayer sessions and start to study the Bible to learn God's word. I thought if the people could learn to love then they wouldn't hate each other so much and be in conflict so much. Nobody thought the prayer would help their situation and it was just a waste of time. Everyone thought it would be better to keep looking for food and not reading the bible and praying. Over time though, people got more curious about my work and soon people started to join me in the early mornings to read sections of the Bible that I felt would help them work through these tough times. The people found that the Bible could help them and give them some answers to their issues. It speaks against sins like rage and greed which would teach these people how to not fight over the resources but also not share with the other people around them and not hoard the supplies.

After some time passed the people seemed to work better as a team. The fighting over the food reserves had died down and they seemed to want to find solutions to their problems rather than fight over them. It was looking like we could actually make something good out of this situation and work towards making a thriving camp. People eventually were studying on their own and would bring passages that they thought were impactful to the group to share. This brought unity as it was almost like an event on Sundays when everyone would bring passages they felt were important to the meetings to share with the others. Although not everyone chose to join in these meetings and didn't want to learn religion I felt I had made a difference in those that did as maybe they found more peace in their lives from it.

Spreading my religion is important to me as it helped me find peace in my life at a young age and again during the apocalypse as in hard times when people resort to sin it's important to be drawn back in to the good you can still do in life and how it can personally improve your life to turn from sin and resort to doing good for yourself and others. Even though doing good can seem hard it is always better than taking the easy way out and being a wrongdoer.

Blaire Willows

By Molly Grace Ralph

The zombie apocalypse was scary. It came out of the blue and no one knew this could ever happen. So many people died and you were lucky if you survived. I did. My parents and sister Annie didn't though. A zombie came through our back deck door and got them before they could get away. We were doing fine and all of a sudden it happened. I was able to run out to my neighbors. Oh I wonder if they're ok. Did they die? Such young kids, who had their whole life in front of them. I always enjoyed my time when I got to babysit them.

I'm at my house right now, sitting in silence and I'm crying. I can't believe they're gone and dead! I can't believe this happened! How did this happen? I had 4 other siblings that weren't living at home at the time but I haven't heard anything from those towns other than they were wiped out. Two were in college and the other two were out of college living somewhere else. Whether they're alive or not, I won't hear from them in a while unless they take a trip and come down to Annapolis. My gosh, I loved my family so much and I'll never see them again. I remember fun times with them. Beach trips, times when my siblings came home from college, watching shows together. That's all gone. What am I going to do? The apocalypse has caused so much destruction and everyone's homes are practically almost gone. Our entire roof came off and I'm sitting on a couch in the rubble. I don't know what to do. I decide to go on a walk and clear my mind.

That's when I find this little hangout/beat-up house that's pretty much intact. I hear many voices coming from inside so I decide to go check it out. When I get inside people are complaining a lot and there's this little girl wailing and whining and everyone looks like they want to kill her. Someone sees me and asks me if I need anything and that people have gathered here so that they wouldn't be alone from who they lost in their family. Also, it's practically the only house that is still in it's shape. Well, except for the house next to it which looks pretty good for going through this. Wonder why we're not there. I see a man there. In the beat-up house I'm in, I see neighbors and friends from our neighborhood. I find out that one of my good friends from my school who lives in my neighborhood got attacked and died.

I'm spacing out when someone claps their hands and introduces themselves as Sam. He's a Catholic priest. Everyone else introduces themselves too and says if they lost anyone in the apocalypse. Turns out that little girl who was whining is named Lizzy Roberts and she's 11. I introduce myself and say that my parents and sister who were living with me and that my 4 other siblings that were in other states died and all their towns got destroyed too. I add that practically my whole house got destroyed.

When I'm introducing myself I also ask about the house next door and the guy living there. Sam tells me he doesn't know his name and that they asked if we could stay there for now but he got very mad and said no. He said that for weeks they would go over there and knock and bang on his door and he just wouldn't open the door. One time he did come to the door but he turned them down. Apparently, they also saw lots of food in his house and asked him about it but he got very mad and stubborn and shut the door in their faces. Everyone is suddenly reminded of how awful that man is and how we just went through something that has never

32

happened before and he's not willing to share something all of us really need. Lizzie starts crying again, everyone gets very loud and complains. There's even talk of breaking into his house and stealing his food.

People start cursing and things are getting out of hand. And I think to myself, we can't give up on him. I step up onto a chair and yell, "Everyone shut up!" They all stop what they are doing and I start talking. "Why did we let him just shut the door in our faces? It was partly your guys fault for just thinking, oh he won't let us so I guess we're done with him. No! That's not ok. I'm going over there and I'm going to talk it over with him and he will give us food and supplies." A few other people yell in agreement with me. We all walked over to his house and knocked on the door. When we knock I hear this type of loud sigh and got a little worried. He opens the door and the first thing I say is, "Hi sir, I'm Blaire Willows. We just have a few things to say."

"My name is Zach and I'm not giving you guys anything!" Well, that was the whole point we came over here. So I decided to play it cool.

"Sir, I don't know why you won't join our group or contribute to people's needs after this horrible time when something crazy and out of the ordinary happened. So many people's family and friends have gotten killed and eaten by zombies! You're just gonna let that go? I mean we don't know what to do and we're all starving and we're gonna need food some time if we want to live as survivors of this zombie apocalypse. Now I don't know if you're going through something with your family or if you're just so shocked or something, but you're the only person that we know of right now with a stable house with most of your resources. And it's just mean if you don't even share little morsels with us. I mean why can't you just come on over and see for yourself the love we share and how you won't be alone."

"Fine, whatever. But don't you say I told you so!"

"Thank you so much, sir! And trust me I won't."

We walk over to the house and when we do, everyone is talking and laughing and having a good time.

"See? Look how fun it looks! We can cook a nice meal and it will be even better!"

I turn around, but I don't see Zach. He was just here, but he's nowhere to be seen.

"Zach? Where did he go?"

He completely disappears. Days go past with very little food and we're trying to get by. One day Zach just appears.

"Well, look who decided to join us."

"I'm sorry I haven't been welcoming and nice. I just lost everything and wanted to be alone. When I walked in here with you, I saw everyone laughing and having a good time and it was just overwhelming. But I'm here now, and I have food for everyone and resources that I'm willing to share."

"Thank you so much! You don't know how much that means to us! You won't regret it. Well, come on everybody! let's make a delicious meal and eat!"

Zach

By Zach Boyd

My life was even before the *plague hit*. I had already lost all of my family due to a house fire weeks before. I was on my own. No home. No family. Nothing. Then, the plague hit. I was in a store when I heard the news. I took this as an opportunity to grab as much food and supplies that I could. There was no order anymore so, no need for money. As soon as I got out of the store, I grabbed my bike and I rode it as far and as long as my legs would take me. I ended up near a dark forest late at night. Luckily, I had grabbed a tent and matches from the store for shelter and warmth just for the night I lit the fire, set up the tent and as soon as I got off of my feet, I fell asleep. When I woke up the forest was so much more clear and I was actually able to see my surroundings. But, this didn't help me that much because it turned out I had ended up in the middle of the forest and saw nothing but trees. It wasn't safe for me to stay there so I decided to start looking for a way out. This wasn't that easy though. Every tree was identical to the last and every turn was the same. I didn't know where to go. But, I kept going, kept turning, kept running until I saw a house in the distance. It looked rundown and abandoned so I moved in closer. Then I froze, I saw moving around and I thought it could be some of the *infected*. Turns out, it was normal people. I was shocked. I hadn't seen another human in forever. It was almost *frightening*. I turned to run, and not too far away, there was another house that was completely unoccupied so I decided to move into there.

A few weeks went by and I was still unnoticed. I was prospering by myself and I saw no problem with it. Then, I heard a knock on my door. I ignored it at first but then they just kept banging louder. I crept towards the window to see who was there and there were about four of five people standing on my doorstep. I remained quiet, hoping they would go away and eventually they did. But this wasn't the last I saw them. They came back everyday for weeks and knocked on the door for about five to ten minutes every single day.

I finally answered one day and they asked me how long I had been there. I mumbled, "A few weeks." They asked if they could come inside and I refused to let them in. I had been alone for so long that I didn't want any new people. I guess that's just who I am. Even when I still had my family I liked to be by myself. Never was a people person.

Since I acknowledged them and said that I didn't want to take part in anything they had going on, I thought they wouldn't come back. I was very wrong. They continued to come back over and over. I just wanted them to go away. No matter what I did they would continue to come back.

Eventually, I had enough. I knew rejecting them wasn't going to stop them so I just decided to give in and I went with them. They took me to that house. The old rundown one from when I first came out of the forest. I had originally thought it would be only a few people but it turns out there was an entire community living there. The complete opposite of my ideal living space. After only a few minutes of being there I had already made up my mind. I don't wanna be a part of this community. Then I looked over and I saw all these people laughing with each other, talking, smiling. It almost made me change my mind. But like I said. *Almost.* I continued on my way home and I did not return for a few days. Later on that week I was sitting in my home and suddenly I just got this feeling of emptiness and for the first time since I lost my family I felt… alone.

Days went by and I realized that being alone was not what was best for me. I went back to the community and told them that I was no longer going to distance myself and I would join their community. I would share my resources with them. I would be a part of their family.

Brian

By Brian Hernandez-Ibarra

Con el apocalipsis zombi muchas personas empezaron a perder el control al ver estas criaturas ya que fue un desastre que paso , que nadie se esperaba que podía pasar así que muchas personas empezaron a hacer sus refugios ya que estas criaturas solo aparecían de noche ya que las lastimaba la luz del día, en los refugios quedaron atrapadas personas de diferentes lugares, aspectos, raíces, lenguajes había personas que talvez no se podían comunicar mucho por el lenguaje pero gracias a otras personas se pudieron comunicar entre las personas que había adentro del refuguio ,ya se estaba quedando sin suficiente comida así que había que salir durante el dia a conseguir comida en ciertos lugares se podían encontrar personas que hablan diferentes idiomas así que las personas que sabían un un poco de pocos idiomas se comunicaban tal vez para llegar

With the zombie apocalypse, many people began to lose control when they saw these creatures since it was a disaster that happened, which nobody expected could happen. So many people began to make their shelters. The evil zombies only appeared at night, since the daylight hurt them. People from different places, aspects, roots, and languages were trapped in the shelters.

I found myself in one of the shelters with people who mostly spoke English. I could communicate with them a little. But I was lonely for Spanish speakers. There were people who perhaps could not communicate much by language but thanks to other people they were able to communicate among the people inside the shelter.

38

a un acuerdo de como pasarse la comida y sobrevivir muchos de los vecinos aceptaron y se comunicaban mediante diferentes lenguas.
Después de eso se decidió trabajar todos juntos, sin importar la raza o lugar todos eran tratados por igual para prosperar poder ser más unidos. (Esto paso en Annapolis)

We were already running out of enough food, so you had to go out during the day to get food. In certain places, you could find people speaking different languages, so people who knew a little of a few languages communicated maybe to come to an agreement.

One man, Alfredo, didn't speak any Spanish OR English. But he knew more than anyone about how to grow food. I realized he knew Quiche, which my grandmother spoke when I was little. We were able to talk a little and he told me what we needed to do to grow more food.

I shared with the others how to grow a few crops so we could have fresh food again.

After that it was decided to all work together, regardless of race or place, everyone was treated

equally to prosper to be
more united. (This
happened in Annapolis)

Alfredo

by Alfredo Chavix-Aguin

Era una vez en mi comunidad donde era muy tranquila, las personas eran todas trabajadores y podían divertirse , yo junto con mi familia y mis abuelos, mis padres y yo que me llamo Alfredo el hijo menor de la familia y nos dedicamos a la agricultura y cultivamos café, arroz y lo principal que era el maíz.

En ese entonces pasó algo bastante trágico hubo un tormenta grande donde casi todas las personas perdieron su cosecha y fue donde ellos recurrían a mi familia, porque ellos tenían como mantenerlas personas pero se escucho ciertos rumores de que podría haber una invasión de zombis y mi familia se preparó para poder no salir de la casa.

Pero las personas no tenían suficiente recursos para poder sobrevivir un tiempo largo,

La invasión comenzó y no podíamos acercarnos tanto a las

It was once in my community where it was very quiet. The people were all workers and they could have fun, along with my family and my grandparents, my parents and me. My name is Alfredo, the youngest son of the family. We dedicated ourselves to agriculture and we grew coffee, rice and the main thing that was corn.

At that time something quite tragic happened. There was a big storm where almost all the people lost their harvest and it was where they turned to my family, because they had to support people. But certain rumors were heard that there could be an invasion of zombies and my family prepared itself so that

otras casas por que los zombis estaban por donde quiera pero ellos se acercaban a nosotros a pedirnos cosas pero, no podíamos comunicarnos por que hablábamos el idioma quiché el cian no era usa en mi comunidad todos hablaban español pero de un o otro modo nos pudimos comunicar y podemos hacer un gran equipo para terminar con esa invasión, un dia todo se termino y pudi

Queremos estar como una comunidad unida de nuevo y preparada para otros obstáculos. Y lo bueno de todo es.

Que mi nueva familia aprendió otro idioma para poder dialogar más y comunicarse con otras personas y es más fácil para todos ser unidos. Después y de todo empezamos a trabajar unidos y mi familia les enseño como cultivar de una manera que ellos también lo puedan hacer bien y que tenga abundante cosecha y poder ser mas unidos que nunca manteniendo la hermosa unión entre todos.

we could lock down the house.

But people did not have enough resources to survive for a long time.

The invasion began and we couldn't get so close to the other houses because the zombies were everywhere. But the other people came to us to ask us for things but we couldn't communicate because I spoke the Quiché language. English and Spanish had not been used in my village.

One person at the new house spoke only a little Quiché but in one way or another we were able to communicate and we can make a great team to put an end to that invasion and grow food. We want to be as a community united again and prepared for other obstacles. And the good part is that my new family learned another language to be able to dialogue more and communicate with other people and it is easier for everyone to be united.

After all, we started to work together and my family taught them how to cultivate in a way that they too can do well and have abundant harvest and be able to be more united than ever, maintaining the beautiful union between all of us.

Aaliyah

By Aaliyah Wilson

Hi, my name is Aaliyah. People perceive me as the "Angry Black Woman" but, hey, I've been through a lot in my life. I've had so many losses and have been to so many funerals I can't even count on one hand, I don't have family, I actually don't have anyone for that matter. Everyone I have ever come in contact with has either abandoned me or just died. Going through all of these events in my life has caused me to become angry with myself and the others around me. No, I don't choose to be this angry, it's just who I am. I want to change but what can I do? I am independent and demand the role of leadership and will NOT be told what to do or HOW I will do it.

Honestly, it's been a while since all of this zombie apocalypse occurred. I am stuck with people in a house who can barely understand me (because of a language barrier) and not to mention constant friction between Brian and me. We can never agree on anything, also there is this 11-year-old girl who is SO annoying and ruining our flow. I think it's time for a change in strategy because I don't see us coming out of this epidemic... There is also a blonde-haired boy who I met on the lake as he was learning some kind of survival skills. He's thinking he runs everything and I am NOT feeling this.

I decide that maybe I should talk to Brian and maybe we could resolve things. I see him as he is starting outside on the porch with a mean ole serious face. I lightly tap him on the shoulder, " Brian, ¿podemos hablar?" (Brian, can we talk?) He turns around surprised. "Sí segura, por dentro." (Yeah sure, inside). We sit down at the table.

It's a bit awkward due to the silence. Eventually, the silence is broken. "¿Cómo sabes español? " (How do you know Spanish?) He smiles. " Oye, estamos en una economía basada en la tecnología." (Hey. we are in a technology based economy) He laughs. I ask "cuéntame sobre ti (tell me about yourself) and he replies, "ok". He takes a deep breath before he speaks.

"Nací en El Salvador, mis padres emigraron aquí después de que nací. Mis padres regresaron a El Salvador para un funeral y como llegaron a los EE. UU. sin una tarjeta de ciudadanía, se vieron obligados a regresar. no tuve ninguno, viví en las calles, nunca tuve educación y solo tenía 10 años. Me obligaron a trabajar, me dije a mí mismo que traeré a mis padres aquí. Cuando lo hice, ambos fueron asesinados mientras intentaban regresar a los Estados Unidos. Estaba enojado como si fuera mi culpa. Fui culpable y desde ese día me volví independiente y enojado con el mundo."

"I was born in El Salvador, my parents emigrated here after I was born. My parents returned to El Salvador for a funeral and because they came to the US without a citizenship card, they were forced to return. I didn't have any, I lived on the streets, I never had an education and I was only 10 years old. They forced me to work, I told myself that I will bring my parents here. When I did, they were both killed while trying to get back to the United States. I was angry like it was my fault. I was guilty and from that day on

I became independent and
angry at the world."

"Wow!" I reply with sadness after translating every word he
has said, while trying to remain respectful. We have judged
each other so much and realize that we are both angry at the
world for how our childhood affected us. We need to forgive
and let go rather than become angry. I grab his hand gently
and tell him. "*Lo siento, me relaciono mucho con que también me
hayan abandonado. nos juzgamos tan rápido y somos tan parecidos que
no podemos amargarnos. vamos a trabajar juntos.*" (I'm sorry. I
relate so much. I've been abandoned as well. We judged each
other so quickly and we are so much alike, we can't be bitter.
Let's work together.) As we both stand up, we hug and walk
outside, talking freely.

Juliana

By Juliana Lucrecio Aguilar

My name is Juliana and I'm a hispanic female. I am not a very talkative person around certain people, but I can be very helpful at some points. I love being organized about everything, and just doing most things on my own. Before the whole zombie breakout I used to work as a person who organized doctor files and kept everything in place.

Now I help organize this community of people that have settled in a broken house in Annapolis. Like the rest of the people here, I have found a way to use what I know, what I am good at, to help everyone survive.

Mike Watson

By Jacob Kirkpatrick

After the zombie apocalypse I had to live off whatever I could find. For two years I was struggling for food by going through towns and neighborhoods to get food from the vacant houses. I had to break the windows and search through every drawer and pantry. If I got lucky I would get an expired box of cereal or a bag of chips. Over time I became more skilled and had a sixth sense for food. I could find food anywhere. I found many plants along the way and took the seeds just in case I needed them for later. I was planning to search for a house for food inside of Downtown Annapolis. The city had been in ruins ever since the military dropped bombs on it. I used to live here before the apocalypse and was a bit familiar with it still everything was either broken or about to break. I saw the only house without broken windows or vines growing on it and was scoping it out until I heard noises in the backyard. I looked over and saw people. I haven't seen any survivors in over a year! Ever since the bombs were dropped I thought I was the only survivor in Annapolis and that was why I had peace of mind breaking into buildings and houses. I didn't know what to do at first, but then I knocked on the door.

Just before it opened, I thought back to what life was like before the zombie apocalypse. It was a regular day, I was visiting my parents for the day but then I heard noises coming from upstairs, the window was smashed and I looked inside. It looked like a bomb had gone off in the room and my parents were gone. Ever since then I have never stayed in one spot for too long.

The door opened and I was greeted by a man who looked shocked to see me, almost like he had seen a ghost. He told me to come in and I was surprised to see a whole group of people. They were all different ethnicities and ages and I wondered if they would want a thief to join them. Everybody else looked at me and instead of giving me a smug look, they smiled and cheered that they had found another survivor. I was able to talk to one of the people, He said he was the one who started this and got everyone together. His name was Alex. I was interested in his stories about saving people and bringing them here. He asked where I came from and how I got here, but I didn't want to tell him.

The next morning I went out to search for more resources because they didn't seem to have much food in that house, I set up various traps to catch any animals, The traps were poorly made and it took me almost all day to make them, most traps were just a stick holding up a box or a trap that would fall on and animal. After the traps were built I ran back to my stash of seeds in the forest. I always make sure to never go out into the forest at night because It can be dangerous. After an hour of walking I saw the sun start to set, my walking turned into running, I knew I was close and when I got there I quickly grabbed them and started to run back. The sun had gone down and the only light was from the moon, I could barely see where I was but then I heard people talking, The sound kept getting louder and louder until I was finally back. I ran into the house, dropped the bag of seeds, and layed on the floor. All the people looked confused or worried but I didn't care because I was safe. Standing over me was a man speaking an odd language that I had never heard before. He took the seeds and instead of being confused like the others he looked happy. I asked what he was doing but all he said was "Alfredo."

When I woke up the next morning there were no birds chirping and no wind going through the trees. It was so quiet and I didn't like it. There were a lot of people in the house and I could barely get out of the door. The house was too small for over 10 people and I had an idea to help with it. I took a hatchet lying on the floor and went over to the nearest trees. I chopped and chopped until the tree fell over, I took the branches and laid them out in a wall shape. I used the vines to tie the branches together and filled all the holes with the rubble from the buildings. I was tired but I didn't want to stop, my whole life I always persevered and tried to always keep going until I physically could not anymore. It took a long time but by the end of the day I had made a fence that could keep dangerous people out and at least slow down the zombies, if they come back.

After a few days I had doubled the space of that backyard and the people were so excited, they decided to plan a party.

Jack Brown

By Tyreus Brown

Hey, my name is Jack Brown. When I was 4 years old, my plane hit a mountain. My mom and dad were killed. I was found by monks on a mountain. They raised me for 14 years as a teacher in zombie killing because of a prophecy. I knew I was different. When I got older they told me I am American..

2 years ago I realized my talent. I was a killer of zombies. Annapolis was getting attacked so I went right to Maryland. I found a group of kids who live in the city and are trying to survive. I help them to move to get stuff for the city.

I met new people everyday. Their families were broken, too. Some parents got turned into zombies. Their kids had to kill the mom and dad. We set fireworks off to tell others where we are at, to tell people. it is a good place to live.

One day we harvested a bunch of food and had a party. The zombies must have heard the noise and attacked us. We had to fight them off one last time. We won the battle once and for all and the threat was finally over…

Rafael

By Rafael Estrada-Barrera

When I was a kid, I hated school. I had bad grades and was skipping class all the time. I would fake being sick and tell my mom that I had to stay home. I would get suspended for fighting. One day when I was suspended, my dad was cooking and that caught my attention. I asked him if I could try some. When I was done eating, I asked him how he made it. He gave me a list of foods from Guatemala, where my family is from. He started showing me how to cook it. One day, I did it by myself and it felt good. From that day, I decided to practice cooking a lot of different foods.

A few years later I decided to work at a restaurant. And it went pretty well. I became kind of famous, at least for Annapolis. When the Zombie Apocalypse came, my restaurant was destroyed. I wandered for months, looking for any scrap of food I could find.

I was trying to find a place to be in for a while, but while I was searching for a place to stay, my foot got stuck in something. It was something really sharp, and I got hurt really badly. My foot was really injured. as I was trying to get my foot unstuck I saw two zombies coming towards me. I panicked and did not know what to do. So I started to pull myself out as hard as I could. I finally got myself out. I could barely run. My foot was hurting really bad. I finally found a path, and tried to find behind some bushes. They finally got away, and I was at a safe spot.

After a few weeks I was useless by myself. So I tried to find some people to help me survive this. So I searched everywhere and I found this old house. So I decided to go in. I saw like four people inside. I saw that they were all praying together . I decided to go up to them and I asked them, "Hey I know you might not want to do this, but would any of you want to help survive this zombie apocalypse." One of the men that was there hesitated. Only one man that was there said "Yes, I would. We are all in this together". The three other men seemed like they didn't want to, but after a few minutes of them thinking about it they finally said yes. So one of the men there actually knew how to fight,and I told him if he could teach me. He gladly said yes, after 2 weeks of teaching me I got really good at it.

Over time, more people came to join us. The four men told me that we need to stock up on food and a shelter because their home and work got destroyed. So one of the men went to go find food, and others started growing food, including this one Guatemalan farmer who didn't speak English, or even Spanish. But he told me through Brian, who understood a little bit of his language, that there was a problem. We said, "What's the problem?" He said, "None of us know how to cook this.!" They were disappointed. Then I remembered that I do know how to cook. I was a chef at one of the most popular restaurants in the city. They all looked at me and told me "You are?" I said "Yes." They were all so happy to hear that. So I got started right away.

After we were all done eating a really good plate of steak. I saw a bunch of zombies outside our shelter. So we got all of our weapons ready and started to fight them. I didn't really know how to use a weapon so I started to fight a zombie, and thanks to all the training one of the men gave me I was beating the crap out of these zombies and it started to look like it was about to end. So I got rid of the last zombie that was there.

After a few weeks later the zombie apocalypse was finally over, and I went to go thank the four men, and the whole community, that helped me survive this. I told them that I really appreciated it. I headed on my way, to figure out what was next for me.

That was the last straw for the zombie apocalypse.

Kemaunya

By Kemaunya Covert

My favorite part of the story is a food party. I just waited and waited all day to grow fruits and vegetables. I just felt tired and needed a little nap but then the fruits and veggies grew.

3 weeks later I need to wash them nice and clean. Once the fruits and veggies were clean, I needed to make a salad and fruit salad for families and kids. I needed to use this chopper cutter to cut fruit, apples, bananas, pineapples, blueberries, grapes,mangoes, oranges slices and I mixed them all together to make a fruit salad. To make the salad, use a bowl of some lettuce, carrots, tomatoes, cucumbers, celery, everything. Once the salad had mixed, all the burgers,hot dogs, cheesesteaks we had found in the basement freezer at another house were cooked on the grill using gloves. Be careful! Safety first! When the burgers, hot dogs, cheesesteaks were done, I put hamburger bread, hot dog bread, cheesesteaks bread and put them nice and straight.

I decided to take a little nap before the party. I started to dream...*I was getting a lot of food, balloons, streamers and snacks for the party in Party City. I wanted all the kids and family to invite me to my food party by putting up streamers, blowing up balloons, putting plates, forks, spoons on the table, some food and juices on the table and decorated grewing with all things fruits and vegetables.I just wanted to do drawing cards for all the kids and families. All foods were nice and straight until I knew a happy plan. I put balloons and cards in the mailboxes at people's houses. somewhere in my house and put streamers on it. So i here at the door its my family were here i just putting on music they like my food i make delicious fruit salad and salad i made first it is music time I sing to my family what you want to do now*

55

I knew that I was putting snacks on the table once that i made this myself. We partied all night until almost 10:00 once the party was over it's the end of the party. Thank you to my parents. I just put on my gown to brush my teeth and get ready for bed...

...Suddenly I felt a hand on my back. Aaliyah was gently shaking me awake...I came out into the yard and there was my new family, all ready to celebrate and eat our food together. I think everyone is going to be okay.

Epilogue: The Day of the Festival ... Aaliyah

The party started promptly at noon and we partied until 10:00pm that night. *Music playing * We were enjoying the feast and seeing different cultures being represented with tables and enjoying different cultural foods/backgrounds.

There was suddenly an interruption by a few last Zombies, looking for a fight. Our warriors came together and destroyed them in a matter of minutes.

As the party began to settle down, I decided to say a couple of words. "Hope everyone is having a good time. Thanks to the warriors who have protected us. Thanks to the peacemakers who have brought us together. Thanks to Kemauyna, who fell asleep at noon because she was so tired making this delicious food - we have had all sorts of delicious sweets and meals. Thanks to Alfredo and Mike Watson, Kemaunya and Rafael had vegetables and other food to cook for us. And thanks to my now friend, Brian, the rest of our people are able to understand each other. Brian has a great idea, which is to give everyone Spanish lessons once a week so we can communicate. Trying times can cause division. Let's make a promise to stay united - let's give a name to this festival: Unity Day."

As everyone ate and sang together, Brian smiled at me and he mouthed, "Thank you..."

The End

The Old Oak Tree

A Story of Identity and Community

Written by Ms. Pittman's 4A GCC Class Spring 2023
Artwork by Asunti Dears

About the Old Oak Tree Book Project

This project integrates two themes we studied in Global Community Citizenship - Identity and the Stages of Community Formation. We learned about different aspects of identity - language, race, gender, education, personality, family structure, core values, religion, and culture. We also learned and experienced the stages of community formation - forming (coming together, often with some skepticism), storming (experiencing some conflict), norming (beginning to understand and embrace differences), and performing (working together as a team). As an example of both identity and community formation, we read the novel Seedfolks, the story of diverse members of a neglected neighborhood in Cleveland coming together around the building of a community garden.

In this writing project, students in each class collaborated to come up with a context for a story about identity and community (involving a bit of storming in the process!). In this class, students decided to write about an old tree in a fictional Annapolis Park and the lives that came together around its loss to a lightning strike. Each student designed their role in the story, choosing one aspect of identity and one stage of community formation to build their narrative around. Students chose aspects of identity that were meaningful to their own lives, but the characters are fictionalized. We hope you enjoy reading the results of our efforts! We certainly had fun creating these stories!

Herman Winkelstein
by Saul Holton

I was 10 when the brownshirts came to my father's store. They broke the windows of the shop and painted the walls with the word, "*Judenrau*", meaning Jewish swine. They had also looted most of the clothing, burning it in front of our store; the pile of ash and embers was still warm when we arrived. My father was shocked. He had served Germany in the Great War, and believed that despite the Nazi's hatred, his service would have protected his family. But to the government, we were simply Jews, *untermensch*. My sister, mother, and I helped my father clean the broken glass from the floor, and paint over the wall.

When we finished, we approached our synagogue, only to find a pile of smoldering coals. In front, our Rabbi wept. With him were many women and children of our congregation; but no men. That night, the SS and rioters had destroyed Jewish property and arrested Jewish men. By mistake, they had missed our house due to faulty information, and spared my father. Learning this, my father made a decision that would forever change our lives. He decided that we would have to flee Germany.

We returned to our house that evening, only after assisting those in our community with nothing left. At home, we gathered anything we could carry, and left. We had to bribe a train worker to hide us in a cargo car heading for the Italian border. But before we reached the border, the train was stopped by Gestapo officers, searching for Jews. When my father heard them coming, he instructed my family to run. When we jumped off of the car and ran to the woods, he pulled out a revolver from his service and fired upon the officers. He was shot dead. But his distraction allowed us to escape. And after searching for weeks in Rome, we found a ship to America.

When we arrived in the United States, my family had nothing. And although a synagogue offered us assistance and housing, they would still need 2 weeks to make the arrangements. Fearing life on the streets of a city, my mother took my family to a local park. In this park, she found a small tree for us to sleep under. For 2 weeks, my family lived underneath this tree. And when the synagogue provided us with housing, I almost felt bad leaving the tree behind.

Recently, I heard on the news that a tree in the park I had lived in was struck by lightning. Perhaps out of nostalgia, I returned to the park to see the spectacle of the tree, and relive memories. But when I saw the tree, I had a realization. The great big tree that was struck by lightning was the very same tree that I had slept under all those years ago.

I saw a crowd of people and joined them. They were arguing about what was to be done with the tree. Rather than speak out, I stepped back. I joined another man who seemed to be anxious about all of the other people. I grabbed his hand and we watched together. Watching peacefully, I appreciated the discourse; if only the people of my nation had spoken to each other so civilly.

Julian

by Julian Hernandez

I am Julian, and I am 21 years old. I didn't do too well in school, I would struggle a lot in school no matter how hard I tried. I was bullied, harassed, and it would hurt me emotionally. Every day after school, I would go to the tree to calm down and relax. I love that tree, it helped me power through every day at school. The tree was the highlight of my day, although I struggled in school, I would power through and remain confident in what I can do. And that mindset powered me through as I now live comfortably with a nice job and house.

One day, there was a nasty storm, winds howling, and lots of thunder. I decided I would go around the city during the storm. As I drove by the tree I watched lightning strike the tree. That strike is something I will never forget. The tree was effectively ruined. I drove a mournful drive back home and took some time to think about what had just happened.

The next day I decided to go to the tree and stay with it for the day. I was there for a bit. Eventually people started to show up. I saw a person walking towards the tree. As she got closer, I greeted her. "Hi," I said. She said "Hi." "What is your name?" I asked. She said, "My name is Sarah, how about you?" And I replied with "Julian." Sarah asked, "What are your memories of the tree?" I responded with "I felt like it was my safe space, I grew up with the tree being a big part of my life. What are your memories?" Sarah responds, " I used to study under this tree and to relax."

Sarah

by Sarah Lashar

I always had a dream that I would get into an Ivy League school. I work hard both in school and out of school. Everyday after school I go to the park to study. I sit under the big tree in the park and do my homework. I like the silence and the wind on my face.

I'm about to graduate from high school and go to college. I have applied to multiple Ivy League schools and got into four of them. I've worked very hard in achieving this and am very happy that my dream is coming true.

When I was at the park, I would sometimes see an old man taking care of the tree. I sometimes talked to him or he would talk to me.

After a lightning storm. I heard the tree got struck by lightning and got destroyed. I went to the tree and saw everyone in the neighborhood standing nearby.

A guy came up to me and said "Hi" to me and I said "Hi" back. He asked for my name and I said "Sarah, how about you?" He replied with "Julian". I asked him, "What are your memories of the tree?" He told me, "I felt like it was my safe space. I grew up with the tree being a big part of my life." Then he asked me what were my memories of the tree. I responded with "I used to study at this tree and to relax."

Kalaya

by Kalaya Hillian

I dated Luis for 4 years. We had dated since we were 11. Sadly he passed away and I continue to visit the tree where we had our first kiss and we carved our names in the tree. I've been visiting it for the past few months with my best friend Maryolin and I would always bring flowers. It hurts me to go there but I can't stop because it reminds me of him. I told my best friend, Maryolin, that sometimes I wished that the tree wasn't there, as if it was gone.

One Sunday around 1:00 pm, I went to the tree as I normally do and my best friend Maryolin canceled on me once again. She'd been distant lately and I wasn't sure why. I came to the tree flowers in my hands, daisies to be specific, his favorite flowers because they were my favorite flowers. I loved daisies, especially the daisies that surrounded the old tree. I laid my blanket down next to the tree and placed the flowers underneath where we carved our names. I sat down, opened a book and began to write, thinking about all the ways that this tree was important to me and my community.

A few days later, I visited the tree again but this time, it didn't look the same. I saw that the tree has been stuck with lightning and it was burning. I could tell because my father used to plant trees and he taught me a lot about trees and I've seen what lightning does to trees . I still hadn't really heard from Maryolin. It was Monday around 1:00pm. I heard a voice and I turned around to see my best friend, Maryolin, screaming "KALAYA!". She seemed livid as if I had done something wrong. She got up to the tree and started yelling at me while crying "KALAYA WHY WOULD YOU BURN

64

DOWN THE TREE?!!" "I didn't burn down the tree, Maryolin. It was struck by lightning." I told her in a calm voice.

"DONT LIE TO ME! YOU TOLD ME THAT YOU WISHED THAT IT WAS GONE BECAUSE IT REMINDED YOU OF HIM." I couldn't believe she would think that I did this to the tree. "YOU KNOW WHAT THAT TREE MEANT TO ME, KALAYA! YOU KNOW WHAT IT MEANT TO US!" she said. "I'm not lying to you, it was struck by lightning."

A friend saw us arguing while the tree burned. She tried to get us to stop arguing. She called 911 and a few minutes later firefighters came and so did the cops. They arrested me and Maryolin because they thought we started the fire and because we were arguing. We were not compliant when the cops tried to arrest us.

Yesenia
by Yesenia Aguilar

My name is Yesenia Aguilar. In my neighborhood there is a big tree and that big tree was my favorite tree and Maryolin's and Kalaya's. We've all played on the tree when we were little. I've loved that tree because that was the tree were my mom and my dad became boyfriend and girlfriend. In that tree my dad asked my mom out and that was my favorite tree since I was little. I always like to be honest with everyone until one way I was honest with Maryolin. I came up to Maryolin and I told I heard Kalaya and her boyfriend broke up and I also told her that I saw Kalaya heading to the tree were Kalaya and her boyfriend carved their initials in the tree. The reason why they carved their initials in that tree was because that tree was where they met and when I told Maryolin that Kalaya was heading to that tree she FREAKED OUT she said "SHE IS PROBABLY GOING TO TRY TO BURN THAT TREE, SHE CAN'T BURN THAT TREE THAT'S MY CHILDHOOD TREE!!!" Maryolin headed out her house running to the tree I followed her because I knew something was going to go wrong because that was Maryolin's favorite tree, she ran for 3 minutes and then she stop because we heard a loud BOOM! We got there at the tree and we saw the tree burning and we saw Kalaya all worried and nervous. Maryolin's reaction when she saw the tree was shocking she started screaming "KALAYA WHAT DID YOU DO WHY DID YOU BURN THE TREE???" Kalaya said, "What are you talking about? The lighting got on the tree and caused it to burn it!" Maryolin said, "STOP LYING YOU BURN IT BECAUSE YOU AND YOUR BOYFRIEND CARVED

66

YOUR INITIALS IN IT AND Y'ALL JUST BROKE UP!!
YOU HAD NO RIGHT TO BURN THE TREE! WHAT IS
WRONG WITH YOU!?"

When I heard them screaming I tried to stop them from arguing and I couldn't. I called 911 because the tree was burning. I was going to throw water at the tree because I didn't know how to stop the fire. But then I remember 4 years ago I had studied about being a firefighter and learned to not put water intently in the flame because it is just gonna make the fire get bigger and it's going to cause more danger. A few minutes later the firefighters came and the cops did too and they arrested Mayolin and Kalaya because the thought they burned the tree and because they started fighting and both of them disrespected the police.

Maze

by Maze Agbonhese

Since I was little I've always liked to be by myself, it's peaceful and quiet but that peace gets disturbed by my own thoughts. I was raised by parents who believe that friends are just distractions that shouldn't be a priority, so I also started to think that way too. I even gave myself a moral code: "never show, never fail." I still believe in that and remind myself of it any chance I get. That's why, to this day, I still question how I ended up in this situation.

At the beginning of this year, I became very close with three girls. I attended school with Maryolin, Kalaya, and Yesenia. Our favorite hang out spot was this big tree but recently, that tree has turned into a war zone. A few days ago, Maryolin and Kalaya were on their way to the tree, but to their surprise, there was a huge crack down the tree's trunk and burn marks. I remember getting a text from Kalaya that day that said, "Come to the tree ASAP!!!!" I rushed to the tree as fast as I could. When I got there it wasn't just Maryolin and Kalaya, Yesenia was there, too. I was expecting to see warm smiles and hear laughter but I couldn't be more wrong. Maryolin and Kayla were arguing with each other and Yesenia was trying to separate them. I was so confused that I just ended up watching with no idea of what to do. A few minutes passed by and Yesenia and I were able to calm them both down so they could tell us what all the fuss was about.

Maryolin immediately blamed Kayla for what happened to the tree saying that Kayla hurt the tree because she was angry with her boyfriend and took it out on the tree. Kayla replied back with "Just shut up you don't know what you're talking about." I quickly realized what was happening so I got up and left. This kind fo drama was exactly what I warned myself not to do. I stayed away from them for a while to hide the fact I was actually really upset about the tree but more upset that my friends wanted to go at each other's throats right now. I even heard the police were involved too. That just gave me another reason to stay away. A week passed since the incident and I missed them, so I finally picked up my phone and asked them all to meet by the old burned tree and chat, and let's just say that day was the best.

Max

by Max Anagnos

10 years ago, I used to be just like the rest: poor. But from a young age, I always knew I would be rich; to be free from the fate of indefinitely slaving away at a job for inadequate wages which everyone else would be subjected to. After graduating from high school I started multiple businesses, and over a few years became extremely wealthy. I am now able to go anywhere I wish whenever I want in my private jet, and I have bought nearly a dozen mansions in multiple countries around the world.

As I talk to the construction workers who are currently working on building my 12th mansion, they quickly inform me of a big problem. Part of a counter of the mansion requires a specific, very rare type of wood which they have not been able to find elsewhere. My personal assistant reminds me that I have a meeting with some friends in Washington. As I climb into my Bugatti to drive to the airport to get on my private jet, I tell them to keep looking for places this tree can be found around the world. Right before landing, I receive word that the wood I need has been located in a big tree in Annapolis, so I promptly contact the mayor and ask about the tree. He tells me that many people in the vicinity really love that tree, and he won't be able to do anything to the tree without losing a sizable number of votes in the coming election. A natural cause would have to bring down the tree.

After the meeting with some of my business associates, I get one to charter me a special plane loaded with silver iodide and have it fly over Annapolis, and I tell one of my hired servants to drive to the tree and place a copper rod on top. A perfect natural cause. A while later from my 7 star hotel I see in the distance through the midnight sky a massive lightning strike hitting what I could only assume to be the tree. My assistant, who was in the vicinity, extinguishes the fire and confirms that the tree had been greatly damaged.

The next day I call up the mayor and inform him that the tree has conveniently been damaged by a lightning strike, and tell him I'll donate $1 million to his campaign once I am able to hire someone to harvest the wood I need without interference. Very bribable. With this superb campaign the peons will surely vote for him again, and his corruption will be easily accessible for me in the future.

Before another important meeting my assistant tells me of a mob organized by a significantly poorer rich man, who have been protesting against the removal of the tree for hours. He personally wants to keep the tree there to improve the value of his properties in the area. He sends me a message saying that I will regret trying to destroy the tree. Instead of being at their 9 to 5 jobs where they belong, these brokies are protesting over some tree and arguing over what to do with it. Everyone in the mob is arguing over what to do with the tree. The woodcutters I contracted won't be able to disperse the crowd, and I can't get my bodyguards or the police to intervene.

The next day I am informed that there was an old man who used to care for the tree, and he just died from a heart attack or something. An associate tells me that someone wants to carve the tree into a bench. Since it would leave enough wood behind, I have no objection, and tell an associate to collect the leftover wood and ship it to the construction guys.

Richard

by William Lopez-Escobar

I´m Richard. I grew up poor. I always loved to help out my community even though I wasn't the richest person there. But all of a sudden I was offered a job at a community organization as a reward for my donations to the poor. When I arrived there I was greeted with many people and they wanted to advocate about poverty. As the years went on I was recognized for my speeches and I started to receive money. As a result of this. I became one of the top richest men for my speeches.

I'm now a businessman who is trying to save a tree that was struck by lightning so a rich man doesn't cut it up and make a house out of it. I heard on the news that a rich man was trying to cut down the tree and was close to my location. I then interacted with the man and told him to stop his evil plan "before you regret it." As I said this, I provoked him and he sent people to cut up the tree ASAP. I decided to organize a protest, which got much bigger than I expected. People started to shout and scream about the tree.

James

By James Kendrick

I've never been good with people. I don't look them in the eyes when I talk and I don't look at them when they talk. My parents say that's rude. My parents say that I should look them in the eyes to be polite. But the old man doesn't mind. I met him a couple months ago. I was on a morning walk when I saw him watering the town's tree. He must have seen me cause he called me over in some language. I didn't know why I was compelled to but I walked over to him. I helped him take care of the tree from then on out. He doesn't speak much English to begin with so he doesn't mind that I don't talk with him. Then, all of a sudden, he stopped showing up. Apparently he was admitted to hospice care. Without him, I started to water the tree by myself every morning and afternoon. I didn't mind but it didn't feel right without him.

Then the storm happened. The tree was split down the middle with lighting. The tree had lost half of its leaves and the bark was now a pale gray from ash and death. I'm glad the old man wasn't there to see it, he would have been heart broken. It turns out his heart really did break. The old man managed to leave the hospice he was staying at to water the tree but found it ruined. It's rumored that he died of a heart attack on the spot. Out of respect for the family, I decided to go to the funeral. When I went to his funeral I didn't talk with anyone, let alone look them in the eyes. I started to take care of the tree by myself, I placed new soil, uprooted weeds, and gave it fresh water and fertilizer all in a hopeful attempt to keep it alive. It was back to just me again, but this time it didn't feel right.

That's when all the people started to show up. A bunch of people from the town started showing up at the tree leaving gifts and planting new flowers, some just came to argue about what to do with it now. But I couldn't believe my eyes. Everyone before wanted nothing to do with this tree and even wanted to uproot it, at least that's what I heard.

I guess someone must have seen me because they started to wave me over. When I didn't move they walked over to me without hesitation. They started to talk to me asking me if I was the one always watering the tree and talking with old man. Apparently she was the hospice nurse who took care of him. I simply nodded to her questions without looking at her eyes. She started to usher me towards the others at the tree. I started to sweat as everyone started to ask me questions and talk to me. I only nodded and shook my head. This became the usual after a couple days. I got more used to it and even managed to talk to a few people about gardening tips. One of the days, an old Jewish man noticed I was anxious and grabbed my hand in an attempt to calm me. And that's when I noticed it, everyone, after a long time finally had started to get along.

Elvis

by Elvis Alfaro-Bonilla

Having a nice family. I am sad because the trees have lightning and my friends helped me. I feel lonely because I don't have friends. Then, I started to make no friends and I started crying for having no friends. Afterwards, the teacher said I was crying a lot in school because I have no friends and my mom is saying, "Why are you crying?" Last, people wanted to be friends with me and they said yes, so that means I have friends and I will be so happy that I have friends. The tree will make me happy because I have friends. My family said that I have friends and they said making friends is very important for everyone. Everyone is listening to me because it is important to have friends. The tree has friends but not in real life. When I was younger, I had friends at elementary school. Everyone likes me because I don't want to be alone right now. The tree helps me to make friends. I don't feel alone because I like to make friends with everybody. The tree helped my friends because everyone knows me. Then, I was outside walking and I saw my neighbor and I said hi to him. I like the tree because it helps me survive the Earth.

Romie

by Eromose Longe

I have a lot of time on my hands, but my Nigerian dad makes it so that I don't, by finding something for me to do. Heck, I often forget where to go when I have too much to do. So I try to organize all the things I do, resulting in a horrendous perception of time. After doing dishes one night, I was washing and folding clothes, and talking with some friends on my phone. But while everyone was sound asleep, I heard a massive boom nearby... and my first instinct was to put a hoodie and a pair of shoes on, and pop out of the window to check it out. Without even realizing, I was the first (or so I thought). There it was. A giant old oak tree, split in half like a 2 of diamonds. "Woah... what happened?" A vivid flash of light fills the night sky and seconds later, BAM! A thunderstrike then brought upon me my answer. I took a picture just in case I needed to prove an unbelievable story. I then left and slept soundly. Interrupting my 5-and-soon-to-be-9 hour sleep, My father busts into my room; "Hey guys? People are gathering outside." Then, both me and my brother hopped out of our beds, and put some clothes on, and went outside.

The look on everybody's faces were confusing. They looked... distraught? I wondered why people had such negative expressions on their faces. Turns out people were deeply connected with the tree. Looking back at last night, I did notice cupid carvings on the tree. Quite a lot of them actually. Considering that I didn't really have a connection to the tree, I felt left out.

But what happened next was painful. People then started to clear a path. An old man showed up, distressed. I knew that he had watched over the tree for ages, but that was something I also could never wrap my head around at the moment. The old man fell to the ground and went into cardiac arrest. And I just stood there. Petrified like I saw Medusa. And not to sound comical, but my body thought it was a good idea to widen my field of vision. I didn't feel left out anymore. It was like my chest started constricting itself. I grew short of breath. See, I don't have a connection to the tree… but I did have a connection to the old man. When my dad was back home, and I was too young to take care of myself, my mom would ask the old man to watch over and take care of me. After I knew how much the old man loved the giant tree, I knew I had to repay him. The only problem I had… was figuring out how.

Kadiann

by Kadiann Isaacs

When I was 13, a lady saw me eating a hot dog in an alley, and she went up to me and said, "Hello there, young lady, may I ask why you are sitting here all alone? You know it's not safe to be outside without a parent with you." I told her all about how my father had left me and my mother without a word, and how we couldn't pay the bills. I had always told my mother we would be fine without him, but now we weren't, and I didn't know what to do. She told me, "If it's money you need, I'll be glad to help. I am a Surgeon and I make a lot of money." I was in shock. I let out a big happy scream and I instantly took her to my home. When we got there and I called my mother downstairs, the lady said, "Hello, I'm so sorry to intrude, but your lovely daughter here was telling me about the problem at home, please don't be upset at your daughter she may have told me but I was the one who kept bugging her to tell me what she was upset about. Oh, and my name is Kinsley." I said "Mom, Miss Kinsley here is here to help us with the bills, she has money and can help us pay off everything." Miss Kinsley then pulled out $3,500 out of her purse. She handed my mother the money and my mother bursted out in tears thanking Miss Kinsley.

A few months passed and my mother met this guy named Richie, the worst person to exist. The guy I almost killed. The reason I am being sent away to a mental institution. He's always been terrible to her. He would always lie to her about where he was, he would not comfort her when she needed it, and he was always ignoring her every time she spoke to him. Every time I tried to help my mother, I couldn't. Richie would always be saying that if I tried to help or call someone or scream, he would kill me and my mother. So I never did, I never tried to help my mother or scream.

Except one time I tried to help. I knocked Richie upside the head with the baseball bat that I used to play baseball with my dad but Richie didn't get knocked out. Richie stood back up and grabbed me by my hair and got a knife from the kitchen and threatened me and my mom. My mother told me that I was insane and I should just stay away from her and my stepfather. She truly loved him even with all of the things he did to her. She told me to go to my room and pack my things so in the morning they can send me away. I was sitting on my bed and was waiting till everyone was asleep so I could sneak out. Once everyone was asleep I left my room and went downstairs to go outside.

Since I had nowhere to go I had decided to go look for Miss Kinsley. I went around the neighborhood walking and then I heard this woman outside of her house around the corner of this park call my name saying "Kadiann? Kadiann Is that you? It's me, Miss Kinsley!" I rushed over to see if it was actually her and I was so happy to see her. She told me to come inside before I get a cold. She went and gave me a blanket and some tea. I had a sad look on my face and told her "I'm sorry if I'm bothering you Miss Kinsley but I really had no other place to go!" She looked at me concerned and asked me "I'm sorry Kadiann. I don't quite understand? Did something happen? Are you and your mother okay?" I told her what happened with my mother and Richie, and how my mother was sending me to a mental institution. Miss Kinsley told me that I could stay with her as long as I liked. We were together after that.

After a few days had passed and I decided to take a walk. While I was walking outside I stumbled around this park area and when I continued walking I passed by this big tree where I saw a little girl sitting under it all curled up in the cold rain. I went up to her and sat next to her holding my umbrella above her head and asked "Hey, Are you okay?" She replied back, "No, I have been sitting under this tree for a few days now and I had nowhere to go." I then told her that I have been staying with a nice lady who lives just by the corner and I told her my name is Kadiann and that I have also run away from home. She told me her name was Lily. I took her to the house.

A few years passed and I moved out of my home with Miss Kinsley and I had my own home and I had my own pets. I had found a job as a florist and eventually started my own shop. I was now 21 and I was in my room when I remembered that this is the day me and Lily are supposed to meet today. I rushed out of the house and went to my car and drove to the park. When I arrived Lily was already waiting for me. I got out of the car and I went over to her, we started to walk over to the tree but we noticed that the tree was cracked in half. I was in shock but then this woman supporting an old man caught my eye. They were both walking up together. When the man saw the tree, he suddenly crashed down to the ground.

Lily
by Lily Horning

When I was 14, I came out to my parents as gay and they kicked me out of the house. They told me that no one like me could live in their house. When I packed up my bags and left the house, I realized that I had nowhere to go.

I walked around for a day or two when I came across this park and this big tree that was in the middle. It covers lots of space. From that moment on I decided that I would live under that tree.

A few days later it started raining when this girl walked past me with an umbrella. She noticed me just sitting there soaking wet. She came over and sat next to me holding her umbrella over me and asked me "Are you ok?" I told her, " No, I have been sitting under this tree for a few days now and I have nowhere to go." She told me that she had been staying with a nice lady who lives around the corner. The girl told me that her name was Kadiann and she ran away from home. Kadiann was saving up money to buy a bus ticket to get to her dad who lived a town over. She brought me to the lady's house. When she saw me she brought me inside and gave me a blanket and some food.

A few months later I saw something, I saw a carpenter's workshop and I noticed a sign in the window that said Help Wanted. I went in. I looked around the store for a few minutes when I pulled the courage to go up to the counter and ask them for a job. When they said yes I was ecstatic, I started my job the day after that learning how to carve and build stuff out of wood.

Later in my life I bought a house looking at a tree in the middle of the park. Kadiann and I were planning on catching up at the park. We met at the tree, as always, but when we got there we saw that the tree was burned and cracked in half. That is when we saw a young woman and an old man walk up together. But when the man looked up at the tree he fell down. Later that week I was told that he died of a heart attack. I decided that I would make something beautiful out of the tree. It took a few weeks but I carved the remains of the tree into a bench. And I put a plaque with the old man's name on it in memory of him.

Chris

by Christopher Monrroy-Mariche

My name is Chris and I am seven. I always have to help my Dad translate because he only speaks Spanish. It's kind of annoying. One day we were walking down the street and we saw this broken tree. Some people were carving it into a bench. My dad is a woodworker from back in Mexico, so he wanted to watch. I noticed a lot of people were sad. My dad asked me what was happening. And I told him that people were sad because the tree got struck by lightning. He had this idea to carve little necklace pendants for people and asked me to ask them if he could have some wood. I didn't want to ask them for something - that felt rude asking for the leftovers because that was part of the tree that got struck by lightning. But I did it anyway. The lady who was carving was named Lily and she said yes! So we took the wood home, and my dad carved about 40 tiny trees and strung them on string. When we went back the next day, my dad started giving them away. People loved them so much. I felt more proud of my dad that day than I ever have. He knows stuff that makes people happy.

Brittany

by Brittany Villalta Mendoza

The old tree in the park was struck by lightning and an old man died. We finally are coming together to make sure we honor the old man. I've personally been wanting the old man to get some type of way to honor him, the tree was really important to him and I can relate to his love towards the tree. My Honduran grandfather is a very passionate farmer back in Honduras, his plants mean so much to him. When I've gone to visit I can see his love towards his plants, just like the old man, something not many may admire. Elders can have a long history with plants, like my grandfather. I know my grandfather would be so upset as well if something happened to these plants he has so much love for, and that if something were to happen to him, as a family we would make sure his beloved plants stay well taken care of in honor of his memory.

Many arguments have been going on about what should be done, but it's now time to come together and honor the old man. I will do my best to make sure this happens. I was on my way to see the tree when I also saw another girl there. I'm not a social person but I knew that in order to make this happen we need to work together as a community, so I needed to go up to her. I asked her name. "My name is Ariana," she said. After some small talk, I eventually told her about my plan to honor the old man. She felt the same so we decided to work together to make this happen, we would make sure to talk to people in the community about our purpose. The goal is to get as many people as we can to help us find a way to make the honoring happen. Everyone has their own story about this tree, many happy memories that mean a lot to them, in which we should keep these memories alive by making sure our community-wide loved tree is remembered, as well as the old man who loved this tree.

Ben

by Ben Browne

I come from a "rough" family to put it frankly. My dad was an alcoholic. My mother left when I was 6, so I don't really remember her that well. It was mostly just me and my brother growing up and we would spend time together by playing catch or we would play by an old oak tree in the park.

When we would come home each night, we would always hope our father was out of the house or asleep because those nights that he was home and not asleep he would beat us over the smallest things. He was always upset with us for no reason, we figured it was because mom left. I knew that in order to get out of this situation I would have to try to further my education. I always had a keen interest in learning new things and would often read many books when I was young.

When I was 17 my brother died in a car crash, and his death destroyed me. I struggled throughout college because I had to deal with the grief of my brother and had no one to go to because he was the only one whom I would talk to. When I came back to my hometown after college, I found out that my father had died while I was in college. I didn't know how to feel about this.

When I was walking in town I saw the same old tree in the park, it caused me to remember how sometimes me and my brother would sneak out of the house and go to the tree in the middle of the town to watch the stars. I could see that it had been struck by lightning and heard there was going to be a new tree planting in honor of the old one. I was taking in what I was just told, because it was one of the last memories that I had with my brother.

Once I thought about it, I decided to go to the tree planting because after I got a major in biology I knew a lot about trees, so maybe I could help out. When I arrived I met a group of people. Among them was a teenage girl who seemed to be taking the lead of the project. So I approached her and I found out her name was Elina and I explained to her my ideas on how to take care of the tree in the future and the best way to keep it healthy and strong. This event brought me closure about my brother's death. Moreover, I was able to use my education to help the town and move on.

Elina

by Elina Czarapata

Today my community gathers. We will plant the sapling in the park where the old tree once was. I watch as the people of our town come together all offering something to our new area of connection. We are all brought together to build the foundation for a beautiful community.

As a little girl I was always insecure, I was surrounded by people that didn't really look like me. I remember all I wanted was to be more like them. If I looked like them I thought I'd fit the standard of "beauty". I started getting body hair much younger than all the other kids around me did. That became one of the first things I didn't like myself for. As I grew older I began to collect more and more little things I didn't like about myself, forming this self hatred. I began to think that I had to be perfect to be loved. That I would only be accepted by others if I got rid of all the flaws of my character and physical appearance. I relied on someone else to affirm me. I let my opinions of myself be determined by what someone else told me that day. I let that control me. I was desperate. I was weak. And if you had asked me at that time what I wanted in life, well, I probably wouldn't be able to think of anything.

That lack of self-worth ultimately was what walked me straight into a toxic relationship. As I look back now I can explain what happened with clear eyes. I thought that somehow he could be a good person even though there was an endless list of horrible things he was doing to me, himself, and others. I cared so much for him to the point where I slowly began to betray myself. I gave up my time, my attention. I dedicated my life to someone else. I relied on someone else and that person constantly let me down. I was sad yet I couldn't see why. I led myself to not expect anything anymore, causing my life to crumble. It would've kept getting worse and worse as she would keep sabotaging herself in a relationship that wasn't good for her. But then a miracle happened: he left. And I was free. He left behind deep scars. Eventually I would be able to heal them through a long process. Though on his side was a short process of quick dopamine leading him down a deeper darker path. He was dead to me, but still his effect stung.

In the time of pain and healing I found myself laying at the base of a beautiful tree in our local park. It was a place I felt comfortable in. I felt comfortable letting out all my emotions underneath the bountiful canopy of leaves. But yet, instead of sitting in my puddle of tears, something about the strength of the tree and its support from the ground inspired me to pick myself up. I kept a little journal that helped me progress and day by day I slowly got better and better. I reflected on the things I experienced and I learned from the causes of my past beliefs and values. I began to grow just like the tree once had. I became stronger, but also I finally felt love for myself.

The tree reminds me of myself in a way. I was living my life separated from my true self. I never embraced it, when something caused that part of me to break I woke up, just like when our beloved tree was struck by lightning.

I used it as an opportunity and I planted something new and now it grows fully embraced and loved. Just like the sapling we have just all planted together. The tree in our community brought us together. Everything that happened hurt in the moment but in the long run it caused us to form much stronger relationships, not only with ourselves but also with each other.

I'm enjoying our celebration of planting our new tree, making sure I can contribute as much as possible. Everyone seems to be thriving in their own individual ways. A lot is going on and everyone in the community is contributing. We used some of the wood to build a bench to honor the old man whose passing caused us to realize the value the tree brought us. A florist is planting flowers, making the environment begin to feel so much more vibrant. Everything feels like it's coming together truly so beautifully.

I decided to use some leftover wood to make a little mailbox-like container. It can be a little place where people of our town can feel comfortable to express something they might be feeling or going through without any judgment. Writing down on a piece of paper and putting them in a little box beneath the safety of our tree probably won't solve anyone's problems immediately like magic. However sometimes just letting emotions out of our heads into the ether helps us to stop suppressing our emotions. Eventually we'll be able to understand ourselves a little more. Enjoying the environment around the tree is just so naturally healing which is why I want to make sure everything is taken care of properly. I met a neighbor who would be able to help me with that. Ben was a newly graduated biology student which was why I immediately knew he would be perfect for taking care of the town sapling. We discussed how we would maintain the health of the tree as part of our commitment to this new space. We both worked together to make a plan of how we will care for our new sapling. Everything that happened through our experience with our tree created the start to something beautiful.

Here I am now living my life the way I love, I know its purpose. I watch as all the people of our town stay joined together. Our values will grow stronger everyday. We all have our own ambitions, by taking the action to build a strong foundation of what ties us together we started our new beginning. Our town holds a great future.

The Writing on the Wall

A Story of Identity and Community

Written by Ms. Encarnacion's 1B GCC Class Spring 2023

Marce

By Astrid Amador

Soy Marce y vengo de Honduras. Mi vida en Honduras es muy diferente a mi vida actual. Yo vivía en una población pequeña pero agradable. Había muchas playas y tiendas alrededor con muchas personas amigables donde te saludaban al mirarte; todos eran conocidos.

En Honduras yo hacía muchas cosas divertidas con mis amigos y pasaba mucho tiempo con mi familia y amigos. Mi familia era muy unida y pasamos mucho tiempo juntos. Los domingos mi familia se reunía en casa de mi abuela. Los sábados yo iba a visitar a mis primas e íbamos a las playas, comprobamos sodas, comida y dulces para llevar y comer en la playa. Y nos reunimos con algunos de nuestros amigos de la escuela para pasar la tarde juntos y era más divertido.

I am Marce and I come from Honduras. My life in Honduras is very different from my current life. I lived in a small but nice town. There were many beaches and shops around with many friendly people where they greeted you by looking at you; everyone knew each other..

In Honduras I did a lot of fun things with my friends and spent a lot of time with my family and friends. My family was very close and we spent a lot of time together. On Sundays my family would gather at my grandmother's house. On Saturdays I would visit my cousins and we would go to the beaches, we would buy sodas, food and sweets to eat on the beach. We got together with some of our friends from school to

Los días de semana yo iba a la escuela. Algunas tardes después de la escuela nos reunimos con mis compañeros en casa de mi abuela para hacer proyectos de clase que nos dejaban los maestros. Todo era divertido hasta que me vine a vivir a Estados Unidos y mi vida cambió mucho.

Yo llegué el 1 de enero del 2022 a Annapolis. Y el 9 de febrero entré a la middle school. Conocí muchas chicas de El Salvador y sus culturas eran muy parecidas a las de Honduras y me sentí feliz al conocer personas con culturas similares a las mías.

Me estoy adaptando a esta nueva vida. El 29 de agosto del 2022 entré a la High School y me perdí porque la escuela es muy grande. Algunas chicas de grados más altos que el mío me ayudaron a llegar a mis clases y me sentí muy bien de encontrar personas buenas.

Tengo amigos aquí pero me gustaría tener más

spend the afternoon together and it was always fun.

On weekdays I went to school. Some afternoons after school we met with my classmates at my grandmother's house to do class projects that the teachers gave us.

Everything was fun until I came to live in the United States and my life changed a lot. I arrived on January 1, 2022 in Annapolis. And on February 9, I entered middle school. I met many girls from El Salvador and their cultures were very similar to that of Honduras and I was happy to meet people with cultures similar to mine.

I am adjusting to this new life. On August 29, 2022, I entered the High School and got lost because the school is very big. Some girls from higher grades than me helped me

94

amigos para compartir culturas con personas diferentes. Por ejemplo personas de diferentes países. Ahora que estoy en Estados Unidos me gustaría compartir mi cultura Latina. Y conocer nuevas culturas de Estados Unidos y otros países Latinos.

  Quiero empezar creando un graffiti educativo en la escuela y hablando de mi cultura. Quiero hacer un graffiti en la pared de la primera entrada de la escuela porque ese lugar se ve muy aburrido sin nada en la pared. Me gusta ese lugar porque muchas personas se reúnen ahí a esperar a sus amigos. Yo espero siempre a mis amigas ahí para irnos juntos para el bus y miro a muchos estudiantes más esperando a sus amigos para irse juntos. Yo pienso que es un buen lugar para que las personas miren el graffiti y miren las culturas de nuestra escuela.

  Yo tenia mucho miedo al hablarle al director sobre mi idea de crear un grafiti, tenía

get to my classes and it felt really good to meet good people.

  I have friends here but I would like to have more friends to share our different cultures. For example people from different countries. Now that I am in the United States I would like to share my Hispanic culture. And get to know new cultures from the United States and other Latin countries.

  I want to start by creating educational graffiti on a wall at school and showing my culture. I want to do graffiti on the wall of the main entrance of the school because that place looks very boring without anything on the wall. I like that place because many people gather there to wait for their friends. I always wait for my friends there to go to the bus together and I see many more students waiting for their friends to

miedo a que me dijera que no. Pero al final me di cuenta que no tenía porqué tener miedo porque mis intenciones son hacer un graffiti representando el arte colaborativo. Y al director le agrado mi idea y me dijo que si podía hacer el graffiti porque él también pensaba que se miraba muy aburrida la pared sin nada.

Quiero hacer una comunidad unida y más sociable porque quiero compartir algo sobre mi vida y mi cultura. A mi amigo Vicente le encanta la música y canta y es de México. Lo conocí en un parque y él estaba cantando. Me agrada mucho cuando lo mire porque me pareció un chico que sigue sus sueños y no le avergüenza cantar en público y eso me admira mucho. A los chicos de ahora les da pena cantar o hablar en público y a él no. Entonces yo le hablé y le pregunté sobre él y le dije que me admiraba mucho de él por el talento. El me dijo que a él le

leave together. I think it is a good place for people to look at the graffiti and look at the cultures of our school.

I was very afraid when I spoke to the principal about my idea of creating a graffiti wall. I was afraid that he would say no. But in the end I realized that I didn't have to be afraid because my intentions are to make graffiti representing collaborative art. And the director liked my idea and told me I could do the graffiti wall because he also thought that the wall looked very boring without anything.

I want to make a united and more sociable community because I want to share something about my life and my culture. My friend Vicente loves music and sings and he is from Mexico. I met him in a park and he was singing. I

encanta cantar por eso lo hacía y no le avergüenza.

Luego que pasó un mes yo empecé a crear el graffiti en la pared de la escuela. Tenía 1 día de haber iniciado a crear el graffiti y mi amigo Vicente iba saliendo de la escuela con su novia. Ellos miraron mi graffiti y me dijeron que les gustaba y que ellos podían ayudarme para terminar más rápido. Me agradó mucho la idea de su ayuda. Terminamos super rapido el graffiti y nos quedó muy bonito que los maestros nos felicitaron por nuestro arte.

Me siento muy feliz de haber terminado el graffiti con mi amigo Vicente y su novia. Y me gustó mucho el final de nuestro graffiti. Me siento feliz porque siento que estoy creando algo diferente en la escuela y a muchos estudiantes y maestros les gusta mi arte y eso me hace sentir bien.

liked him a lot when I looked at him because he seemed like a boy who follows his dreams and is not ashamed to sing in public and I admire that a lot. Today's boys feel embarrassed to sing or speak in public and he doesn't. So I spoke to him and asked him about himself and told him that I admired him a lot because of his talent. He told me that he loves to sing, that's why he did it and he's not ashamed.

After one month passed I started to create the graffiti on the wall of the school. The day after I started to create the graffiti, my friend Vicente was leaving school with his girlfriend. They looked at my graffiti and told me that they liked it and that they could help me to finish it faster. I really liked the idea of his help. We finished the graffiti super quickly and it was very nice that the teachers congratulated us on our art.

I feel very happy to have finished the graffiti with my friend Vicente and his girlfriend. I really like how it turned out. I feel happy because I feel that I am creating something different at my new school and many students and teachers like my art and that makes me feel good.

Emily

By Catherine King

Apparently I am considered a "weird" person, I don't talk to a lot of people which is fine in my opinion but not really to my mom. My mom is an extrovert which means she can talk to anyone she wants to and isn't scared. Maybe that was one of the reasons her and my dad got a divorce. She always tells me to just put myself out there and express myself but I can only do that through my art. Art is probably my best friend. I can spend hours just working on one painting and I would be so happy. I can be myself when I am creating art, definitely not in any social aspect though. That must be one of the reasons high school is so hard, everyone likes to get in everyone's business (not that I have any business).

I go to Annapolis High School and I am 15, probably one of the roughest times. Two thousand people go to my school and I have yet to find one decent friend. My mom is forcing me to go to this art thing at my school on a Saturday which isn't how I would've liked to spend my Saturday but we are making a graffiti wall. I am terrified. Not for the art part but just for the socialization part. Like what if people judge me, or I do something wrong to make everyone laugh at me. I think I might've always had that fear of socialization. For some reason I think that the world is going to fall apart if I mess up or make a mistake in public. This is how me and my mom are so different and how she doesn't really understand where I am coming from. She tries to be able to understand and relate but she just can't, how I want her too. I definitely would never show my face again, I would move schools, maybe even a state if that happened. Okay well that was a bit dramatic but you get the point. I get to the school and they tell us that we have to add to a graffiti wall and I instantly grow a smile.

I love just being able to do anything I want, using my own ideas and creativity. But then the teacher says "but you have to do it incorporating something you learned from GCC". My mind instantly goes into panic mode because I took GCC last year and I barely remembered what we learned because in that class I just worked on my art projects and didn't pay very close attention.

But I do remember one thing we learned and that had stuck with me which was about collaboration. We have collaborated in our class garden by planting with other people and learning about new plants. Also we have collaborated between different people and different languages, trying to come up with answers and resolutions to GCC topics. I think if I wasn't so shy and scared to talk to new people or frankly any person that wasn't my mom or my pets that I would be really good at collaborating because I definitely can listen to other people and think of resolutions. I always get mad at myself for being so introverted and shy because I am missing out on the "high school experience" but I never understood what that really meant. After I heard about this GCC component in my art, I really wanted to go home but there was no getting out of this.

I began to blank out my thoughts when I suddenly realized I could just do the most basic thing which would be people holding hands in a circle. That represents collaboration right? Anyways I am just going to go with my thoughts. Once I begin to start painting the graffiti wall I am not scared or stressed out anymore. I have my airpods in and I am just listening to music so I can't even hear anyone if they are trying to talk to me. That's what I normally do in school. It always helps me with stress and anxiety because music is impactful. I am in my own little world when I am listening to music. It's sort of a type of comfortability and it feels normal with it.

About an hour goes by and I finish but I just want to keep "touching" things up because I don't want anyone to bother me, but my plan doesn't work out . A girl named Lia comes up to me and asks if I could help her and give her some advice about her part on the wall. I stuttered but she looked like she really needed some help so I took a deep breath and I very quietly said "yes".

Lia seems like someone who talks a lot to fill silence which definitely happened. She kept thanking me before I even started. I didn't peep a word before I started because I was shaking so much that people probably thought I had frostbite. I felt like I was going to cry, and my heart was going to beat out of my chest. Once I start helping her I begin to calm down and then she says "Wow you are so good at art how did you learn to do this". I blurt out "oh thanks but I am self taught". What did I just do? Did I just talk to her? And why did it feel so normal? She seems stunned that I even responded to her but then our conversations keep going and they get longer and longer.

Since interacting I realized it was so much easier to make friends. Once I finished helping her she considered me one of her friends. Friends? I was so excited to talk to my mom about it. Talking and trying to figure out what would be best for Lia's art piece really made me comfortable and it made me realize that I can talk to other people and that it is okay to be nervous but never to degrade yourself for not being able to make friends. Lia was so sweet and nice. She made me so comfortable. Lia and I have become best friends. Lia will always be my best friend, but since then I have made some other school friends. Which is amazing compared to how I was and how my friendships used to be. Talking to Lia and becoming friends with her helped me gain confidence in myself and my painting. I can help people with their art completely now and I think I want to become an art teacher. Collaborating with Lia was probably the best thing to happen to me.

One day, I saw this girl named Jane who was so outgoing and social and I wanted to be like her because she seemed super nice. She went up to talk to me and it made me feel seen and happy, and by becoming friends with Lia it made me realize how important friends are. Me and Lia normally visit the wall just to remind ourselves of where it all started and reminisce about how scared I was. I promise that any time we go we always see people creating friendships and expressing themselves which makes friendships in lots of different ways. I am always so grateful for that graffiti wall because me and my life would be so different without it.

Riyi

By Estefany Ixcaco Sunun

Soy una joven hermosa como las estrellas cada noche. Tengo 17 años y hablo el idioma Español. Soy de Guatemala y me mude a Estados Unidos por la razón que no había trabajo en mi país y pues por mi edad era tiempo de salir adelante yo sola. Quería sacar adelante a mi madre y mis hermanas.

Yo vine a Estados Unidos con mi tía pero no nos llevábamos tan bien cuando yo estaba con ella. Comencé a trabajar duro para salir adelante, era complicado para mí. No tenía a quien contarle mis cosas, mis problemas, y me sentía sola y me sentía disgustada y sabía que me iba enfrentar si yo me salía de mi casa y de mi país.

Pasaron los días y conseguí un trabajo y pues había unos de mi país del mismo lugar donde vivía en mi país. Éramos compañeros de la escuela en mi país y pues me sentí contenta

I am a beautiful young woman. I'm like the stars at night. I am 17 years old and I speak the Spanish language. I am from Guatemala and I moved to the United States for the reason that there was no work in my country and because of my age it was time to get ahead on my own. I wanted to support my mother and my sisters.

I came to the United States with my aunt but we didn't get along so well when I was with her. I started working hard to get ahead. It was complicated for me. I had no one to talk to, or tell my problems to. I felt alone and upset and I knew what I would face if I left my home and my country.

The days passed and I got a job and well, there were some people from my country, from the same

103

porque pensé que nos íbamos a llevar tan bien como cuando estábamos en mi país. Pues no fue así.

A pesar que convivimos varios años juntos ellos se portaban de lo peor conmigo, me humillaban. Me ponían a hacer sus trabajos mientras ellos no hacían nada y me sentía tan mal. Dure en ese trabajo como una semana. Luego conseguí otro trabajo ahí me trataban tan bien y pues me sentí tan bien.

Luego comencé a estudiar en la High School. Era un poco aburrido pero hice buenos amigos cuando llegué. El primer día vi a Miguel afuera, cerca de una pared. El estaba poniendo un dibujo sobre un grafiti de su comunidad y pues me dio una idea de poner mi propio graffiti en esa pared sobre mi comunidad .

Luego de salir de la escuela me iba a trabajar y estudiar al mismo tiempo. Era complicado hacer las dos cosas a la misma vez. Llegaba a la

place where I used to live. We were schoolmates in my country and I felt happy because I thought we were going to get along here too. Well, it wasn't like that.

Despite the fact that we lived together for several years, they behaved in the worst way with me, they humiliated me. They made me do their jobs while they did nothing and I felt so bad. I only lasted a week in that job. Then I got another job and they treated me so well there. I felt so good.

Eventually, I started studying at the high school. It was kind of boring but I made some good friends when I got there. The first day I saw Miguel outside, near a wall. He was putting a drawing over a graffiti from his community and he gave me an idea to put my own graffiti on that

escuela con sueño, no quería hacer nada pero lo hacía para tener buenas notas porque mi sueño es graduarme. Trabajé, estudié y estoy sacando poco a poco a mi familia.

Ahora que tengo 21, estoy apunto de graduarme y me siento tan bien porque hice el mejor esfuerzo para sacar buenas notas y apesar que pensaba que no lo iba a lograr.

wall and share about my community.

After leaving school I went to work. Studying and working at the same time was difficult. I came to school sleepy, I didn't want to do anything but I did it to get good grades because my dream is to graduate. I worked, studied and I am gradually getting ahead and helping my family.

Now that I'm 21, I'm about to graduate and I feel so good because I tried my best to get good grades, even though I thought I wasn't going to make it.

Corey

By Decker Coale

My name's Corey. I'm just your average delinquent in A-high yet none of the staff expects it because I tend to pay people to do my work in class. I don't tend to have healthy habits, I can't help myself from skipping school and I'm only 15. I don't have any real friends, just kids I skip school with. One day I snuck out of my house with a couple kids in my neighborhood. The original plan was to go into the forest near our neighborhood and ding dong ditch,which we did. As we were walking back home we realized the high school was about a 20 minute walk away. Now it was only 11:00 and I had to get back home at 12:30 because I had baseball practice the next day and I needed some sort of sleep.

Anyways, my friend had a couple of spray paint cans in his bag.So I got the idea to go X out that graffiti wall at the school. I hated that wall. Everyone always talked about it like it was the greatest thing ever and how it helps everyone "cope." What a load of bullcrap. I just got tired of hearing it. Everyone acted like it was so important and helpful when really it was just a wall. So anyway I told this to my friends and some of them didn't like the idea so they went back home. Two people went with me to the school. I'm not going to say their names because I'm not a snitch.We walked to the school and it looked like no one was there, until a light popped out of the left corner of our eyes. Someone *was* there. He started chasing us so we assumed he was security or something. You could probably guess what we did next,we ran like the wind to the back of the school where the woods are, and we made it there. But I didn't have enough stamina to hop the fence. The man grabbed me by the collar. I tried to break free,but he was much stronger than me. Turns out it was a security guard. Shocker. So I got caught and the security guard had to call my parents. I was hoping I got a nice security guard, but no.

My mom came to pick me up and it was a rough car ride home. My mom said I wasn't allowed out of the house for a while. The next day I had to go to school and meet with the principal and he told me I was suspended for a month for vandalism. I was so angry. I didn't even mess up the graffiti wall. *I think* I kind of made it look better. I also had to go to Phoenix Academy, a school for special kids and kids who got suspended too much. I never got suspended before but I still had to go to some sort of school "because of the seriousness of the offense". That didn't make any sense. That month flew by though. I didn't talk to anyone, and my mom kept her promise of my not leaving the house. I wasn't allowed to even speak to her sometimes.

Eventually I got to go back to A-high, I was a lot more happy when I got there. I felt way more comfortable. I guess I was just glad I didn't have to stay in Phoenix forever. I also started to get "ungrounded" if that's a thing, and I started to think about the graffiti wall and how it looked kinda cool. I still vaped and got into trouble now and then, but I felt kind of grateful for my privileges. I stopped paying people to do my work for me and started doing it myself. It felt good. I also got to play baseball again but only for a little because it was close to the end of the season. I started to think about the graffiti wall and how it looked kinda cool and how maybe things got better because of it.

Jose

By Flor Palacios Pleitez

Yo soy un chico de 17 años, hijo de padres salvadoreños. Mi nombre es Jose.

Mi idioma materno es el español y soy de raza blanca. Mis antecedentes son salvadoreños.

Nacido en Annapolis, en los United States, provengo de una familia grande. Mi madre decidió viajar a the United States, porque pasaron cosas muy terribles antes de que naciera yo. Mataron a mi papá y mi mamá tenía mucho miedo. Se sentía muy insegura en su país y decidió viajar a otro país.

Ahora mi mama se siente mejor pero también la veo triste por la muerte de mi papa. Yo trato de consolarla. He hecho lo posible por hacerla sentir bien, hemos llorado y hemos reído juntos. No me imagino mi vida sin mi hermosa mamá.

Yo estudio en Annapolis High School y quiero superarme y darle una vida mejor a mi familia. Estoy estudiando

I am a 17-year-old boy, the son of Salvadoran parents. My name is Jose.

My mother tongue is Spanish and I am white. My background is Salvadoran and I was born in Annapolis in the United States and I come from a large family. My mother decided to travel to the United States because some very terrible things happened before I was born. They killed my dad and my mom was very scared. She felt very unsafe in her country and she decided to travel to another country.

Now my mom feels better but I also see how sad she is about my dad's death. I try to comfort her. I have done my best to make her feel good, we have cried and laughed together. I can't imagine

108

ingenieria y también estoy estudiando un poco de cocina. Quiero ayudar a las personas en lo que pueda y contar mis experiencias y valores que en la vida nada es imposible todo se puede lograr con esfuerzo y valentía que aunque hayan días malos hay días buenos también.

Todos en el colegio me dicen que soy diferente, que soy tímido y no hablo mucho. Pero yo me estoy preparando para mi futuro y a ayudar a las personas que lo necesiten. Yo trato de ayudar a mi familia y superarme yo y demostrarles que todos podemos superarnos. Si me lo propongo puedo hablar más, compartir opiniones más, hacer amigos y ayudarnos mutuamente porque no tenemos que cerrarnos en nosotros mismos. Todos podemos, tenemos derechos y valores en la vida todos merecemos ser respetados. Tenemos derechos, valores y dignidad para sentirnos seguros de nosotros mismos.

Yo ahora tengo un nuevo amigo y estuvimos conversando.

my life without my beautiful mom.

I study at Annapolis High School and I want to improve myself and give my family a better life. I'm studying engineering and I'm also studying a bit of cooking. I want to help people in whatever way I can and tell about my experiences and values. I want to share that in life nothing is impossible, everything can be achieved with effort and courage. Even if there are bad days there are also good days.

Everyone at school tells me that I'm different, that I'm shy and I don't talk much but I'm preparing for my future and helping people who need it. I try to help my family and improve myself and show them that we can get ahead. If I set my mind to it I can talk more, share my opinions more, make more friends and help others. We

Tenemos muchas cosas en común, por ejemplo, los valores, ambos tenemos familia grande entre más. Yo no hablo mucho pero estoy seguro de que puedo cambiar a ser más sociable.

Porque todo se puede, todo es posible. Un día cuando iba para la escuela junto con mi amigo vi un graffiti en la pared y me detuve a pensar. Me pregunte porque todos agregan cosas al grafiti y pense por que no escribo algo y yo también quise escribir algo de mi a dar a conocer un poco mis experiencias de mi familia y valores.

A Alex lo inspiró su amigo y familia lo inspiraron a hacer el graffiti. Yo conecte con él porque nos inspiró la familia a ambos. Y eso me hizo querer compartir los valores de mi familia.

don't have to close in on ourselves. We all can get ahead. We have rights and values in life, we all deserve to be respected and have dignity to feel sure of ourselves.

I now have a new friend named Alex and we were talking. We have many things in common, for example, values, we both have a large family among others. I don't talk much but I'm sure I can change to be more sociable.

One day when I was going to school with my friend and I saw a graffiti wall and I stopped to think. I asked myself why everyone adds things to the wall and I wondered why I don't write something too.

I wanted to write something about myself to make my experiences and my family and values known a little.

Alex was inspired by his friend and his family to do

110

graffiti. I connected with him because our large families inspired us both. And that made me want to share my family's values with others. When I saw that my friend was sharing the story of himself in graffiti it inspired me to share too.

Jane

By Beverly Sura

My name is Jane, I'm a girl and I am 17 years old. I am from El Salvador. I lived in El Salvador with both of my parents for 6 years. After 6 years of living in El Salvador my parents didn't wanna stay there anymore because they didn't earn enough money. I have 2 uncles and 3 aunts. One of my aunts on my mom's side lived in Annapolis in the United States, and my aunt suggested my mom move to the United States too since my she was living there. She had told my mom they had jobs that paid more than they did in El Salvador.

After a couple of months we moved to Annapolis, Maryland. I was going into 1st grade since I was about to be 7. After a while of going to school I learned how to speak English because Spanish was the only language I knew. During all my school years I was very outgoing and I loved making friends and loved talking. Many people loved coming to me because they knew I was very dependable and very supportive towards them.

Throughout all my years of high school I was in my last year of school in Annapolis High School. One day I was running late to school and around 7:55, almost 8 I was walking towards the front door and to the right I saw this wall that had caught my eye. I saw there was this graffiti wall that everyone was adding to. After I was done looking at everyone's graffiti I knew I wanted to add something about my personality, and that was because I love my personality and it was what people recognize most about me. After thinking about what I wanted to write or draw, I chose to write down the word gold and the words loyal, caring and dependable around it.

When I was at the graffiti wall I saw this person adding something to the wall while I was there and this was how me and her connected. We became very fast friends.

Bryan

By Erick Cruz Garcia

I am Brayan, I come from the state of Mexico, in Mexico. I lived with my parents and brothers in a very small ranch where everything was peaceful. I went to a school that was half an hour from my town. I helped my father with his work in the mornings and in the afternoon I went to school. Everything was fine. After about a year and a half I started to have problems at school. Sometimes I no longer went to school at all because it was so far away.

It was then that I decided to travel to the United States. I suffered a lot when I emigrated but I finally managed to get to an aunt who lived in Annapolis, Maryland.

I was 17 years old when I got here and I saw that everything was different from where I lived. I started working in a restaurant. I was hoping to understand what life was like here and my aunt told me that I was going to join the school to learn English.

We came to the school one day to ask how I could register. They gave us some documents and told us where to go to complete the paperwork.

The day I started school I was nervous because I didn't know what school would be like. *El día que empecé la escuela había un estudiante que me ayudaba a encontrar mis clases y después de una semana ya había aprendido todas mis clases y todo iba bien.*

One day when I was coming to school and I saw a group of students doing graffiti on a wall and my friend Alex was there. I went up to him and asked what the graffiti was about and he told me that one of the students made a drawing that represents the identity of each one of them and I found it very interesting. I asked if I could also collaborate on the graffiti and they said yes but I needed a drawing to add to it. I thought of adding some Roman numerals that represent the people who lived in Mexico to represent my culture. I like how it turned out. In the end I was proud to have contributed to other people and all the students upon entering the school were able to see the graffiti we had done showing our identities.

We all like how the graffiti turned out and how we help each other.

Liam

By Liam Conklin

I'm just another student that attends A-High. I'm a 14 year old boy, and I enjoy working out. I enjoy school, not really for the learning part, but to spend time with my friends and to go to the weight room. Just for me, one day blends into the next, it feels like each day goes by faster than the last.

That's until I saw the wall. It all started a couple months ago. I was walking into school just like every other day, but today something caught my attention. There was a little drawing on the wall outside the main entrance. There wasn't a whole lot of color, and it had to be only the size of a notebook. But I didn't really think much of it, so I didn't go over and check it out, but each day, the drawing grew bigger and bigger. After a couple weeks, the drawing was covering almost a third of the wall. So I figured I would check it out.

Instead of a couple big drawings, there were many small ones. It seemed like the themes were all related to community and identity, but each one was different and special in its own way. There was one drawing I thought was neat, and it was the earth, and there were people on the edge and they were all holding hands, all the way around the world. Which I thought was neat.

It seemed like multiple people all came together to add their own little picture. But there wasn't any description saying who or what group was doing it. So, the next couple days I was listening around in the hallways at school and I found out from a conversation two students were having that the GCC class was doing it. I had never heard of GCC before, so I looked it up and it stands for Global Community

Citizenship, and essentially they work on growing the community and relations with other people. I stopped by that class, and I asked them who can all add to the wall. And they said anyone was welcome to contribute, which I thought was cool, that they weren't gatekeeping.

I went home that day and started thinking about what I wanted to add. It took awhile, but eventually I came up with it. I was gonna draw 3 chain links linked together. With the story behind it being that we all need to work together, and we need each other to help one another succeed. Just like the chain links, alone, they don't really accomplish much, but together, they are strong and benefit each other. So the next day, I went to school with my supplies, and I painted the chain links on the wall. The GCC teacher caught up to me halfway through the day, and thanked me for contributing. I had a couple people come up to me throughout the week and shared that the chain links opened their perspective even more about being a strong and successful community, which I thought was cool.

Because I felt that this connected me to the community and I started to be more active with the wall. This is how I met Audrey. We both had gone to the wall at the same time to contribute to it. And we also introduced ourselves and I found out she didn't go to our school, which I thought was very interesting.

Roberto

By Jonnatan Donis Fajarado

,

Hola mi nombre es Roberto y me gusta salir afuera para jugar soccer. Tengo muchos amigos y una gran familia, me gusta la naturaleza, los animales, y los árboles. Me gusta la escuela y conocer mas personas y hablar con mas gente.

Vine a Annapolis de Guatemala cuando yo tenía once años. Mi mamá, mi papá, mis hermanos y yo venimos a vivir aquí porque el hermano de mi papá vivía aquí y nos dijo que viniéramos. Cuando llegué aquí, me gustó el lugar porque había muchos árboles y era exactamente como yo imaginaba.

Los primeros días en la high school me perdía porque la escuela era tan enorme como un aeropuerto. No sabia donde ir para llegar a mis clases. Un día iba a mi clase de ESOL donde aprendo el inglés pero no me acordaba cómo llegar. Mientras iba perdido, vi una

Hello my name is Roberto. I like to go outside to play soccer. I have many friends and a large family. I like nature, animals, and trees. I like school and to meet more people and talk to more people.

I came to Annapolis from Guatemala when I was eleven years old. My mom, my dad, my brothers and I came to live here because my dad's brother lived here and he told us to come. When I got here, I liked the place because there were a lot of trees and it was exactly as I imagined.

The first few days in high school I was lost because the school was as big as a giant airport. I didn't know where to go to get to my classes. One day I was going to my ESOL class where I am learning

pared con muchos dibujos. Me llamó mucho la atención una familia que alguien había pintado. Mientras miraba el dibujo vi a un joven de 25 años. No sabía si hablaba español entonces le dije hola a ver si me volvía a decir hola de regreso. Me saludó y me preguntó mi nombre. Le dije "Roberto" y así empezó nuestra amistad. Hasta hoy en día somos amigos.

Después de algunos días Alex me invitó a hacer un dibujo en la pared. Quería pensar en qué tipo de dibujo haría. Decidí hacer un dibujo de un papá regañando a su hijo por no prestar atención en la escuela y que le decía que se portara bien en la escuela, y que fuera respetuoso y amable.

English but I couldn't remember how to get there. While I was lost, I saw a wall with many drawings. A family that someone had painted caught my attention. While looking at the drawing I saw a 25-year-old man. I didn't know if he spoke Spanish so I said hello to see if he would say hello back to me. He greeted me and asked my name. I told him my name is Roberto and that's how our friendship began. To this day we are friends.

After a few days Alex invited me to draw a picture on the wall. I wanted to think about what kind of drawing I would do. I decided to draw a picture of a dad scolding his son for not paying attention at school. He was telling him to behave well at school and to be respectful and kind.

Joshua

By Josue Alvarado

Hola, mi nombre es Joshua y vengo de Honduras. En mi país estudiaba en el Instituto Gubernamental Cultura Maya. Actualmente tengo 16 años de edad y me vine de mi país a los Estado Unidos hace 3 años. La verdad es que no me quería venir de mi país pero yo quiero aprender un idioma nuevo y aprender nuevas cosas. En este nuevo país actualmente vivo en la ciudad de Annapolis con mi tía. Mis papás se quedaron en Honduras.

Luego una semana después de haber llegado a la ciudad de Annapolis, me inscribieron en la high school. Una semana después un día martes 2 de marzo del 2023 llegué por primera vez a la escuela y cuando iba entrando en la escuela lo primero que vi fue una pintura de graffiti. Muy asombrosa era la pared de graffiti y estaba muy colorida. Tenía muchos detalles buenos.

Hello, my name is Joshua and I come from Honduras. In my country I studied at the Mayan Culture Government Institute. I am currently 16 years old and I came from my country to the United States 3 years ago. The truth is that I didn't want to come from my country but I want to learn a new language and learn new things. In this new country I currently live in the city of Annapolis with my aunt. My parents stayed in Honduras.

Then a week after I arrived in the city of Annapolis, they enrolled me in high school. A week later, on Tuesday, March 2, 2023, I arrived at the school for the first time and when I was entering the school, the first thing I saw was a graffiti painting. It was amazing and the

120

Había muchas personas observando la pared de graffiti justamente en la entrada de la escuela. Todas las personas que llegaban la quedaban viendo la pared de graffiti. Vi que tenía un mensaje sobre los idiomas.

La pared de graffiti explicaba que todos los idiomas no son difíciles de aprender siempre y cuando tu tengas un interés por aprender algo nuevo cada día. Fue en ese momento que decidí agregar un graffiti en la pared sobre unas letras japonés. Decidí poner letras japonesas porque a mis amigos también les gusta el idioma japonés y el graffiti quedó muy bien en la pared.

graffiti wall was very colorful, it had many good details. There were many people looking at the graffiti wall which is right at the entrance of the school. All the people who arrived stared at the graffiti wall that had a message about languages.

The graffiti wall explained that all languages are not difficult to learn as long as you have an interest in learning something new every day. It was at that moment that I decided to add graffiti on the wall. I wanted to put Japanese letters because my friends also like the Japanese language and the graffiti looks great on the wall.

Audrey

By Kayla Eckert

Hi, my name is Audrey! I am 17 years old. I am a Cuban American from Florida. I contribute to my community by hosting parades and festivals to raise money for people who need it. There's parents with children, people with animals sleeping in homeless shelters, sleeping on the side of the road and even outside of stores asking for money to help them, their kids and their pets.

It breaks my heart seeing people having to beg because I know how embarrassing it is and how hard it is to ask because I was once in that position. I wish it was as easy as people make it seem to just get a job and buy a house because a lot of these people don't have cell phones, a bank account, an ID or even a ride. I hate when people see homeless people and the first thing they say is "They are choosing to be this way, why don't they just get a job?" because sometimes they aren't choosing to be that way. Some people can't have jobs because they either have a mental illness that doesn't allow them to work or have none of the things I listed.

One day I want to create something for people who can't work for those specific reasons. Everyone deserves to eat and have a home. Nobody should sleep on the ground or be hungry. We need to work harder to see less people begging for money.

I finally got a chance to show this when I found the graffiti wall at my school. I could finally show how much I care and understand by drawing on the graffiti wall and creating something that symbolizes these people. Finally

others in my community can see and understand as well through my art.

When I finished my piece of the graffiti wall, a man walked up to it and looked interested so I introduced myself. The man's name was Jowel Anderson, he then proceeded to tell me how he admired my piece because he was homeless once and he was happy to see that people wanted to help. Jowel was only 18 when he got kicked out of his home and had nowhere to go. He then said that a man found him one night sleeping on the sidewalk and helped him and invited him to stay with him since he was so young. The man who saved Jowel made him into a great man and put him on his feet and he is so happy that he came into his life. I'm glad that I had the chance to hear his story and to see that there are people like me who want to help.

Miguel

By Leoncio Flores Romero

Yo me llamo Miguel y yo desde que era un niño era muy amigable y me gustaba estar siempre junto a mis amigos o a mi familia. Mi familia es muy linda, es bien amigable con sus amigos. Mi papá trabajaba mucho para sacarnos adelante a mí y a mi hermano. Mi mamá era una mujer luchadora y nos cuidaba mucho. Mi tía había creado una comunidad con muchas personas y me decía "siempre unidos" porque unidos podemos hacer muchas cosas.

Para venir a este país sufrí mucho porque mi familia no tenía mucho dinero y me vine solo. En el camino encontré amigos buenos que me ayudaban en lo que podían y yo les hable de mi comunidad que quería hacer cuando llegara. Ellos me dijeron que les gustaría ser parte de esa mi comunidad. Yo les dije que me encantaría que fueran parte y les hable que yo quería una comunidad buena. Cuando llegué los busqué y

My name is Miguel and I have always been very friendly and I always liked to be with my friends or my family. My family is very nice and we have lots of friends. My dad worked a lot to support me and my brother. My mom was a strong woman and she took great care of us. My aunt had created a community with many people and she told me that we are always together because together we can do many things.

When coming to this country I suffered a lot because my family did not have much money and I came alone. Along the way I met good friends who helped me in any way they could and I told them about the community that I wanted to have when I arrived and they told me that they would like to be

creamos la comunidad y fuimos creciendo. Poco a poco fuimos una comunidad muy grande y fuerte porque siempre estábamos unidos.

Hoy que ya he crecido mi meta es crear una comunidad muy hermosa donde todos estemos unidos y todos colaboremos juntos para que sea una comunidad muy unida porque juntos podemos seguir adelante. He pensado que a mi comunidad la puede representar un grafiti.

Yo estudio en la escuela de Annapolis y mi primer día que vine vi en la entrada de la escuela una pared llena de graffiti. He pensado que puedo hacer un dibujo de un torogoz, es una ave que siempre representa unidad y es bien importante para mi y mi familia y tan bien puede representar mi comunidad y cultura. Es una ave muy reconocida por mi país porque es una ave muy espectacular y solo se puede ver

part of that community. I told them that I would love for them to be a part and I told them that I wanted a good community. When I arrived, I looked for them and we created the community and we grew. Little by little we became a very large and strong group because we were always united.

Now that I have grown up, my goal is to create a very beautiful community where we are all united and we all collaborate together to make it bring everyone together because together we can move forward. I thought that my community could be represented by graffiti.

I study at the Annapolis school and the first day I came I saw a wall full of graffiti at the entrance of the school. I thought that it could add a drawing of a torogoz. It is a bird that always represents unity and

en los lugares que hay mucho monte.

Hubo un día yo estaba mirando la parte de graffiti al mirar el trabajo de todos y mirando la pared de graffiti me encontré con una niña que estaba ahí también. El nombre de ella es Paris, es una niña con pelo rubio y muy linda y empezamos hablar de nuestra comunidad y empezamos a hacernos amigos.

is very important for me and my family and it can also represent my culture. It is a bird that is well recognized in my country because it is a very spectacular bird and it can only be seen in places where there is a lot of forest.

One day I was looking at the graffiti part when I was looking at everyone's work and looking at the graffiti wall I found a girl who was there too. Her name is Paris, she is a girl with blonde hair and very cute and we started talking about our community and we started becoming friends.

Charles

By Mikey Howard

Back in my school days I was not one many would talk to because I was always to myself. I wanted to talk to people but I wasn't good with talking to others face to face in conversations. Now I'm 26, far past high school and now it's super hard to meet people in real life. I believed if I were famous for something I wouldn't have to worry about making friends because many people would know who I am already.

I first started trying to become an artist by drawing realistic faces of celebrities but my proudest piece is a drawing of my dad. It was not appreciated by many of the people because these art critics were too picky. That is when I changed course and decided if I wanted recognition I could try acting and I was given many opportunities for different roles. I was still not recognized for my good acting. Once I was even given a spot in the Hunger Games but they cut me out of one of my only scenes leaving only my shoulder in the scene's frame. I began to lose hope in being an appreciated artist.

Things changed one day when I was walking to a museum for more art inspiration after my car broke down. I came across some people vandalizing a spot outside of Annapolis High School. This was the school I used to go to back when I was in high school. I first believed these people were committing a crime which is why I stepped in to speak to them. I asked "Why are you guys destroying public property?" in an angry tone. A lady said "I am not destroying the property, this is a community graffiti wall for people to express themselves and it's approved by the principal of the school because it helps out the entire community.

I saw many different pieces of graffiti art expressing how these people feel and how they can connect as a community. I saw many different pieces of art like pieces showing many different themes. I saw examples of ethnicity, collaboration and family, among others.

I saw this as a chance to connect with people who wouldn't normally connect with me. I purchased some spray paint and went to work on a visual demonstration on how I want others to be able to connect with me. I drew an abstract art piece about how sharing common goals, like a graffiti wall can help begin new relationships with others you wouldn't normally speak two. After contributing to this graffiti wall I now feel a part of something great and I can relate and speak to so many people like myself.

After I added to this wall I finished my piece. People began to understand my message and even appreciated my artistic skill. And a lady came up to me asking about this graffiti wall. Her name was Paris. I told her all about it and she told me she had a deaf sister who attended this school and she would like to add to this wall. As more people came across the wall the more people there were that wanted to help me. Even Paris helped by writing her number on the ground so we could talk on the phone. We talked for hours about what we had going on in our lives and how we can help each other achieve our dreams.

When you have a community or family for support it becomes a lot easier to achieve your goals. They compliment you when you are at a loss of confidence, are there if you need assistance and they care how you are doing. With the community I have joined and friends I have made I can ask how my drawings look to others in the community and get proper advice on what needs to be adjusted or changed. I can rehearse my lines for my roles in movies and shows with people with experience or that care. My art pieces are now being bought for good prices and I'm getting more important roles in my acting career. I tried out for an upcoming movie and after all of my revising and support I was given my own character in the movie who mattered. The movie was a horror movie called "Last of Grads' '. My role was one of my proudest achievements. This movie and my presence on social media like Youtube, Instagram, and Twitter and my pieces of art have made me a well known person.

This simple little art piece outside of a school has completely turned my life around. I made friends, I have fixed my acting career and my art has now become appreciated by those of good taste. I now have become a known person on the internet and a small celebrity in a way because of the support of my community. I am so grateful for this community and what they have done for me and am going to give back to those in my community with the money I have received as a thank you for what they have done. Hopefully I can help them as they helped me!

Ethan

By Leo Braley

My name is Ethan Rommano. I got my name from my mother who is from the United States and my father who is from Italy. I have always been unsure where my origin is truly from. My parents split up when I was 9 and my dad moved back to Italy so now I live with my mom in the United States. I still see my dad occasionally, just a month each year during the summer but that's fine.

I am happy here in the United States, I have some great friends here.

I got a job around 2 years ago at a fast food restaurant. It's not much but it does help my mom. She has been really busy lately holding many jobs and then also taking care of me. Not to say that we aren't happy. We have seen a lot of things here in the United States like when we visited the Grand Canyon, or when we went to Mount Rushmore.

I am a 9th grader and recently started to go to Annapolis High School. I have made a lot of great friends and I hang out with them most days after school. Recently I have been taking a Global Community Citizenship class.

We work on finding where we can fit in with others and to find what personal values are important within ourselves.

In my community we are creating a collaborative graffiti wall and I figured because of my very unique background that I can illustrate to other people how having a complex background doesn't have to be a personal burden and how it can help build themselves up for a better future. I made a person peacefully and happily rising upwards because it is like an angel rising above all their problems and ultimately becoming a better person from them.

Alex

By Pablo Hercules

Yo soy *Alex* y vengo de *El Salvador. Yo vivía con mi mamá y vivíamos en un rancho con mis abuelos y mis hermanos. Vivíamos muy cómodos disfrutando de la naturaleza muy apartados de la sociedad yo convivía con mis abuelos hasta que un día que el destino me quitó a mi abuelo.*

Convivia mucho con él, éramos una familia muy unida y vivíamos en el campo. Éramos agricultores y yo le ayudaba con los quehaceres del rancho a mi papá y a mi abuelo.

Un día decidí irme para Estados Unidos porque en el rancho no nos alcanzaba para todo los gastos de mi casa y en qué trabajamos toda la semana no nos alcanzaba para las necesidades Como familia decidimos buscar nuevos horizontes, nuevas oportunidades de vida en los

I am Alex and I come from El Salvador. I lived with my mom and we lived on a ranch with my grandparents and my siblings. We lived very comfortably enjoying nature very far from society. I lived with my grandparents until one day fate took my grandfather from me.

I lived with him a lot, we were a very close family and we lived in the countryside. We were farmers and I helped my dad and my grandfather with the chores on the ranch.

One day I decided to go to the United States because at the ranch there was not enough for all our household expenses and even though we worked all week there was not enough

Estados Unidos. Un día me dio una oportunidad de estudiar y prepararme para ser una persona con buen futuro ya que en mi país no tenía oportunidad de estudiar y en los Estados Unidos me está dando la oportunidad de estudiar. Pienso ser un buen alumno y aprovechar la oportunidad que me está dando este país ya que en El Salvador no tenía la oportunidad de estudiar porque mi familia no alcanzaba a pagar mis estudios.

Yo llegue a Annapolis el 1 de enero del 2023 mis primeros días eran raros y me sentía raro llegar a un lugar que no conocía. Pero todo cambió cuando fui haciendo amigos y cuando empecé a ir a la escuela. Hice nuevos amigos y empecé a convivir con mis amigos de la escuela y me empecé adaptar en Annapolis. Después de acostumbrarme a Annapolis todo fue diferente porque ya no siento raro vivir en Annapolis y mi vida cambió mucho. Estoy muy alegre de estar aquí.

for our needs. As a family we decided to look for new horizons, new life opportunities in the United States. One day an opportunity arose for me to study and prepare myself to be a person with a good future since in my country I had no opportunity to study and in the United States I could. I plan to be a good student and take advantage of the opportunity that this country is giving me since in El Salvador I did not have the opportunity to study because my family did not have enough to pay for my studies.

I arrived in Annapolis on January 1, 2023. My first days were strange and it felt strange to arrive at a place that I did not know. But everything changed when I made friends and when I started going to school. I made new friends and started hanging out

Un día que llegué a mi escuela vi a mis amigos y cuando los fui a saludar vi que había una pared de grafitis ahí. Veía que muchas personas estaban compartiendo su historia con la comunidad y decidí compartir mi historia con las demás personas. Agregue mi historia en la pared para compartir con los demás así como ellos lo hicieron y conocieran más de mi personalidad y mi historia.

Mientras hacía mi dibujo conocí a un amigo que estaba compartiendo su historia y comenzamos a interactuar. Teníamos mucha historia en común. Él tenía una familia muy unida igual que la mía y por eso decidí compartir mi historia. Más que interactuamos más vi que tantas cosas teníamos iguales

Al ver la pared de graffiti, conocí las historias de muchas más personas y eso hizo más fácil mi vida porque entendí que no era la única persona que tenía una historia así. Que

with my friends from school and I started adjusting in Annapolis. After getting used to Annapolis everything was different because I no longer feel weird living in Annapolis and my life changed a lot. I am very glad to be here.

One day when I arrived at my school I saw my friends and when I went to greet them I saw that there was a wall of graffiti there. I saw that many people were sharing their story with the community and decided to share my story with others too. I added my story on the wall to share with others as they did and so they could learn more about my personality and my story.

While doing my drawing I met a friend who was sharing his story and we started to interact. We had a lot of history in common like that he had a

había muchas más personas que compartían la misma historia en la pared de grafitis y eso me hizo mucho más fácil mi vida. Ya es más fácil convivir con las demás personas y conocí muchas más historias diferentes de otras personas de otros países.

very close family just like mine and that's why I decided to share my story. The more we interacted, the more I saw that so many of us had the same backgrounds.

Seeing the graffiti wall, I got to know the stories of many more people and that made my life easier because I understood that I was not the only person who had such a story. That there were many more people who shared the same story on the graffiti wall and that made my life much easier. It is now easier to live with other people and I learned many more different stories from other people from other countries.

Paris

Megan Sale

I first came to America looking for a better life. My mom paid with what little she had to send me and my sister Mia from Poland off to the United States. My parents both agreed to send us off because they didn't have enough money to support my entire family. They wanted to give us a better life and more opportunities. They sent us because they knew me and my sister would get along well and that we had the best chance of getting by.

I'm the eldest of 5 siblings, 3 sisters and 2 brothers. Me and my second oldest sister went to America to "reproduce and replicate our family heritage" as my mom would say. She kept my oldest sister Kas to watch my other siblings while I was in America. Supposedly, it was temporary and I'm supposed to go back. Now that I'm here, I don't know if I want to go back home. This place is my home now.

I started renting a townhouse in the Annapolis Gardens so my sister and I could stay near my work and her school. I got a job at Tsunami Sushi and work there as a chef, 11 to 11 six days a week. I planned on biking there every day to work. Half the money I make is sent back to my family in Poland, to help them survive. We lived in poverty, paying late rents and moving in and out of apartments to find something inexpensive. "The cheaper the better" as my mom would say.

While I work, my sister Mia goes to a public school called Annapolis High School. It's this open place with lots of programs and opportunities to experience. I'm glad she goes there, as there is a special program for those with disabilities.

Mia is fully deaf in one ear, and 75% deaf in the other ear. It started when she was a baby. She was born with one deaf ear, and the second got worse as she grew older. Her condition is called Pendred syndrome. She has to wear hearing aids to hear and even that doesn't fully help. I've found it super helpful to learn sign language so I can better understand Mia. At first, we could talk normally even with her deaf ear. But as time went along, her other ear only got worse and I couldn't always talk to her anymore. That's why my family learned sign language. We could understand Mia better afterwards.

Mia developed a skill of lip reading to help her understand people that she can't always hear. Sometimes I even look up to her even though she's my younger sister. I love how she's learned to push through her syndrome and use it to get smarter and understand the world better. Even though I look up to her, sometimes it was hard to communicate. I would get frustrated when she couldn't understand me, thinking she didn't care even though I knew she did. Occasionally I forget Mia can't hear me, and I speak verbally to her. Those are the hardest moments, remembering that she can't really hear anything anymore.

Some people look at us funny in public. Mia's hearing aids aren't super obvious, but they're still there. She gets super insecure, and has grown very shy. Although people think she's stupid because she is losing her hearing, Mia's really smart. She had to learn sign language at a young age before she learned to lip read, therefore the rest of our family had to as well. Not only did she learn sign language, but she also learned Spanish in school. Mia's always wanted to go to Cozumel and see the beautiful white beaches and gorgeous colorful sunsets. She learned both languages very quickly.

The way our Polish school worked was that you had to take another language to graduate. They offered a variety of languages. Spanish, English, French, Chinese, and even Italian. I took French, but I was never any good at it. Mia however, wanted to take Spanish. She's wanted to visit Cozumel ever since she saw a commercial of the beautiful white beaches and leafy palm trees on tv when she was younger. She also wants to leave our mother, but she hasn't told anyone that except me.

I've found that my mom has had the hardest time with Mia. I swear she's the favorite child, her baby. Ever since Mia's second ear started breaking down, it's as though mom has forgotten about the rest of us. That's another reason we had to come to America, to keep mom's focus off of Mia so she could pay attention to her other kids and her husband.

One of the hard parts about coming to America with just my sister is that neither one of us can speak English. We both speak fluent Polish. This is difficult because Polish isn't a common language spoken here, so it makes it hard to get around. I have to use google translate in the restaurant I work at so I understand which ingredients are which.

Mia's situation is worse. She can't speak to most of her classmates, except in developing Spanish to the few that speak it. She's a smart kid, but doesn't know English just yet. I've found that her easiest class is art class, since she doesn't need to speak any language to do art.

Even though she isn't comfortable yet, I know Mia will do well. She's 17, a hard age to start an English dominant school.

We recently went to her school one Saturday morning to take her SAT. Mia was super worried, because the test was entirely in English. It was like asking a fish to climb a tree, as Einstein would say. She didn't want to get a bad score on the SAT because English wasn't her first language, but maybe that was the case. I came up with the idea that she could ask for the test in Polish or in Spanish so she could understand it better. I've never been to her school before.

In the car, Mia mentioned something about a graffiti wall at school.

"I was walking into school yesterday and saw a man spray painting on the front wall by our main entrance. He seemed jumpy, and I just assumed he was trying to send a message to the school's staff members or something. I wasn't really sure, but I'm glad I just ignored it. The last thing I need is to start problems with a stranger." Mia said.

"I'm glad you did what you did," I said, "I'm sure I can find out more about this man."

"Thanks Paris!" my sister replied.

As I was walking to the front entrance, I noticed a man spray painting the front of the building by the main entrance.

This has to be the man Mia was talking about! I thought.

I wasn't sure whether or not he understood Polish, so I asked Mia to translate it to Spanish for me.

"Hey you!" I said, "What do you think you're doing? This is a high school, not an abandoned building! You have no right!"

He turned towards me, and that was when I saw what he was really doing. This man was spray painting a picture on the building. Mia translated my words for him, and he looked a little surprised.

"Yes I do! This is a community graffiti wall. The school opened it up for anyone to add to it. You're welcome to contribute." he replied in Spanish.

Phew, I was hoping Mia and I could figure this one out. Luckily he spoke Spanish so she could lip read and understand him.

"What's your name, sir? I'm Paris, and I'd love to help." I said.

"My name is Charles. Please help, I need all the hands I can get!" he said.

"Ok," I said, "I need to drop my sister off inside because she's taking the SAT. I'm going to run to the store and grab everything I need so I can finish my section. I'll be back."

"Got it, any chance you have a phone so we can use google translate?" he said.

"Yes," I replied, "I have one right here. Now we can understand each other! I'll be back, don't worry."

I walked off with Mia, excited that I might've made a new friend. We talked with cheer, eager to find out more about this man.

I dropped Mia off outside the SAT room, and walked back outside to Charlie, that's the nickname I call him by. I pulled out my phone, and translated that I was going to the store to get paints.

After I got back, I noticed he was gone. In his place was a phone number spray painted on the ground, clear as day in black with a heart next to it. I smiled, thinking to myself how exciting this was.

I dropped my bag of paints on the ground, grabbing the hot pink spray paint. It took a bit, but I finally figured out what to do. When I was done, I stepped back and saw the intricate and colorful designs I had created. Proud of my work, I signed my name at the bottom right hand corner.

Suddenly, I realized Mia would see my work. I didn't want that to happen, as I added elements of our family to it. She doesn't like talking about us, embarrassed by her deaf traits and how her family feels about it. It couldn't hurt to bring her by though, maybe it can help her.

I waited by the testing room for Mia, and led her through the front door to my car. As we walked out, I prayed Mia wouldn't see the mural. She did, and I was surprised how she reacted. First she looked irritated, then asked why I created this. After I didn't answer, she looked it over again and said she loves it.

Mia looked tired, but she went up to the mural and traced her fingers over our family's heritage. I'm definitely proud of showing her. I had to tear her away from the mural to get her to go. When we got home, she went straight to bed and fell asleep. While she was sleeping, I called the number left on the floor by the graffiti.

Charles picked up on the third ring, and we talked for hours (through google translate of course). I'm starting to feel more at home here already. Family doesn't have to be related, they just make you feel good about yourself. It can be anyone off the streets, even someone you just met.

Josue

By Kenneth Freire Noboa

Me llamo Josue y tengo 24 años, soy mestizo y latino. He tenido un pasado oscuro y delictivo por diferentes circunstancias como el manejo de droga entre otros. Por eso, mi familia me desprecia y me margina.

Cumpli mi condena en la Prisión Ferdera de Anápolis, saliendo dos años más temprano por buena conducta y me dirigí con el poco dinero ahorrado a una comunidad muy cerca del colegio de Anápolis, en busca de un lugar para dormir. Me tope así con una muy humilde y sencilla y decidí que ese sería el lugar perfecto para pasar la noche. Al día siguiente me dirigí a la sala en busca de mi desayuno y una niña muy emocionada hablaba de una pared de grafitis que se iba a poner en el colegio de ella. Yo pues sin darle importancia me dedico a comer.

My name is Josue and I am 24 years old, I am mixed race and Latino. I have had a dark and criminal past due to different circumstances such as drug addiction among others. For this reason, my family despises and marginalizes me.

I completed my sentence in the Federal Prison in Annapolis, leaving two years early for good behavior. I went with the little money I had saved to a community very close to the school in Annapolis, looking for a place to sleep. Thus, I came across a very humble and simple place and I decided that this would be the perfect place to spend the night. The next day I went to the living room to get my breakfast and a very excited girl was talking about a

Luego fui a comer para irme a conseguir un trabajo. En la sala de comida me encontré con niños, personas adultas, ancianos y jóvenes compartiendo también su desayuno. Me acerco y con una gran voz todos me gritaron "bienvenido, aca esta tu desayuno!" Al acabar de comer y tener una pequeña charla con algunos de los que estaban presentes en el desayuno me dirigí en busca de trabajo. Al despedirme así de todos con una sonrisa, yendo preguntando y preguntando en restaurantes y no consigo un trabajo pero me topo con un amiguito que ya creció mucho se llama Roberto. Fue un chico de 13 años que me tope en inmigracion. Nos saludamos y me contó que estaba acabando de estudiar en el colegio de aquí y trabajando para ayudar a sus hermanos. Me despedí y ojalá algún día lo vuelva a ver.

Llegando en la noche cansado y muy enojado el anciano y dueño de la graffiti wall that was going to be put up in her school. Well, without giving it much thought, I went to look for something to eat.

After eating I would go to look for a job. In the food hall I met children, adults, the elderly and young people also sharing their breakfast. I approached and with a great voice everyone yelled at me "Welcome, here is your breakfast!" After eating and having a little chat with some of those who were present at breakfast, I went looking for work. When I say goodbye to everyone with a smile, asking and asking in restaurants and other places, I don't get a job but I run into a little friend who has grown a lot called Roberto. He was a 13-year-old boy who I met at immigration. We greeted each other and he told me that he was finishing his

142

comunidad me pregunto muy amablemente si quiero el trabajo de conserje ya que el anterior había tenido unos problemas con las drogas. Yo, desesperado, inmediatamente accedí a tomarlo con una voz alegre diciendo MUCHÍSIMAS GRACIAS!! El anciano sonriendo se fue a descansar .

Al siguiente día muy temprano empezando por cortar los árboles y las malas hierbas ya que hace un buen tiempo no se daba mantenimiento y me di cuenta que había pasado un poco de tiempo. Decidí ir a comer un poco para continuar después con lo que estaba haciendo , conversando y contemplando la sonrisa de los más pequeños. Vuelvo a retomar mi trabajo pasándome así el día y recibiendo mi día de trabajo por parte de la recepcionista, corriendo muy desesperado voy en busca de mi adicción .

Todos tenían el conocimiento de dónde venía y el expediente delictivo pero les

studies at the school here and working to help his brothers. I said goodbye and hopefully one day I will see him again.

Arriving at night tired and very angry, the old man and owner of the community asked me very kindly if I wanted the job as a janitor since the previous one had had some problems with drugs. Desperate, I immediately agreed to take it with a cheerful voice saying THANK YOU SO MUCH!! The old man smiling went to rest.

The next day, early, I started to cut the trees and weeds since maintenance was not given for a long time and I realized that a little time had passed. I decided to go eat a little to continue later with what I was doing, talking and contemplating the smile of the little ones. I go back to my job spending the day

daba recelo decírmelo supongo, pasando la semana en mis labores una niña en la hora de comida en toda su inocencia se acerca con una voz suave y me dijo qué es eso huele mucho! Se puede sembrar las personas quedándose calladas se pusieron tristes. Yo en ese momento, muy avergonzado, me voy sin tomar mi desayuno y decir una sola palabra y prometer en mi por el bien de esta comunidad dejar mi adicción.

Pasaron los meses y conocí a una chica muy linda lo que me puso muy nervioso ya que hacía mucho tiempo que no tenía contacto con una mujer. No estaba allí a menudo debido a su propia adicción, pero rápidamente se convirtió en mi novia. Debido a mi adicción tuvimos una discusión y estuvimos a punto de romper. ¡Estaba tan enojada que decidió irse sin decírmelo primero! SI ME QUIERES TANTO COMO DICES, ¡DEJA ESA VIDA ATRÁS! Yo,

like this and receiving my day's work from the receptionist, running very desperately, I go in search of my addiction.

Everyone knew where I came from and my criminal record but they were wary of telling me, I suppose. Spending the week at my work, a girl at lunchtime in all her innocence approached me with a soft voice and asked me what smelled! At that moment, very ashamed, I left without having my breakfast and saying a single word and promising myself for the good of this community to stop my addiction.

Months passed and I met a very pretty girl which made me very nervous since I haven't had contact with a woman for a long time. She wasn't there often because of her own addiction, but she quickly became my girlfriend.

muy frustrado, respondí tartamudeando: "No sé".

Los dos no nos dirigimos la palabra por días, un fin de semana habían organizado la comunidad una comida yo ya reflexionado fui decidido a pedir perdón a ella y a la comunidad por exponerlos ante todo esto. Era tanta la confianza de dejarlo que desde ese día nunca más he probado ningún tipo de droga ni sustancia de ese tipo llevo ya 5 meses.

Un dia limpiando el jardín me dirigió la palabra una nina me dijo que si le podía dar una idea para poner en su graffiti, era un trabajo para acabar el semestre y el año, me dijo que podía ser lo que sea un dibujo pensamiento, frase etc. Le di una idea de una frase muy bonita que a mi en lo personal me gusto mucho la frase era, "El amor puede cambiar sentimientos y pensamientos", ella muy emocionada me agradeció y se marchó ya muy tarde. Muy contento me fui a

Because of my addiction we had an argument and were on the verge of breaking up. She was so angry, she decided to leave without telling me first! IF YOU LOVE ME AS MUCH AS YOU SAY, LEAVE THAT LIFE BEHIND! I, very frustrated, answered, stuttering, "I don't know."

The two of us did not speak to each other for days. One weekend the community had organized a meal and, after reflecting on it, I decided to apologize to her and the community for exposing them to all this. I was so confident to quit that since that day I have never tried any type of drug or substance of that type again for 5 months.

One day while cleaning the garden, a girl spoke to me and told me that if I could give her an idea to put in her graffiti, it was an

145

dormir.

assignment to finish out the semester, she told me that it could be whatever, a drawing, thought, phrase, etc. I gave her an idea of a very beautiful phrase that I personally liked a lot. The phrase was, "Love can change feelings and thoughts," she very excitedly thanked me and left very late. Very happy, I went to sleep.

Our Community Table

A Story of Identity and Community

Written by Mr. Cover's GCC Class Spring 2023

Leah

By Abigail Gorzkowski

Hi I'm Leah and I live in downtown Annapolis with my best friend. We are both 21 years old and one afternoon in June we received a flier in the mail inviting us to a community meal at Sandy Point beach on June 17th at 2 pm. We decided to help the community more by bringing food. We made my grandma's apple pie and her mom's potatoes. Community is really important to us because it makes everyone more connected and that is why we are bring our ancestors' food. When we arrived it was a very beautiful day. The sun was shining, the sky was blue and everyone was running, playing and enjoying people's company. We met 2 older ladies and they were the sweetest people we have ever met. We talked a bunch and we even found a small table and we sat together.

When it was our turn to get food I grabbed a Chinese dish that I thought looked good. I found out this dish was made by Millie Kim so I went over to ask her how it was made. I found out it is one of her ancestor's dishes and I loved that because she also cares a lot about family just like me. Then I started to ask a little bit about who she was. I found out she just finished high school and is going to college next school year which is funny because I am a junior in college so I gave her some advice about college. She told me that her goal for being there is to help support the community before she goes to a different state, so we went to ask the head coordinator if we can sign up to clean up the beach after the event and she happily agreed.

By this point I was getting hungry so I went back to the table and met up with my bestie and discussed how our evenings were going. I told her about signing up for cleanup and she thought it would be a great idea but right when we were about to go let the coordinator know she held a community meeting. At this meeting she explained to us her mission and why she is holding this event. She said that she is hosting this to bring together the community and make it so everyone was included. Then she brought out a student choir; they were all wonderful and it was a great show.

One little guy looked to be about 7 or 8, and he was fabulous. He was in the front and was full of confidence. Even though I don't know his name he really inspired me to go out and just feel confident about everything I do. I later found out he was an orphan also volunteering and he found his family at the event that made me even more inspired. At this point we were nearing the end of the event when it started to sprinkle. After that everything got crazy. People picked up their stuff and ran in the building that was nearby, everyone was starting to leave except for the people helping with beach cleanup. This also helped the community because it made the beach a cleaner and safer place. After the cleanup we all went home but I made lifelong friends from one meal.

Antonio

By Alex Jodon

My skin was balmy to the touch as the warm light of a morning sun shone through the window. The crackle of the pan on the stove filled the apartment, and the smell of fresh oranges and vanilla wafted through the cool air. An alarm in the kitchen began to beep as I was whisking the egg mixture needed to make french toast. I quickly dropped the whisk and ran across the kitchen to turn off the timer on the oven. I pulled down the door and the sweet smell of bacon flooded the kitchen. I went to grab the bacon pan before hastily recoiling with a hiss as I realized I forgot to put oven mitts on. I grabbed my mitts and set the bacon down on the counter on top of a towel and went back to making my famous orange and vanilla french toast. After dunking all of the bread slices in the egg mixture, I began flipping them on the stove. The Beatles blared in the background as I cooked, surely loud enough that my nearby neighbors could hear. Suddenly, My phone began to ring in my pocket. As I rushed to grab the phone from my pocket, I dropped my spatula on the ground. I checked the call, and seeing that it was from Sage, I answered.

"Where are you?!?" Sage yelled into the phone.

"What are you talking about? Where am I supposed to be?" I asked.

"You're supposed to be here at the Graduate Hotel in Downtown Annapolis. For the Sandy Point Beach Environmental and Education committee meeting..?" Sage

150

trailed off. I could hear a conversation happening on the other end of the phone, one that was not directed at me. Sage finally turned her attention back to me, continuing on as if she had not been interrupted at all,

"These committee members are getting impatient, and if you don't get here soon, I can't keep defending you."

"Of Course! How could I have forgotten? I am so sorry Sage! I'll be there as soon as I can!" I hastily hung up the phone, not leaving time for a response from Sage. Grabbing aluminum foil from the cabinet, I hurriedly wrapped the plate of french toast and grabbed the bowl of freshly made whipped cream. Running out of my apartment with plates full of food in my hands, I almost forgot to lock the door. Only later did I remember the bacon that was left forgotten on the counter, its warmth dissipating in the air without anyone there to eat it.

* * *

Pulling into the parking lot, I parked his car and dashed to the door, almost tripping over myself and dropping all of the food. The front doors slid open, taking much too long. I quickly sped past the receptionist and into the expansive room hidden behind the doors that sat on the far wall. Inside, the ballroom had been converted into a meeting room for the committee. Long wooden tables had been assembled in a U shape upon the soft, blue carpet and spinning office chairs had been lined on either side. Within each office chair sat a man or woman, all impeccably dressed compared to the casual outfit I had shown up in. The office chair in the center spun to face me first, and the middle-aged woman that was sitting there stood up and approached me.

"*Finally!* I was worried you wouldn't make it, after hanging up on me so quickly." Sage exclaimed as she gave me a warm embrace. "What's all this you brought with you?" She gestured to the dishes I was carrying.

"Well, I was in the middle of making breakfast when you called, so I figured I would bring the food with me, to share with everyone." I unveiled the french toast, and a mouthwatering smell flooded the air. I began to plate the french toast, unstacking the pile of dishes that I brought with me. The sound of twenty people eating filled the room as everyone received their plates.

"As I was saying, I believe that Antonio would make the perfect Head Chef for our community meal" Sage bellowed across the room. Nods of encouragement came quickly from the committee members.

      *   *   *

I felt honored, I truly did. I had been working my entire life for a chance like this. To be not only a chef, but a Head Chef? It was unbelievable to me. This was my chance to pay back the debt that I owed to my neighbors, and friends. The only problem was: What would I make? I had never had trouble before coming up with new dishes to make before, and yet for some reason, all my ideas had drifted away from me like a river. I started my car and began the short ride back to my apartment.

Hopefully that forgotten plate of bacon could inspire me while I ate it.

Back in my kitchen, a mountain of dishes awaited cleaning, and by now they were sure to be much harder to clean now that the food had time to harden onto the pots, pans and other utensils. It was only 1:45 in the afternoon and I already felt exhausted, but the dishes had to get done. At least the apartment still smelled of bacon and french toast. I began to scrub the dishes as hard as I could, for what seemed like hours. When the massive pile of dishes was finished, I finally had a chance to begin the long and tedious process of designing a new dish, just for the event. I had to make this food special. It had to have a *BANG!* to it. This would be my big chance to show everyone how grateful I am, how important their sacrifices meant to me. How much their contributions helped me grow to become a better version of myself. But I guess that wasn't enough to inspire me.

Stacks of dirty dishes covered the long surfaces of granite in my kitchen. Plates with only partially eaten and quickly spit out dishes, bowls with an array of soups that disgusted my tongue, and platters of plain, boring, and easily forgotten appetizers. *UGHHH!* Why couldn't I find anything that was worthy of this community meal? Everything I tried was either too plain, too absurd, or just downright disgusting. For the second time today, my phone began to ring in my pocket. And when I answered, it was just the kind of inspiration I needed.

"Hola Hijo, how are you?" An elderly woman said.

"You're actually just the person I wanted to hear, Mom. I've been having a really stressful day." I replied. She responded with the same worried voice I remember from when I was a young child, when I had just come home bruised, and scraped up from playing outside,

"Oh no, what's wrong, Antonio? Did something happen at your job? Do you need me to call your boss? Or was it your Apartment? Did they evict you Sweetie? Oh, is it that your laundry machine broke? Do you need me to do your laundry? Or did your car break? Do you need me to fix it or give you a ride somewhere?--" I cut her off with a quick reply,

"No Mom, I'm fine. It's just that I was chosen to be the Head Chef for the Sandy Point Community Meal, and I can't seem to come up with a menu to make for the event. They're relying on me to make the food for this event, and can't help but feel like I'm letting Sage and the others down. I'm still trying to make it up to everyone for helping me pay for culinary school, but I'm worried that if I can't come up with something good, then everyone will think I wasn't worth their help." I let out a deep sigh.

"Oh Mi hijo, you will not disappoint them. They all helped pay for your tuition because they watched you grow as a little child into a capable young man who is one of the best chefs in the community. They did it because they wanted you to achieve the dreams they knew would become a reality. They didn't do it to be paid back."

"Thank you Mom, I needed that."

"I'll tell you what– I have an idea that might help with your menu troubles. El libro de cocina familiar has been passed down through our familia for generations. It has recipes that come from my mother and my grandmother, from before we immigrated from Cuba. I'm sure you can find something great in there. I used to make these meals for you when you were just a little boy, who would always beg for seconds!" Mama began laughing to herself, reminiscing of the old times when I was still a hungry little boy.

"I'll be at your house in just a moment to pick it up!" I said excitedly. I finally found it! My inspiration.

* * *

After arriving back at my apartment, with the cookbook in hand, I began to flip through the pages, looking through all the magnificent, mouthwatering dishes that made my stomach growl. When I saw it, I stopped flipping the pages. With a few little changes from me, This meal would be perfect! I had found my menu.

By A'lia Ajayi

My family and I just moved to the neighborhood, my brother Mike, and my mom and dad. We were just invited to the community meal on June 24th . They also asked if we could contribute to the event in any type of way, so I'm gonna make baked mac and cheese for the event. So now we have to just wait till the morning of the event to make the food.

So it is now the morning of the event and my mom and I are going to work together to make the food. While we were making the food, my mom asked me, "are you ready to meet new people at the event?" I replied to her saying, " Ehh. Not really, I would rather just stay to myself. "Why?" she said. "Because what if those people are weird? You never know," I said, laughing. My mom said, " You can't just judge these people, you don't even know them. "Ok mom. I might give them a try. "Maybe," I said . Then we continued back to just cooking. Once we finished cooking I went upstairs to my room to change into some good clothes and get ready to leave for the event. As we're about to leave my mom stopped me at the door and said "make sure you at least socialize with one person." "Ok mom," I said.

We get there early so we can bring the food while it's still hot. As we're pulling up to the house I just see how huge it is. From the car you can see the view is so beautiful. When we get out of the car I stay close to my mom since I don't know anybody here. While we're walking into the house I notice how there's so many different types of people inside the house. My

156

mom and I go put the food where the rest of the food was. Then my mom leaves me alone and she tells me to "go outside and talk to somebody." As I'm walking outside I see a girl struggling to set all these things I guess are for a kids corner, so I go over to help her. I asked what her name was and if she needed any help. She replied "Yes, please." So I began to start putting together the toys as fast as I could before the kids got here. When we finished Jessica thanked me and I went back into the house to find my mom to tell her what I just did.

"Mom, I just helped somebody named Jessica," I said. She replies, "Wow! You actually talked to somebody! How did you help her?" "I helped her set up the games for the kids because it seemed like it was too much for her to do alone," I said. Then my mom says, "I'm proud of you!" You met a new person and you helped her out."

Once the event was over and everybody was cleaning up, I saw Jessica and she came up to me and said, "Hey, I just wanted to thank you again for helping me out earlier. See you at school Monday."

At the end of the day I realized that I made a friend.

Alice

By April Wevodau

The cupcakes on the table look almost perfect. Perfectly proportioned icing, perfectly spaced sprinkles, perfect bronzing of the cake. It's perfect. If only life could be perfect. I find myself drooling over the cupcakes and have to quickly stop myself from looking. I don't need any more sugar so instead I go to the salads at a different table.

I quickly grab a small serving of the salad and as I take a bite, I can taste the crisp, coolness of the lettuce leaves. I look out at the Severn River as it glistens from the setting sun. I notice the cars crossing the bridge as they zoom across.

I'm suddenly snapped from my trance when I notice a young teenager carrying a nicely decorated chocolate cake with frosting decorating the cake like a crown. They had short dreads and wore a blue sweatshirt, black sweatpants. It looks perfect. Just like the cupcakes. I notice an air of familiarity about this person. *Something familiar*. I suddenly realize that they also need a place for the cake. I decide to approach them

"Is that cake for the potluck?" I ask. I *had* to offer...after all, it was my job today. They nod in response, And that was all the indication I need to take the initiative. The teenager exchanged words with their parents as we started towards the food covered tables. I then offered to help them carry it over. After Jaime accepted the offer we brought the cake over to an empty spot on a cloth covered table. I helped them gently lower it on the table next to the plates of perfect cupcakes and bowls of brightly colored fruits. I softly slide it near the center of the table. They gave a soft thanks as I adjusted the now wrinkled tablecloth. I introduced myself, "I'm Alice."

"I'm Jaime," they returned. There was something familiar about this person, though I have never met a Jaime.

"You know you have a lovely name, what part of town do you live in? I haven't seen you around before?" I inquired.

"I just moved here recently from California so that might explain it" They elaborated.

"Well I think you'll love it here. Though, look out for this weather. It could be 60 degrees one day and snowing the next!" I Laughed.

"It's mostly just hot in California," they responded. Boy I wish it was the same thing here.

Not ready to end the conversation, I asked "Well since you're new here have you made any friends?"

"No, not yet." I was shocked. They seem like such a lovely kid. Something I used to have.

Now I know who Jaime reminds me of. I missed him making his birthday cakes from scratch not even using the mix boxes from the store, even if it wasn't perfect it was still good. I miss the crazy things he would say, the fun games and the unwavering optimism... and the mischievous smiles too. I giggled to myself. I miss the imperfections.

I suddenly remembered I still have things to do and so, "it was a pleasure to meet you Jaime."

"Thank you" they said as they left, and set off.

I traveled back over to the dessert table and observed all the cakes and pastries once more. This time I noticed all the imperfections, the creases in the frosting, the dents in the sprinkles, the varying colors and texture of the cake. It's imperfect. Maybe life isn't always perfect and doesn't always go as planned. I look back to where the conversation had taken place to see Jaime had returned to the dessert table and see them talking to Benji who is stuffing his face with the chocolate cake. Maybe this is what I need. Maybe having someone like Jaime around would be good.

Jessica

By Araaf Zahid

It was one week until the Sandy Point Beach picnic and one week before the last day of school. I couldn't wait because everyone from the neighborhood was going to be there and we were coming to do a lot of fun activities together. On top of that, we wouldn't be stuck in school with all of this good weather going to waste. I was heading over to my best friend's house, JP, after school to hangout when I saw a new family moving in a block away from my house. Though it was only a mother and a daughter that looked about my age. In my culture we are very welcoming to everyone so I decided to go over and introduce myself. She was busy unpacking so I went and knocked on the door. Her mother answered the door and called her down. Her name turned out to be Kiara and she was 16. I told her that she can be comfortable here because it's her new house and that there are a lot of people to become friends with. Afterwards I told her about the picnic and really encouraged her to go. Then I texted JP that I was going to also bring her over and he said it was fine. It was really awkward at first but then they eased up on each other and got closer.

Everyday after school would end I would go over to Kiara's house or I would wait for her at mine so we could get to know each other more. She became really comfortable with me. She had a lot of excitement and was a really fun person to hangout with. We got close really fast and we shared things about each other that no one ever knows. She told me that her

161

dad had left when she was young so she doesn't really know a lot about him. Though we were different in certain ways, we had this connection that I always wanted in a friend. On the day before the picnic we came together and met up at JP's house to prepare for the picnic the next day. We made blasted music and danced while making cookies. I prepared chocolate strawberries and JP decided to bring juice boxes and not make anything. At the end of the night me and Kiara left and talked more about what we are going to wear and do once we get to the beach tomorrow. She really wanted to go and swim but it was still really cold outside.

On the day of the picnic I brought my strawberries and Kiara brought the cookies. She was nervous because she thought there wasn't going to be anyone her age in this neighborhood but there turned out to be. When we got there I introduced everyone to Kiara and they were all very welcoming to her. Then I went over to JP because that was the only other person that knew Kiara other than me. They had a lot in common because JP also lost his mother today when he was young on this day. He wasn't really feeling like doing anything and was very quiet because of it. Throughout the night Kiara said that she was having so much fun and everyone was so nice and welcoming. We played games like volleyball and soccer and danced a lot. Kiara made a lot of new friends and got to know more people. We ate food and talked a lot until the sun went down and everyone left to go their separate ways. Kiara and I went home together and we decided to have a sleepover. Kiara was now a part of this neighborhood and knew everyone. She brought excitement and a new member of this community. Most of all it brought everyone together and made the community stronger.

By Caleb Lenham

The day was a normal day but there was something special about it - the community meal that was planned at the end of it. I was looking forward to this for many reasons but especially because I was going to bake a pie for it. I love to bake. I had enjoyed baking for a long time. To me a warm baked treat was like a cozy fire. It helped me relax and to wind down after a long day and helped me refocus my mind.

I just got home from school and was starting the process of baking. I grabbed the sugar and the flour and started to cut up some apples. I said hi to my parents and all seven of my foster siblings. I enjoy having a big family but sometimes having so many people gets on my nerves. I was adopted, and my parents had passed away a long time ago. They died in a car accident traveling from London to Leeds. I am 17 years old and have lived in Maryland ever since the accident, and I was adopted by the Clemsons.

The Clemsons are an interesting family. My mom was a bio engineer who worked for Abbott. My father stays at home to take care of all of us; there's a lot to do for 8 kids. I had previously lived in the UK. The community meal that we would soon be leaving for was being hosted by a family that lived in a house overlooking the bay. They had gotten rich doing some sketchy things but that's a story for another time. It was going to start at seven o'clock.

I had just finished baking my pie when it was time to leave for the meal. Me and my family loaded into the van. We had bought the van a couple years back. It was a relic from the '60s. It had some cool designs on it, but it didn't run very well. We were planning on getting a new one soon but we didn't know what type we wanted.

We made it to the house around 7:15. I went around back to put my pie with the other desserts on the dessert table. There were chocolate chip cookies and those gross but really good store bought cookies. The ones that have the frosting on them. There were also a couple of cakes, but mine was the only pie. I then went looking to find something to do. I looked around and there were a lot of options. There was Can-Jam and Croquet. The adults were playing drinking games in the further areas of the yard. After seeing all this I settled on a game of Cornhole. I went over to the Cornhole pit and started talking to the girl that was running it. We exchanged greetings. Her name was Melanie. She has black hair and dark brown eyes. I asked if she wanted to play a game, she said yes. We went on to play a few very intense games of Cornhole. I would get a beanbag in the hole and then she would get one in. I would land mine on the board and she would knock it off. The ending score was Melanie 3 and me 2. "Good game," I said.

After the games were finished they went over to the dessert table. "Would you like to try my pie?" I said. " Yes I would," replied Melanie. They went over to try the pie but it was all gone. A man approached and said,"that pie was so good that it got eaten almost immediately." I apologized to Melanie about not being able to eat the pie but she didn't mind. The day was wrapping up and I began looking around for my family.

The air was getting cooler, it was a bit chilly. The last light from the sun after it had set was fading. I found my parents and was going around saying his goodbyes. I walked over to Melanie and said goodbye. I then got in my parents van and we began to drive home. I began to reflect on the day.

I had begun the day waking up and going to school. I ended the day with a new friend. I had always felt like a bit of an outsider being adopted and from another country. But after today I felt closer to my family and better about myself as a whole. I started to feel like I could fit in in this community. I was happy that I went to this meal and was happy that everyone enjoyed my pie. The van arrived at their home and I headed to bed happy and tired.

Kinsley

By Catherine Kammeier

I'm Kinsley Wilson and this is my story. I have two daughters, Sadie and Summer, twins, 17. I love them so incredibly much, but they're a reminder of my husband, everything from their facial features to the way their laughs sound. Ever since he left me and them, a part of my happiness has been gone. I don't think I'll ever get it back. Some days I'm left wondering why he left, why he left our two daughters. What I did wrong, but here I am still in the bakery I built with him making cakes just as I was 12 years ago.

It's 11am and I'm just now finished with the cake I was baking. My two daughters Sadie and Summer were invited to an event for charity for the beach foundation, which I of course have to bake food for. Summer and Sadie occasionally help me out, but more Summer than Sadie because she is a bit more of a people person. We three have always been close, not the traditional teenager angst towards parents (well in this case, parent), but, we're always there for each other.

I'm not upset about having to bake 30 cakes, I do love raising money to help the environment, I'm just running low on time.

Finally, I get them all done! Well, 29 of them...Summer accidentally sold one to a customer, but 29 is still plenty. Thanks to the delivery truck, getting them there was so easy.

The set up at the beach is beautiful, the tables are arranged nicely and someone so sweet placed out napkins all around just for my cakes. Being here feels so much more like home, that bittersweet feeling I haven't felt since my daughters were five and it was a family of four. But I know it won't last. I'll leave here the way I felt coming, because nothing ever stays, it just washes away after I've become attached.

I walk around enjoying the view of the beach and enjoying the company of the other people volunteering. Who would have thought just being at an event like this helping others can bring so much joy. After everything is set up I look at my watch and it's 20 mins till everyone is going to start arriving. And there they are my two pretty daughters with their pretty floral dresses on.

"Hey, mom," Summer says in a smiley way.

"Hi, Summer and Sadie! How was the drive?"

"Oh it was good we stopped and got some more utensils for the tables." While Summer's talking I noticed how joyful Sadie looked. Sadie and I are very similar, we both keep things to ourselves unlike Summer, but Sadie looks at peace. Yes, not very talkative but less shy and more relaxed. Ever since I found that flyer the little boy gave to Sadie, I knew this would be the right event to go to. Even if it doesn't bring me that much joy I'd still be satisfied if it benefited one of my girls.

One by one, more and more people start to arrive. More food than tables. And so many children. One nice lady set up a game of Corn Hole, which has been where most of the kids wandered off to. Another family brought a football and the ball already went into the water. It got a laugh out of many when the dad ran into the water, and submerged himself, but luckily someone brought towels. The event is full of laughter and smiles and it feels like I'm in a dream.

While I'm walking I notice a kid forcing himself to engage, forcing a smile. I notice his behavior because I've had experience from Sadie. I go to introduce myself.

"Hey I'm Kinsley, what's your name?"

"My name's Sawyer" he doesn't make eye contact, he just plays with an old orange bracelet, tied around his wrist.

"Who gave that to you?" I point at his bracelet. He looks up at me, then at the bracelet.

"I'm not really sure, I've had it since as long as I can remember. I think my dad might have given it to me and I've kept it on waiting for him to come back." I'm sitting here listening to this poor kid, and I realize, how am I here upset over nothing while he's having to surround himself with happy families. I have my daughters...how could I be so selfish?

The little guy continues and says that apparently this fundraiser is connected to the orphanage. We continue talking and slowly his eyes turn sparkly and you can see his real smile seeping through. The rest of the event I show him around. Summer and he played Corn Hole together, then Sadie painted in the grass with him. But while they were having fun, one of the founders of the orphanage approached me.

"Hello I'm Emily, I noticed you were talking to Sawyer, are those your daughters?"

She points to Sadie, Summer and Sawyer doing cartwheels in the sand.

"Yes, that's them. Sawyer said he was an orphan, has anyone been wanting to adopt him?"

"No unfortunately not, all the older kids have been adopted but he normally stays behind and doesn't make himself known. He's happy with you though, he normally doesn't smile around many people." I didn't know what to say. Is this what I need? Is this what I was looking for?

I'm sitting at the table with Emily, Sawyer and my two daughters, they're all laughing and Emily and I discuss that if I want to adopt him, she would need to know that if I was the right fit. I think I am.

Everyone's gathered around the table, I've gotten many compliments on my cakes, which means more customers. Everyone in the community is happy and I feel so uplifted, so joyful. This feels like home.

It's August 21st, nearly three months since the charity event. Sawyer just finished moving all of his stuff to his room and he's now going to the same elementary school my daughters went to. Sadie and Summer are getting ready for college and the poor kid I knew three months ago, helps me in the bakery, and is so thankful for his new life. I'm thankful for my new life. From now on I'm promising myself to go to as many charity events as I can, because you never know what life-changing things can happen!

JP

By Chris Cruz

June 17, 2013, Was a very tragic day, it was raining and there was thunder. My Mom died that day. After that day I've always felt that things were not the same after her death. Sometimes I would cry because I missed her so much.

One of the things I missed the most was the amazing food she would make after I came home from school. She always had food ready when I came from school because she was home all day cleaning and tidying up. I've lived with my dad ever since her death because they had been separated for a while. I would ask my dad if he remembered any foods my mom would make for him and he would always tell me that he didn't care what my mom made him, just that her food was just so good, he wouldn't even pay attention.

My childhood was a very interesting one because my Dad would try to remember my Mom's food but he couldn't because he just couldn't remember. He would also burn all the food so a lot of times we would just get take-out. In school, I didn't have a lot of friends but this one girl turned out to be my best friend, Jessica.

Jessica was very nice and welcoming to me. Jessica was the only person who would talk to me because we both loved our mom's food. Jessica has been my friend from elementary school to our high school graduation. Now it's June 13, 2023, School just ended and I'm walking home. I started to smell a familiar aroma that reminded me of my mom. I saw a window open and I saw one of my mom's friends from back in the day. I went and knocked on her door and she opened it, she hugged me because she hadn't seen me in so long since my mom's funeral.

She asked me how I'd been and told her everything that has happened to me. After a while, I asked her what she was cooking and she said it was soup. I asked her why that smell is so familiar. She told me that it was one of my mom's old recipes that she had given her before her death. I asked her if I could try some of the soup and she said, "Yes! Of course!"

When I tried the soup, I started to cry because I hadn't tried my mom's food in over ten years. She asked me if I wanted the recipes for some of her dishes. I told her "Yes, Please!" I left her home with so much joy because I knew that now I can make my mom's food that I haven't tried in so long.

When I got home I tried one of the recipes and after I finished making it I had so many memories of the times when I would get home and have food waiting for me and my mom always had a smile on her face. I had an idea and I felt that I should go out and share my mom's food with other people who have also lost a mother or father and they missed their cooking. I decided to contribute by giving out food and copies of my mom's recipes to people in my community who have lost their mom or dad. I wanted to do this because I know what it feels like to lose a mom and the feeling of having to move on with life and missing them every day.

172

Two days go by and I get an email from my school saying that they are hosting a charity meal for a community fund called the Sandy Point Beach Foundation for Elementary Schools. The email says that it will be hosted at Sandy Point on June 17, on a Saturday at 2 pm. The email told us to bring as many dishes as we wanted. This sounded like a great idea — I could make my mom's dishes and bring them to the event and share them with other people.

I went to check what I could bring to the event. When I was looking through the recipes I found recipes that were about pupusas and Empanadas. I felt excited and I couldn't wait until the event. I decided to text Jessica and Kiara to come to my house to try and make some food. The last time I saw Jessica was when she came to my house to hang out after school. She brought Kiara and she told me that she had just met her as well because she was new to the neighborhood and wanted all 3 of us to get together to hang out. That day was a great day because we got along so well. When I told them about the idea of coming over to cook some food they said it was a great idea.

When they came over I asked them what they wanted to make and Jessica said pupusas sounded like a good idea because she and I were from El Salvador. Kiara said that sounds delicious and agreed to help out. The day of the event came and Jessica, Kiara, and I had our dishes prepared.

We went to the event in my car and when we arrived there were already so many people there with stands. I started to set up our stand so people could come and try our food. When

I was finished setting up I noticed a stand by itself...it looked a little isolated from the rest. I went up to the stand and I met Millie.

She was giving out Kimchi, Kimbap, Bulgogi, Korean corn dogs, tteokbokki, and more. I was so shocked when I saw how many different dishes she had that I had to call over Jessica and Kiara to come and meet Millie and try some of her food. We all started to talk about the different foods we brought and we had a great time. We decided to go around and go and grab some food that different people were giving out.

After we grabbed some delicious food we decided to sit down at a table and go and eat our food. We sat with other people and we all ate together. By the end of the event, I was so full of all the different delicious foods I had. June 17 was the 10th year since my mom's death and It was also the day of the event so this day will forever live in my heart.

Dave

By Del'Mari Hicks

Hi, I'm Dave and I'm 26. This is a story about the best cookout of my life.

It all started one day in mid-June when my family and I went out to eat. While we were eating my mom said, "Let's have a cookout on June 24th with a free fireworks show and invite everybody in the town." So being the social people my family can be, we all agreed.

We decided to have it at a huge house overlooking the Severn River So later on that week everybody had jobs to do to set up the party. My sister was in charge of finding the location. My dad was in charge of getting the food. My mom was in charge of getting the party decorations, and my brother was in charge of getting fireworks. But then they realized they needed someone to do the invitations. So I ended up being the one to do them. I was fine handing out the invitations because I'm a pretty outgoing person.

The first invitations I started to send out were the online invitations because they were easiest ones.Then later on that day I started to hand out invitations in person. The first store I went to was a coffee shop named la cafe. It's a famous place in my neighborhood. A lot of people like to hang out there. Then after that I started handing them out to people on the street and my friends then later on that night. A lot of people were replying to my online invitations saying they would come and bring their favorite food there too.

On the day of the cookout I saw a lot of different types of food — one of them being sushi. It tasted amazing. I loved it and everyone else did too. I had met this girl named Sarah. She was just like me so we got along. Pretty quickly she made some food of her own to bring to the cookout, and when I tried it, I liked it.

At 8:00 o'clock we lit the fireworks. The firework show was fantastic and the big fireworks lit up the sky.

Everyone had a smile on their face the next day. And that's how I knew my family and I threw the best cookout. As people were leaving they were talking about how much fun they had at the cookout. It was the only thing people were talking about for a week!

Cristiano

By Emerson Garcia-Rivera

About two weeks ago I received an email from the Make-A-Wish Foundation. The email read, "Hello Cristiano Ronaldo! It would be a pleasure to have you in our community meal at the Make-A-Wish Foundation House," and gave me all the event details. I read the email and thought to myself I would make a child's day if I went. I responded to the email by saying "It would be my pleasure to come and hang out with you guys at this community meal!" I quickly rushed to the store and ordered about 500 meals for everybody attending the Community Meal. I met many fans at the store and took pictures with them! I even ran into a fan from Make-A-Wish Foundation. He was super cool and was excited that he would see me at the Community meal. A week has passed and I am super excited to meet the children.

Today is the day I meet the children. I am so excited. It was around 6:00 PM and I packed up my stuff and Flew from Portugal   to the community meal. On the way there I also stopped by to get some drinks and some outdoor activities such as Frisbee. Since I was the first one who arrived, I set up all the tables and greeted everyone at the door.

It was 7:00 PM and everyone was here. I saw and met all the children from Make-A-Wish Foundation. They were so excited to meet me they teared up. They told me how I was their inspiration and their idol. We then gathered for the community meal outside and we started eating. We had a fun time eating and doing activities. We then gathered to take some pictures after they finished eating.

The parents stayed outside while some of the children of Make-A-Wish Foundation invited me to their room to play FIFA 23 . They chose to be Argentina and I chose to be Portugal. The first half went by and it was 0-0. The second half started and I scored the opener, so I was winning 1-0 and when I went to celebrate they quickly scored on me. The game was then tied 1-1. It was about the 90-minute mark and he fouled me outside the box for a late shocking free-kick. It was about 25 yards out and I smashed it in! I then went on to win the game 2-1 in the last minute and I did my famous celebration SIUUUUU. We played a few more games and before we knew it, it was about 10:00 PM.

We then went back downstairs and then said our final goodbyes to all the Make-A-Wish Foundation children and parents. They thanked me so much for coming and having a fun time with them and the children. The parents called me over right before I opened the door to leave, and said WAIT! I looked, and it was a drawing from a child who drew it for me. It was wonderful! It was a drawing of me scoring a last-minute free-kick just like what happened in the FIFA game. He then told me he didn't want to hold him up for too long and gave me a hug and told me goodbye.

Sadie

By Erin Bower

My name is Sadie Wilson. I live in Annapolis, Maryland with my Mom and twin sister, Summer. My mom owns a bakery downtown, where my sister and I work. Summer works in the front taking orders, because she loves talking to people. I, on the other hand, like to stay in the back and help my mom bake; I tend to keep mostly to myself for the most part. Talking to my people isn't my thing I guess. Summer and I have a lot of differences but that's what makes us work.

One day it was just me and my sister working because my mom was out running errands. It was a really hot day out — it was the week before the summer break. The drink of the day was lemonade, so a bunch of people came in to quench their thirst. I could hear my sister in the front talking to people, making simple conversation. I thought to myself, *How? How can she just simply talk to someone? Even if she doesn't know them?*

"Sadie!! It's getting backed up here. I really could use your help!" said Summer. Before I could even think of any excuse why not to help I felt Summer grab my arm, pulling me to the front. "Summer! You know I can't do this. I can't just go out and talk to people like you." "Fine," she said. "I'll do the talking and take orders, you just need to work the cash register."

As I was working up front a little boy came in with a flier, and said: "Hi my name is Sawyer, I'm here handing out papers for the Sandy Point Beach clean-up fundraiser run by Sandy Point elementary school."

"Oh, thanks" I replied. I shove it to the side not thinking anything about it.

A couple of days went by, and it was three days before the big event (that I completely forgot about) When my mom found the paper "Sadie! Summer! Why didn't you guys tell me about this event?!"

'Oh god I forgot...' I think to myself. My mom wanted to bring something to show that she cared about our community, so she decided to make cakes. She worked 15 hours on each of the three days just to finish in time. She (of course) made us help. I didn't mind because it was kinda my fault we were behind on making all of this. If only I just didn't forget.

It was the day before the fundraiser, and Summer accidentally sold one of the cakes. Mom was pissed. She eventually got over it, but it took a lot of "I'm sorries" on Summer's part. Summer is always kinda getting in trouble you could say. Maybe because she doesn't overthink everything and just does what she wants. We are just the complete opposite.

Today is the day of the event! We finally finished baking around 11 am. We packed up all of the cakes and put them in the delivery truck. We drove to the beach and set up the cakes on this very long table. We got there very early, so all we could do was wait. Summer and I decided to go on a walk to make time pass by. We eventually went back, and that's when a bunch of people started to show up.

Usually being around a bunch of people stresses me out, but today was different. I was at ease. The last time I felt this calm (and not anxious) was before my dad left me and my sister and mom. So I decided to branch out and talk to people, and break out of my shell.

I went to try to find someone to talk to but first I had to start easy, talking to people that are younger than me is SO much easier. I walked around for a while trying to find a familiar face when I saw Sawyer, the kid who gave me the flier like a week ago.

"Sawyer right?" I say, trying to start a conversation, "Oh hey! You came! I never got your name," he said. "Oh my name is Sadie, It's nice to see you again!" Sawyer and I walked over to Summer and the kids she was playing with. I sat and watched her play with the kids. I talked with a few of them here and there. I got hungry so I went to get a plate of food and sit down.

I filled up my plate till there was no room left, then I went to go find my mom to sit with. I couldn't find her anywhere. I walked around for a couple of minutes, but still no sign of her. I give up on trying to find her and try to find at least an open seat. I find a seat next to a group of people I have never seen in my life. I start to get anxious. These people seem to like to talk, because right as I sat down they started a conversation.

"Hey there! I'm Sarah." I tried to sit in silence, but then she asked me what my name was. "I'm Sadie," I said quietly. The conversation went on even though we were completely different people. She was loud, I was quiet. She reminded me of Summer and I felt a sense of peace. I could tell we were going to become friends. We talked for a while. I felt like the reason we became friends so quickly was that she embraced our differences.

Being at this event was fun, I had to admit. I think being finally a part of a community made me break out of my shell. Oh and fast forward a while, my Mom ended up adopting Sawyer, so we warmly welcomed him into our family. (I had no idea he was even an orphan). I started to help Summer up front more frequently, and Sarah and I became best friends. We hang out every day.

Vivi

By Gabriella Alvarez-Hernandez

Vivi immigrated from Mexico where she used to be an assistant. She had a son which is one of the main reasons why she immigrated to America to try to give him a better life. When she immigrated to America at 40 she didn't speak any English and was struggling. After settling in she began working in a restaurant in the dessert/salad area. Everything was fine until the head chef began to make snarky comments about her age. They would argue and one day one of her co-worker told her that she heard him say that he wanted Vivi gone and would start cutting her hours to make her quit. Now Vivi wasn't someone who let anyone walk all over her. Sadly one day his comment made her walk out and find a new job. When she clocked in he told her "He wished she'd "hurry up and leave because she was too old." She was only 54. She tried her best not to cry but tear after tear began to stream down her face as she walked out. She felt mocked like the work she did and the contribution she made to restaurant wasn't valued at all

She decided to leave and find somewhere new where she could be accepted. When Moving from Farragut St. She decided to rent a room in Eastport. While looking for a new job, she met a man named Mike and began to talk to him. She told him about her old job and how she was discriminated against. Mike was intrigued by her and especially by her restaurant skills. So he offered her a job at his restaurant. She would work in prep. When she walked in at her new job she was accepted immediately, everyone was respectful and in their little bubble. when she got critiques they never criticized her about her age which made her feel like she belonged. A lot of the younger people loved to ask for advice because of how wise she was and one of them even told her that although her hands were rough as stone her touch was gentle as a gem. After two years of working there, they all began to call everyone mama Vivi out of respect they had for her.

While working in her garden she realized how disconnected all her neighbors were. Then suddenly she had an idea of hosting a cookout where she would invite the whole neighborhood. She asked Mike to help her put flyers around the neighborhood to invite everybody. To invite as many people as he could and that she would do the same. In the flier she wrote she wanted everybody to bring something homemade so it felt more welcoming. On the day of the cookout she was absolutely stunned to see how many people showed up and how many people she got to meet. Even some of her old friends showed up. There was music, people were dancing and enjoying each other's food and all was great. Vivi has never felt so free and welcome before. She had earned the respect of her community. They all knew her as Mama Vivi, the one you can go to if you need help or advice. She decided to start a group of older people and share their stories of discrimination against them. On March 26th, 2023 she finally declared that she's home and in her community.

Sage

By Hayden Haynes

My name is Sage Willow, and I am a Community event planner and host.

Today I woke up in a rush of excitement and nervousness. I can't believe it came so soon. I have to prepare myself for the big meeting today. I get out of bed and instantly write down my to-do list for today. Let's see...

> #1 send out the reminder message
> #2 Gather the attendance sheets
> #3 Gather my speech index cards
> #4 Arrive before everyone else!

Okay! I think I'm ready. About 30 minutes have passed and I'm in my car on the way to the meeting at the Graduate Hotel down the street. When I arrive I am the first one there! Perfect! A few minutes pass and people are starting to arrive.

Some of the committee members are arriving. The main person I am looking for is the main chef of the committee, Antonio, but I don't see him. A few more minutes later Antonio is still nowhere to be found. I text Antonio asking where he is. And finally start the meeting off.

Later that day - The meeting was very successful! I put out all the information necessary and I think the committee is also most excited as I am. The Sandy Point Community Lunch will be the best community event yet!

Days have passed and the Community Lunch date is coming closer and closer. But on June 5th, with only 12 days before lunch, the worst possible thing happened. Driving to gather more supplies for lunch, I see a car approaching a light that is just about to turn red. The car is going a little extra fast. It is my time to turn the block when that car comes racing through the light and hits my car right into the driver's door. The rest is a blur.

I woke up in the hospital with a cast on my left arm and right leg. As my vision comes back I realize that I am surrounded by people all around my hospital bed. Flowers, cards and gifts are in each person's hands. The people I am surrounded by are all committee members and people from my community. Joy fills my heart seeing everyone's faces. But the first thing that comes to my mind is how will I still be able to finish setting up for the community lunch. Stress flows through my head. I must have shown the stress on my face because Antonio came up to me and told me everything will be okay and the committee will have everything taken care of. But being me, I really want to have a say on everything that is planned. The doctors tell me I should be out and back in shape before the day of the Lunch. Relief is all I feel now.

June 15th, I am out of the hospital with just a boot on my leg! Immediately I get back to planning and updating the community. June 16th, The day before the Community Lunch. I am so stressed but also so excited to see how everything will come together. Once I see the smiles on the community's faces everything will be worth it. Just being able to come together with some many volunteers and kind people all supporting a cause has made this all worth doing.

June 17th, the day of the Community Lunch! I can't believe the day has come. I plan on being the first one at the beach! So I woke up super early just to get ready, pack up and have some time to mentally prepare. Driving up to the beach, The parking lot is already full of cars? Think maybe there are just beach cleaners. I grab a few things from my trunk and walk down to the beach. But when I get there....

Almost the whole committee is there waiting for ME! All the tables, chairs, tents, food, decoration is all set up. At first I looked at all of this and didn't even know how to function anymore! But after taking it all in I just smiled so hard I could feel my cheeks burning. I greeted and thanked everyone in the committee. I am forever grateful for this amazing community that I have. Now time to wait for the rest of the community to arrive so we can all celebrate together.

Rosa

By Jennifer Lawrence

Rosa is 16 years old. She was born in the U.S.A but her mom is from El Salvador and the Dad is from Mexico. Rosa has a little sister named Anna. Rosa goes to high school and she is in 11th grade. Rosa is going to bring a friend to the community meal to meet new people because Sofia came from El Salvador just to see her best friend Rosa.

When Rosa was nine years old she went to El Salvador and she became Sofia's best friend. Sofia asks Rosa if she can teach her how to speak Spanish. Rosa and Sofia were talking about what to take to the community lunch and they both want to take pupusas, so they are making pupusas because pupusas are the best food in El Salvador.

When Rosa and Sofia went to the community meal Sofia saw Marella, a girl that she saw at the store. Marella speaks a little bit of Spanish. Marella and Sofia said hi, then Sofia said to Rosa I know Marella. I saw her in a store, but I did not know Marella was in the community. Rosa said she was going to get the pupusas. Sofia said, "Ok...do you need help to get the pupusas?"

"No, I don't need help," said Rosa.

Pupusas are imported from El Salvador and they are stuffed corn-flour tortillas grilled up like pancakes and they are a staple food in most Salvadoran households, and a symbol of home for immigrant Salvadoran communities worldwide. Rosa and Sofia are talking about how they make pupusas that are made from masa harina (cornmeal flour) or rice flour that are mixed with water to make a corn masa mixture. They are usually stuffed with delicious things like refried beans, shredded pork or cheese. All of the people are going to like the pupusas. So that is why we like pupusas and why we made them to help make others from El Salvador feel a part of the community.

J'den

By Jordan Hicks

I had always been fascinated by basketball. As a toddler, I remember I would crawl around the house with a plastic ball in my hand, passing the ball with my big brother, and dribbling it seemingly naturally. My auntie, who had played basketball in college, encouraged my young love for the sport. She bought me miniature basketball hoops and took me to local games. As I grew older my aunt's encouragement turned into pressure. She saw the potential in me and pushed me to train harder and longer, up to seven days a week. Even when I would be crying in the car unable to catch my breath from anxiety, she'd still drop me off at the front door of the gym. Every time.

I really did still love basketball. I still had the passion but it was no longer fun. It was a job, and I had felt as if I had no other option but to keep balling. Despite the pressure, it honestly paid off. I continued to excel on the court. My natural talent combined with the non-stop rigorous training led me to become the MVP on my school's varsity team. College scouts came to watch my games, and many were already offering me scholarships before I even finished my junior year. But my success came at a cost. I had no social life outside of basketball, and I was constantly stressed from the pressure to perform at my best everyday.

My auntie was always relentless in her pursuit of my success, and I felt trapped in a life I no longer enjoyed. While shooting hoops alone at a local park, I met a group of kids my own age who were just playing for fun. A girl named Jordan invited me to join in. I admit I was hesitant at first. I had always been told that playing basketball for fun was a waste of time, and that I needed to focus when training. But something inside of me wanted to feel the freedom and joy of playing without the pressure to win, and maybe find a friend. So I joined in the game, and for the first time in years, I felt truly free on the court. Over the next few weeks, I continued to play with the kids at the park. I also started to skip some of my training sessions, much to my aunt's dismay. She scolded me for my lack of dedication, but I didn't care. I had finally found a way to enjoy basketball again, and I wasn't going to let anyone take that away from me.

One day when I was meeting up with Jordan and the group, she asked if I wanted to join in a community meal. Over the last couple weeks I learned to be more open, more free, so I said yes. I came home and started thinking about it. What should I wear? Should I bring something? What if they don't accept me as part of the community? As my anxiety-coated thoughts swept through my mind I heard my doorbell ring. I opened the door and to my surprise it was Jordan holding a pie crust, some fruit, and some other baking supplies in a tote bag. I looked at her and asked what she was doing here.

"Oh I thought we could bake a pie together for the community meal...unless you don't want to, which is fine." She looked away and frowned at that last part. Who could say no to her with a tone like that? I let her in and we set up to bake.

Turns out two teenagers trying to bake by themselves with no prior knowledge is not a good idea...but it *was* a very good time.

As the clock struck 10 pm we were finally done. We put the pie in the fridge and she was walking out of the door. I grabbed her arm and gave her a hug. "Thanks for coming over, Jordan. I had a really great time with you." I had never been a bold person. Always listening to others and always holding my tongue. But with her, with my community, they had taught me to be me.

"Thanks, J'den, I had a great time as well." She smiled at me and left.

The community meal was great! We ate and laughed and played games. Everybody enjoyed the pie. I met some new people as well. As the end of my senior year approached, I had a decision to make. I had offers from several top colleges, all of which promised me a future in basketball. Over the last few weeks I have learned to love basketball in a different way. The community taught me how to turn something bad into something I can truly enjoy.

Jaime

By Julia Scott

Outdoor Community Potluck
7pm, June 24
Cliffside on the Severn
Yard games, pool, fish pond, and dinner!
Everyone MUST CONTRIBUTE to attend!

I reread the invitation that came for my family in the mail a few days ago. The paper wrinkles in my hand and I look out the car window. My parents and I moved to Annapolis a week ago, right after school ended. They were so excited to see this potluck invitation in the mail, since we don't know many people here. The invitation says that it's mandatory to help out with the event, either by bringing something, or by helping to set up. So I decided to bring a cake to the event.

"You okay, Jaime?" I look up. My mother is staring at me with a concerned look on her face. I hesitate for a moment.

"I'm fine, Mom," I say. I keep staring out the window. "Just nervous."

I can feel my anxiety building up inside me, and my palms getting clammy. This potluck is a good chance for me to make some new friends before the school year starts, and I'm so nervous about messing it up. I hear my parents discussing the directions to the potluck in the background, and my nerves spike. Before I know it, we're pulling up to the building.

The house is huge, with a gigantic yard filled with picnic tables and yard games. I see a few kids younger than me playing a game of cornhole, and a group of about six or seven adults having a conversation near the middle of the yard. Two adults are lecturing two kids who look like their children, as the two kids look down in shame. I notice a soccer ball in the branches of a tree on the other side of the cliff, and it suddenly makes sense why they're in trouble.

My parents look around the potluck. My dad rubs the back of his neck, and my mom shuffles her feet a bit as she looks around, but I notice that a smile never leaves her face. I glance around, feeling incredibly awkward at this party full of strangers. A couple dressed in matching cerulean blue outfits walks up to us. The man smiles at us wearing a blue long sleeve t-shirt, and I notice he's so tall I have to crane my neck to look up at him. The woman is wearing a knee-length dress of the same color. She offers my parents her hand.

"Hey! My name is Beverly, and this is my husband, Jonathan, it's lovely to meet you both!" she says. Her voice is high pitched and fast, with a slight southern accent. I look at my parents. My mom looks a bit surprised, and my dad looks as awkward as I feel.

"Hello, it's so nice to meet you! My family just moved here from California! My name is Dana, and this is my husband Scott, and my kid, Jaime," my mom gushes. "I really am glad to meet you, we haven't been here that long, so it's good to meet people in the community."

Beverly nods. "We moved here about four years ago, so I can understand how it is. Can I ask why you moved?" Her eyes widen with curiosity.

"My job required that I move here, so we waited until school was over for Jaime before moving here. It's a nice area to live in though, so..." My mind drifts off. I've been carrying the cake in my hands for a while now, and it's starting to feel heavy. I furrow my brow, and scan the picnic tables for a place to put it. "You okay, bud?" my dad asks. I nod, "Just seeing where to put this cake."

I see someone walking towards me. She looks elderly, with silver strands of hair tucked behind her ear. She smiles at me. "Is that cake for the potluck?" She asks me. I nod. "Let me help you carry it, it'll go on that table right over there."

"Ok," I say. She grabs the other end of the cake container. "I'm going to put the cake on the food table," I say. My dad nods, and my mom keeps chatting with Beverly. I see her wave at me as I walk away.

The older woman guides me to the dessert table. There isn't much on there. There are a few bowls of fruit, and a tray of cupcakes. We set the cake down on the corner of the table, and she pushes it a bit so it ends up near the middle of the table. I smile at her.

"Thank you," I tell her. She smiles back at me, but when I look at her eyes, they seem sad. "Of course," she says.

She turns away from me and strides away. I watch her go for a moment.

I walk back to my parents. They're still talking to Beverly and Jonathan. I hear them all laugh loudly as I approach. My mom looks at me as I get closer. "Hey Jaime, you need something?" she grins. I shake my head.

"No, I'm just going to get something to eat," I tell my mom. She nods, and as I leave, she jumps back into the conversation. I can feel the prickly grass on the lawn poking my ankles as I head to the food table. The table is four picnic tables pushed together, and I look at the vast amount of food and the countless scents around me.

First things first, get a plate and utensils. The nearest end of the table is covered in different kinds of meat. Beef, chicken, turkey, and all kinds of shellfish, with a few others I can't quite place. They all smell like a kitchen in a restaurant, covered in different seasonings and herbs. There's a dish so covered in cilantro that you can barely see what's underneath. The plates and utensils are squished between a baking tray of pork chops and what looks like a crab stew. The forks, knives and spoons are standing alertly in red plastic cups, so packed in that the cup almost falls when I try to grab some.

I grab the tongs sticking out of a tray of hamburgers and put one on my plate.

The middle of the table is filled with vegetables and bread. Green beans, broccoli, carrots, rolls, sourdough, and hamburger and hotdog buns. Why they're not with the actual

196

hamburgers and hotdogs, I have no idea. I grab a roll, and scoop some sliced carrots onto my plate. I look at my plate. At least three things, although it could be more, depending on what's on the last table.

As I get to the last table, my plate filled, I see a kid much younger than me, probably no older than six. He's wearing glasses, and a slightly stained shirt with a carrot on it. I look across the table. This table has condiments at the edge, with fruit in the middle and cakes to the left. I spot mine, and notice it hasn't been touched. I feel a little sadder. I also notice that there are more desserts here than before. I take a look around the lawn, there's more people there than I remember.

I take a fork and put some cantaloupe and strawberries on my plate. I look around a bit more to see if there's anything else I'd want to get.

As I'm considering my options I notice something out of the corner of my eye. The little kid from earlier, cutting the biggest slice of cake I've ever seen out of the cake I brought. It's at *least* a quarter of the cake, and I gawk at this tiny kid taking a whole quarter of it. He notices me staring, and smiles at me, like he has no idea why I would be staring at him.

"Hi, my name is Benji," he says. "What's yours?"

I feel frozen for a moment, still in a bit of shock about the cake. I look back and forth between this *tiny kid* and the gaping hole in my cake. I realize he spoke to me and look back at him. "Sorry, missed that, what'd you say?"

"I said, my name is Benji. What's yours?"

"Jaime, my name is Jaime," I say. He smiles at me, and holds up his slice of cake.

"See how much cake I got? It's chocolate cake, and chocolate isn't my favorite, my favorite is carrot cake, but I like chocolate too. This cake looks good, you should probably try some, but not some of mine, because I've already got it."

My head feels like it's spinning. I take a deep breath. "Are you sure you can eat all that cake, Benji?"

He looks down at his plate. "Yeah, I think so," he says. He swipes his finger on the side of his slice, and licks it off his finger. He smiles. "The icing is good!"

I laugh a little. "I'm glad you like it. That's the cake that I made." He looks down at his cake, then back up at me.

"Thank you!" He says. "Are you new here? I don't think I've seen you before..."

I fidget with the string of my hoodie. "Uh, yeah, I just moved here a week ago. From California." I say. I can feel him looking at me as I crumble the edge of my hoodie. It feels quiet for longer than it should.

"I thought you looked unfamiliar! You moved here from California? That's really far away. You haven't been here that long, I bet you don't know anyone here yet. I can introduce you to some of the other kids here if you'd like?" Benji offers.

I can feel my heart hammering in my chest. This is as good a chance as any to make some friends. But what if I mess it up? I could say the wrong thing, and I don't know anything about the people here. What if I say something wrong and offend someone? I doubt I'd have any friends then.

But strangely, as I look across the lawn, at all the people at this gathering, I see my parents, Jonathan and Beverly, the woman who helped me move my cake, the golden light of the sunset, the soft pink of the clouds, the light bouncing across the grass and shimmering off the bay. I feel a sense of calm wash over me at the sight of these things, some familiar, some new, all supporting me. I feel a cool breeze, and a grin spreading across my face.

I look back at Benji, his face hopeful and expecting. I still feel nervous, and my heart is still beating loudly, but the people I'm going to meet, and the friends I might make feel less daunting to me. I turn to Benji.

"Thanks, Benji, I'd like that a lot."

Millie Kim

By Litzy Luengas-Mendoza

May 27th! I had finally finished high school. I graduated as valedictorian in my class. My dad and I went out to eat at one of my mom's favorite restaurants - a famous Korean BBQ. It gave us a warm feeling of how things were like back home when we celebrated things. Maybe it was that the adults were drinking suju, or the kids digging their little toothpicks through their dalgona, something just made it feel nice. Though when we got there I didn't feel as joyful as I expected.

When me and Appa sat down at the table I began to tear up a bit. Eomma wasn't here with us to celebrate. She had passed away midway through my senior year in a car crash. Appa saw my tears and told me "Eomma would've been so proud of you...I brought a couple of pictures from a photo album that we had and thought, since you had graduated, we could look back at your first times here in the U.S with Eomma." He pulls out a little box filled with pictures and shows me one. It was middle school with me and my Eomma. We were sitting down on a bench while I was holding my lunch box. I looked a bit sad though. I stared at the picture for a bit and remembered, it was because the kids at the school made fun of the tteokbokki Eomma made for me that day.

Her food was always the best. I always preferred to eat the traditional foods from my home country but since my first day of school I forced myself to eat the food that the American kids would like. So from that day forward I told Eomma to only

200

pack me foods that the American kids liked. Eommawas confused but she went along with it. The amount of Pb&J's I had eaten in middle school was crazy, I tried so hard to like them but I couldn't. They weren't for my taste buds.

I asked appa if he knew how to make the dishes that Eommamade for us back then but he told me he didn't. I felt a little part of me get sad hearing that. Had I known that she would die that day I would've asked her to make me a meal one last time. "However, she did leave a bunch of card recipes," I heard my Appa say. I looked up at him and gave him a relieved look. "She made them and planned to give them to you when you went to college, just in case you craved some of her food while you were away. I can show them to you when we get back home if you'd like." I of course said that I'd like to look at them. I felt a bit better while eating the food after hearing those words.

While waiting to get responses from the schools I applied to, I was constantly in the kitchen trying to perfect the taste that my Eommahad created for me. I remember only cooking a few times with her but the memories are a bit vague. After a few weeks of constantly making her dishes I finally managed to match her taste in a way that reminded me of her. And by then my college acceptance letter came and soon I was off to live on campus in Towson University. I was sad about the fact that I had to leave my Appa all alone but I told him I'd visit often. We have other Korean neighbors that live around us so he'll have a bit of company.

After a bit in college we got our summer break. As I was scrolling around some websites around Maryland I noticed that there was a fundraiser going around in Sandy Point. It was started by an elementary school that was having a reunion and wanted to start a fundraiser as well. On the page it asked for some help or if there is anyone interested to help sell some food to raise. I thought I should help out since I had no plans to do much over the summer and I still had my mother's recipes. I could cook a meal to help raise money for the fundraiser!

I went to apply and waited for the day to come. Saturday June 17th came, I went to prepare a bag to leave and packed the stand I was going to set up along with the ingredients I needed. Driving to Sandy Point Beach took a while but when I got there the sun shined bright and the nice cool breeze coming from the ocean felt nice. Since the event started at 2:00 pm I started to set up my stand and began to prepare the ingredients.

I saw people rolling on the beach and getting food from other stands but no one really came to mine. A couple of people came to my stand, some gave stares, others were actually invested into my culture but I didn't see a face of enjoyment when they tried out my food. Suddenly I felt like I was back in my first day of 7th grade. Everyone just looking at me and my food stand kind of made me feel a sense of deja vu all over again. I was beginning to debate if I should pack my stuff and head back home but then I saw someone in the distance coming over.

I try to look a bit more presentable so that at least the last person I serve can have a good meal.

"Hey, welcome to my stand! Would you like to try out some of my Korean dishes?" I say politely. The boy comes up, gives me a smile and says "Hey I'd like to order a couple of things from here! I've never tried any Korean food before so this will be a cool experience, My name is JP by the way." "I'm Millie, what would you like to order? We have kimbap, tteokbokki, Korean corn dogs and other Korean food!" I say back.

He ordered quite a lot of food so I asked him if he was ordering for anyone else. He told me that he had a couple of friends waiting and wanting to order from my stand. I was in a way relieved that other people wanted to try my food, so I happily made the large order. "I think you should move your stand to where people come from more often, That way you get more people to come." JP says. " Oh really? Alright then!...Though uh I might need a bit of some help. There are quite a few things to carry over." I say back. We both carry the things over near a dock.

There were more people over there than where I was. I was kind of amazed. I just thought that not many people came to the event but there were so many people near the docks. As soon as I finished setting up with JP there was already a line of people. They were all here to buy some of the food I've prepared with my Eomma's recipe. I was overjoyed that there were so many people wanting to try my food. After JP grabbed his large order he invited me to try some of his and his friends' food. So after I finished serving a bunch of people I went to look for JP's stand. He said that he was serving Salvadoran food, so I went to look for a stand that had the Salvador flag.

When I found him there were people around him, whom I assumed were his friends. They were all sitting on a round table set up by the people organizing. I walked over and greeted them. They were all mixed up of different races so I thought that these people had a comfortable environment when I first saw them. All of them introduced me to the different dishes that they had to offer. Some of them being Indian, Russian, Norwegian, Filipino, Mexican, Laotian, and so much more. JP was the last to introduce me to his cultural dishes. He told me to try out a food of his called pupusas. There were ones with different flavors so I didn't know what to pick.

Eventually I ended up picking one called revueltas. It was really delicious! It's appearance made me hesitate in the beginning but its flavor was really good! Looking back at it now it reminds me of how other people must have felt about my food. They may have not put their words in the nicest way but they must have also been hesitant to accept my food like how I was. All the people who JP introduced me to must have also experienced the things I have with their different foods. I know now that we are all different and hold different types of food dearly like how I do. These recipes from my Eommaallowed me to get closer to other people even though we don't come from the same places, and for that I'll be forever thankful.

By Mariah Davis

My name is Mariah. I am 17 and I will be cooking fried chicken for my neighbors to eat at the community meal. I grew up learning new things to cook and my grandfather used to teach me how to cook and I loved watching. I will be teaching Mya, who's 16 years old, how to cook so she can help us out and people can get their food faster. This will make the community stronger because people will be happy and thankful for us that provide good food for everyone. Mya and I are very helpful to the community because we care and I like to cook. I love when people say my food is good.

People will love the event and they will want to keep coming back. We need to keep focusing on collaboration. The party is at 3:00 and everybody is invited. We need to serve the food for the others that need good tasty food. I cook for everyone. I'm very kind and I care about everyone in the community. It's always good to be kind and genuine to people that need help or anybody.

Mya loved learning how to cook and she got the hang of it quick. We could move way faster than if I was by myself because I will cook the fried chicken and she can cook the sides. People will have a good meal and will love how the food tastes. The event will be at a big mansion with tables so people can sit down and eat at the event. My role is to cook good food for everyone. I will be helping others become more happy. I love being happy to help people and always being respectful and kind. At the party parents and children are allowed there and music will be played, people will be dancing and having fun and if they want more food there is *always* more.

When I was younger I used to go to a lot of parties with my family members and we would eat and have fun and dance. I wondered what it would be like if I cooked and how that would feel, I like cooking all the time. I never doubted myself at anything. I always try my best to be brave.There will be cool drinks at the event — there will be a lot of options like Sprite, water, tea, ginger ale, and more. You should always be hydrated! There will also be lots of snacks and candy!

You can wear anything you would like to the party! No one should feel uncomfortable or judged. You can wear whatever shoes you would like to wear or that you feel most comfortable. There will be plenty of TV for people to watch and games to play like Uno cards, chess, checkers, and lots of fun things to do.

By Noah Bishop

Mom says we have to dress nicely for the Community Meal. I don't want to, I'm only 7 after all, I shouldn't have to. Besides, I'm going to be cooking. Don't want to ruin my clothes. We started walking out to the car, It was hot. Really hot. This jacket is uncomfortable. I was singing in the car, mom didn't seem to like it, she doesn't like my singing. When we got to the beach I took off! Running with my feet in the sand, holding my shoes, flying like the seagulls that took off as I came towards them. At least, I was.

I was scooped up off the sand by one of my grown-up friends. "Antonio!" I called out, giving him a big hug. "Hey buddy!" he said to me. "Let's get you back to your mom, ok?" I like Antonio, he smells like french toast and vanilla. My mom tells me to go play while she talks to Antonio. I go and sit on the rocks as I watch the other adults set up the tables, it takes ages for everyone else to get here, but they do. My friends. We go play. The adults finish setting up, and call us over. The two big tables that they were dragging out of the red truck are now standing on their flimsy plastic legs, with an oversized tablecloth draped over each of the tables.

My mom walks up with a big bowl of salad and places it on the very end of the table. As more and more people show up, more and more dishes get placed on the table, to the point where I think it might collapse. No grill though, so I guess I won't be helping to cook. That's a bummer.

As more people start to arrive I start to recognize a lot of them, like grandma! I ran up and gave her a big hug. It's been a long time since I've seen grandma. She came all the way from Rhode Island for this. I give her a big grin to show off my missing tooth, she laughs and asks me where my mom is before leaving to go see her. As everyone steadily trickles in, people start forming into groups of 6-8 and having their own conversations. I walk back and forth between them, talking to my friends and looking for something interesting to do. I threw rocks into the water for a little while, then started building a sand castle. Right when I was almost done with it, mom called everyone over to the tables.

At this point there aren't enough seats for everyone. People were sitting on whatever they could get their hands on. Logs, rocks, bits of driftwood, those sorts of things. Those who couldn't find anything stood. The air was filled with the smell of the food on the table and the bay breeze which today, oddly, didn't smell like dead fish. As my mom finished her boring speech we all started ravaging the food, plates were piled high with everything from waffles to pastelitos. I had some chicken and this weird looking potato and meat dish. Someone started playing some music and that's when everything really kicked off.

People were dancing, singing (badly), and drinking lots of juice. After what seemed like no time at all, it started raining. Not a lot of rain, but just the occasional drop. And then another drop. And another. Pretty soon it was pouring and people were picking up the food and taking it inside. After a little while everyone was thoroughly soaked and dripping on the floor inside. However, most of the food was safe and people quickly got the party rolling again. I sat back down and tucked into my plate as someone plugged in the speaker and restarted the music.

Chalea

By Ny'Liyah Jones

My name is Chalea, and I am 32 years old. I heard about the event from my daughter's school, so I decided to help the school and make some food to help out the community meal. I went home to prepare the food and bring the water bottles and some snacks.

When I was preparing the food I had to also get my daughter from school, so I rushed out the house and forgot to turn the food off, so when we got back home the food was burnt and I started to cry. My daughter said it was going to be okay. We can just start over and do it together. I stopped crying and we got to work.

We finished cooking — we cooked chicken, mac and cheese, greens, and we baked chocolate chip cookies and strawberry cake. We even managed to finish a little early so we cleaned the house a little bit, then we got ready.

We put everything in the car and went to the park where they were having the event. I help put the decorations up and put the food out. We had a great time! There were games, and we played around, ate some amazing food, and I'm looking forward to doing this again next year!

By Sam Bodor

I've always been kind of quiet. Not the kind of quiet where I don't say anything to anyone, but the kind of quiet where it takes time for me to warm up to people. That's why when I found out about the community meal happening at Sandy Point, I was really hesitant to go. I heard about it the Monday before it was happening, and was planning on not going the whole time. When I asked if any of my friends were going, all of them said no. That was enough to convince me to not go.

The day before the meal, I was talking to my friends when they asked why I wasn't going. When I told them I didn't know anyone going, they told me to just go. "You might as well go, worst case scenario you don't meet anyone and leave." That sort of convinced me. That night I was thinking about what they said earlier, and I realized that they were right in that I might as well go because there really wasn't a point in not going. I started trying to come up with ideas for stuff to bring to the meal. Should I bring food? Drinks? Nothing? I had no idea.

That morning, I was making breakfast for myself when I decided to make one of my favorite meals to bring to Sandy Point. One of the first things I thought of was my mom's chicken alfredo. I told myself that I was going to the meal, and I'm going to help contribute to this community. Later that day, I went to the store to get some ingredients for the alfredo.

When I got there, there were quite a few people shopping. Will I see these people at the meal? I would soon see.

I began making the alfredo around 1:30, and I finished around 2. I decided to wait a little bit because I didn't really want to be one of the first people there. I left around 2:10 and got there at about 2:40. When I arrived, I began having second thoughts about going. I was conflicted. Because even though it would be something new and something I don't usually do, I was nervous. What would people think of me? Why am I here by myself? Why am I here at all? I tried to relax by thinking about what my friends had told me the day before. Worst case scenario, it isn't fun and I leave. I got out of my car and started walking, pasta in hand. There were a lot of people there, which I guess I could've expected, but it was still a bit of a shock. I got nervous again. When I was standing there, probably looking like I was going to throw up, about to turn around and leave, someone approached me. "Hey!" they said, "Is that food for the meal? I can take it and put it at the tables if you'd like." "Oh this. Yeah that'd be great, thanks." I said. "I got this." They said, " Go enjoy yourself with the other guests." "Thank you," I said again. As I looked over to the masses of people, I tried thinking about who I would go talk to. There were the people over by the food, the group standing by the water, and of course the multiple groups at all the tables they had set up. Then I saw someone standing alone. I decided to go and talk to him.

"Hey," I said walking over to him, "don't you want to go and talk to some people?" "Oh," he responded "yeah I guess so. I just don't really know anyone here all that well." "What a coincidence," I said "I don't really know anyone that well either. I'm Sam. What's your name?" "Adam." He said. We talked for a while, talking about pretty much anything, what we brought to the meal, where we're from, why we came, our families, and the community as a whole. After a little while I asked if he wanted to get some food and talk to some more people. He said yes. We walked over to the food tables and each grabbed a little of almost everything, including my alfredo. Before we walked over to another group, we toasted, "To meet new people and try new things."

When we walked over to the tables, we decided to split ways. I introduced myself and these people that I had never met before just accepted me with open arms. Even meeting a little orphan boy, that was kind of weird though. I wasn't sure what I was expecting, but I guess it wasn't that. As the afternoon turned into early evening, I talked with many new people, introducing myself countless times, and talking about common interests as well as personal experiences. When I went back to the table to get another cup of water, I saw my alfredo was gone, and I asked the person managing the table what happened to it. "Oh that? That disappeared as fast as it came. Heck, people were even lining up to get a serving." "Wow." I responded. I really didn't know what else to say other than that. Before that meal, I hadn't realized how much community would affect me.

When everyone started clearing out, I noticed how much trash was left behind. I approached one of the workers, and insisted that I help clean up the mess. The workers and I talked for what seemed like hours, all coming together again over picking up trash. We talked about how it's nice that people can join together and become a united group of individuals that can accomplish pretty much everything. As I cleaned, I reflected on the afternoon. I realized that, even though it might not always seem like it, I am always a member of a community, and it may not be the community I'm expecting it to be, and in the end I was so grateful for my friends who convinced me to go. I was now a part of that community, and I always will be.

Justyce

By Saniyah Conley

Hi my name is Justyce Nicole Allen and I am 15 years old. I used to live in Jamaica but then I moved to Maryland when I was 14, over the summer. I don't know why my mom chose this place. I understand she wanted to give me a life where there are more opportunities but why not California where there is Hollywood, sun, flowers, and fun? Now that is a real opportunity. I could have become an actor or movie star but it's whatever, I guess.

When I was younger I thought I fit in well at school, I guess because everyone looked like me and spoke like me, but now that I am in high school it's different. I'm in higher leveled classes and for some reason everyone seems so shocked by that because they assume I'm just a dumb black kid. I'm often stereotyped as the dumb, troublemaking, suspicious, up-to-no-good, dangerous black kid, but my mama always told me that I was as bright as the sun and as beautiful as the sunset.

It's the first day of school and I walked into my English class. I was the only black kid there. I just knew it was about to be a rough semester. As I sat in my seat I felt all eyes staring at me. It felt like forever but then the bell finally rang. Once the bell rang the teacher introduced herself and told us what we would be doing this semester. She then told us to introduce ourselves. I was the last one to go and once I started speaking everyone began to laugh. I was so confused as to why. Then I heard someone say, " Why do you sound like that?" Then I heard another person say, "Can you not speak proper English dummy?" Then everyone started laughing some more. I looked at the teacher and she was chuckling. I headed back to my seat, so embarrassed and ashamed.

At the end of class my teacher told us that we had to write a poem on whatever we wanted and that it was due next class. The bell rang and I went to my last class of the day - AP U.S. History. This was also a higher level class, but I wasn't the only black student this time. There was a girl named Bacardi Noles Carter and the teacher, Ms. Coates, who were black. Ms.Coates looks just like my Mama.

In class we were learning about slavery, which of course led to everyone in the room looking at Bacardi and me. Two minutes before class was over I was walking to the door and I saw Bacardi crying. I asked her what was wrong and she explained to me that she was in charge of planning a community meal and she needs people who are willing to participate. I told her to calm down and breathe in and out and focus on her hands so she could relax. I told her that she should let people know about it on social media. She was able to calm down and thanked me.

When I went home I told my mom about the community meal and I told her that we should make some jerk chicken and Jamaican patties. She agreed and said she would start cooking the morning of the community meal. I went into my room to get started on my poem. I was struggling with a topic to choose or what to even write about. But then I remembered what happened today and that made me think of a name. The name of my poem is "Smarter than you Think."

I was done with my poem in about 30 minutes which was pretty good timing. I then suddenly felt the urge to post it on my tik tok because I felt like my poem was really good and people needed to hear it. Here is what I said.

"Hey Tik Tok, so I came on here to read a poem I wrote on the topic of racism, stereotypes, and bullying. The name of my poem is "Comfortable With the Skin I'm In."

An academically smart black girl, who many view as dumb in this strange world. They say this because of the color of my skin, I just can't win. Stereotypes kill me, it disables me to have more opportunity, this is just the truth to me, but it shouldn't be. My skin shouldn't make others think I'm dumb and don't know how to read. A good teacher and education is just what I need. Not somebody judging me based on my ethnicity and what my background is viewed as unfortunately in this case, just see me as I am within, not the color of my skin or race. My accent and the way I talk isn't even my fault, but just because I sound different, it leads people to the suspicion that I am not the same and trying to succeed on a different mission. My goal is to glow and grow, and let my true talents show. My goal is to make my family proud so they can scream and shout and be loud as I walk across the stage and read off the page because I'm valedictorian, which may seem out of the ordinary for people of my kind, but this is my time to shine. Black girl, you're smart and beautiful, and I wanted to let you know, don't let anybody steal your glow or say you aren't smart when you know you are, you truly are the best and you're that golden star."

I posted the Tik Tok and expected to get no views so I went to sleep so I could wake up early tomorrow to help my mom prepare the food for the community meal.

It was the next day and the sun was as bright as a star shining at night. My phone began to go off. I had so many Tik Tok notifications. When I opened the app there were 9.8 million likes and 200,000 comments. I also gained 750,000 followers. I was so surprised I ran downstairs and told my mom. She was so proud of me.

When I was checking the comments I noticed that CNN had commented and said they wanted to interview me and read my poem on national television. I began to cry. I never thought I'd blow up like that but I did.

I began to help my mom prepare the jerk chicken by marinating it and leaving it in the fridge so when it was 5:00 it would be time for me to cook it. I made my mom breakfast and a cake to celebrate since it was only 10:00 am and I had 9 hours until the community meal.

It was finally 5:00, so I had to take out the chicken and put it in the oven so it could bake. I began helping my mom fix the Jamaican patty. Once I finished cooking, I washed the dishes and then went to my room so I could start memorizing my poem. I finished memorizing my poem and I was very confident. Me and my Mom finally left around 6:00 because I wanted to make sure I was there early so I could set up the food and my station for my activity.

I arrived at 6:30 and the setting was just beautiful. There was a lot of green grass and there was a big house on a hill near the water. I began to set up the food and my station.

It was finally 7:00 and there were a lot of people there. I would be reading my poem at 7:45 pm but first everybody had to eat and everyone was ready! I was afraid people wouldn't eat the traditional Jamaican food that my mom and I cooked. Surprisingly, it was successful and everyone was asking for more and I may have changed people's viewpoints on non-american food.

There were a lot of people so I began to get nervous but I used the method that my mom taught me in order to calm down. I also began to calm down because I saw young black girls and I was hoping that my poem would inspire them. It was 7:45 and there were a lot of people at my station and I think it is because many of them saw my Tik Tok. There was even the news there.

I stood up as tall as a giraffe and I spoke really loud and clear as if I had a megaphone. I read my poem and it was a success, I didn't stutter — not once — and I received a standing ovation! The little black girls in the audience were smiling and looked very thrilled to see someone they could relate to. When I saw them smiling I became as happy as a kid going into a candy shop.

When the community meal was finally ending, over 30 people came up to me and congratulated me. Three little girls even wanted to take a picture with me.

The community meal was a success! I don't even know why I was so stressed. I've never felt so confident until today and I am now not ashamed of my background, I am proud of who I am and where I come from.

By Susie Herrera Aguilar

I don't like people.

Okay, I hear how that sounds but what I mean is my family are the only ones who I can bond with. I have never been able to make friends; my mom likes to say I don't try hard enough to make friends but honestly, I don't understand how people make friends. The amount of times I have heard "oh we met one day and started talking and ever since we have been friends" which I don't understand because it is not specific at all about how they became friends.

Although my mom pushes me to make friends, it never works out. I remember one time when my mom was working at this job and she had made a friend who she invited over to our apartment. The friend had this daughter who looked about the same age as me. I remember she wore this light pink shirt with shorts and her giant smile was like a warm sunny day. I remember saying "hi my name is Melanie, what's your name?" and she responded with "My name is Heather!" I thought that I would like her and that we would become friends because of how nice she seemed but I didn't. I felt like she was forced to get along with me and I could tell she was nice because she tried to make conversation with me but it was very strained as the more we talked, the more we realized we did not like the same things. So after she left with her mom that was the last time me and Heather had a real conversation. We still see eachother once in a while when our moms gather for an event and we say hi to each other but that's about it.

Deep inside, I know a reason why I don't have friends, although I don't like to admit that not having a father has impacted me. I felt it when I was little because I didn't like to see how other kids, especially girls, would get picked up by their dads from school while I had to take the bus. It made me jealous that I didn't have that luxury so it gave me a reason to stay away from others, and yes I love my mom very much. I still am very grateful for her hard work but it didn't change the fact that I felt like that.

I should include the fact that my mom is from Mexico and she had me when she was 18 and I have one brother, who is Bryan, which she had him when she was 26. We were born in the United States as my mom left Mexico when she knew she was expecting me. She told me she wanted me to grow up somewhere nicer so she came here. I haven't really explained much about my mom, but she was planning to go to College in Mexico before she knew she was having me. My mom is very intelligent and am sad she never had the opportunity to go to higher education. I forgot to mention that my father was apparently a part of the first 8 years of my life until my mom had my brother which then he left a week after my brother was born, leaving behind a note apologizing but saying that he couldn't stay. I think the most crucial part was the fact that he left in the middle of the night when I was sleeping and I don't even remember the last day we were all together because I never imagined it would be the last day or that he would leave. He gave me trust issues because one day he was there and then he was gone with no empathy for us.

Now that would be another reason I can't make friends as it is hard for me to be able to trust them enough to build a relationship when I have the fear that they might leave one day as well. So as I couldn't make friends, my mom and brother have been the ones who are there for me and always seem to make me laugh. My relationship with both of them is like a circle because it would never end.

One summer day, my mom told me that our community was having a dinner and that we all had to participate in one way. She told me that I would have to be the one to help out as she works everyday except Sunday and she said that I was in charge of the cornhole game. Which is fine as all I had to do was make sure everything ran smoothly in that area. My mom said I would have to make sure that me and my brother were ready by the time she got home from work.

The dinner was on June 24th, 2023 at 7 pm which was a Saturday and my mom told me it would be held at a place overlooking the Chesapeake Bay. I was really excited to see the view. I was feeling a little anxious as I would be around people I don't really talk to. Anyways the day came quicker than expected and we had 3 hours before we had to be there. My mom was still not home but she had said she was on her way, so I helped my brother and I get ready and was very excited to wear the new outfits my mom had bought us. My mom got home an hour later and we finished getting ready so we headed to the event and we saw the house from when we were on the bridge. It was a stunning house and we had all never seen a house so big and what made it better was the yard it had. Not only could we see the house, but we could see people finishing setting up the tables and chairs and the food.

When we got to the house we were still in shock and the front of the house just added to it. We got to the backyard and there were already many people there doing their parts and I went back to the car, got the cornhole game and took it to the backyard with the help of my brother. I found a nice spot for it and so I started setting up and waited for people to play. Soon enough more people came to play and the sun also started to set. It was the most gorgeous thing ever, especially from the house as you could see the bay and the bridge also as the weather was feeling nice and breezy but still warm.

I got distracted and didn't realize there was someone waiting to play. I turned around and realized there was a very tall white guy with brown hair and blue eyes. He came with his younger siblings. He asked if he could play and of course I said yes and we started talking first about my brother and his siblings but then we just started to talk about other things like the fact that he was 17 and was adopted and so has foster parents. I really liked him because I felt like he understood how it feels to not have a parent even if he has two adoptive parents, he still understands as his biological parents aren't with him, we talked for the rest of the event and got each others' numbers to be able to communicate with each other.

I forgot to mention that the community was very happy with my help and everyone was happy that everyone contributed. The boy's name is Duke Clemson and he and I are now best friends. I am so grateful to have him as my first best friend as he really is the best friend I could've asked for and my mom is also thrilled that I have made an actual friend. I still am close to my brother and mom but now I have one more person who understands me. He has helped me understand that I shouldn't be worried about him leaving because one thing that will never leave is the memories that we share together and now I am trying harder to make friends because he has shown me that there is more to life than holding grudges.

Marella

By Vanessa Leigh

Hi! My name is Marella Sakuma and I am a Japanese-American woman in a family of five (six, including me.) It's me, my mom Hina, my dad Nate, my 10-year-old brother, Akihito, and the twins, Yui and Akio, at six years old. We live in the sweet and quiet community of Sandy Point.

We have been living in this community since I was 8 years old and when my brother was just a newborn . Even though I was born in Japan I feel like I'm not as in touch with my Japanese culture because I started living in America at such a young age. Unfortunately I became as some would say white-washed when I was in middle school. I stopped eating the food my mother made for me and only wanted American food. I stopped celebrating the Japanese holidays we had. And worst of all I only spoke to my family in English because I was embarrassed of our language. This lasted for almost all of middle school, until the summer before my 9th grade year.

My parents decided that my father and I were going to go to our hometown, Nikko, Japan, in the Tochigi Prefecture. Once I heard the news I was so angry. Mostly because I wanted to be with my friends going to the beach and the mall, so I screamed how unfair this was. After I said that my mother for the first time raised her voice to me, telling me I have lost my culture and I need to be embraced by it until I remember where I am from. So as soon as summer break started, me and my father hopped on a plane straight to Japan where we would be

227

staying with my fathers parents AKA my grandparents who lived on a farm just outside the city.

When we arrived, we came up to a big Japanese styled home with tons of shoji doors surrounding the front of the house. On the way to the house we were passing fields and fields of crops, and all of them were so colorful. When we got out of the car an old couple walked up to us and it was my grandparents. My grandma was the first to hug me, tight. I mean it had been almost a decade since I'd seen them. I hadn't been back since we left for the U.S.

As we said our hellos and everything, they asked about our trip up here and I told them about the beautiful fields I saw on the way here, and asked who owned them. It turns out that my grandparents actually own all of those fields, which I was surprised to hear, because we're talking acres of land!

My grandparents helped me and my father with our luggage and showed us to our rooms. My grandma helped me to my room and as we were walking to the room she explained to me that around here everyone will help out with the farm. That was a bit shocking to me. I was unaware other people were living here, but my grandma told me that my Aunt Sara, Uncle Samuru and their 4 kids started living here a couple years after we moved out of Japan. My grandma explained that we would all be waking up at the crack of dawn to help with the crops, watering and weeding and anything else that needed to be tended to. She explained that they don't just sell what they make for profit, they also need to eat so everyone needs to earn their keep. Even the children.

That night my grandmother and my aunt cooked a traditional japanese dish which I was hesitant to try but after one bite I scarfed it down as if I hadn't been fed in days. That night was a little odd in the beginning because I was sleeping in a new bed, but once I fell asleep it was one of the best sleeps I've had in a long time. The entire time I'm there I am helping out on the farm, and hanging out with my family. My family and I also decided to take the long ride to go up to Tokyo for the Fukagawa festival, and I had never seen or been to a festival before.

When we went to the festival I was so happy and mesmerized by everything I was seeing, and it showed me the beauty of my culture and how I should be proud of it. It was a bittersweet departure when my father and I needed to leave but I promised to my grandparents and to myself that I would change. I promised I would become more connected to my culture.

When I got back from my trip the first thing I did was apologize to my mom for all of my rudeness for the past several years. I had a week before school and decided a good way to start my first day at high school would be to be my true self, who now knows and is proud of my culture. Ever since that trip, I asked my mom if we could visit my grandparents every summer, and I decided to be a more empathetic and kinder person.

229

Now I am a fresh graduate from highschool, and I decided that I want to go to The University of California, Berkeley, for an art major such as either photography or realism drawings. My plan to leave was already making my family sad, but when I told them I would be moving across the country, they were shocked. They were ready to tell me no but after some convincing they allowed me on the exception that I call them every afternoon.

I had until fall before I left for college and I really wanted to give back to my community since I wouldn't be back until winter break and I probably wouldn't be living here ever again. I told my mom this so we were on high alert looking for anything we could do, or be a part of.

One day while we were at the grocery store I noticed this girl in the same aisle as us but I paid her no mind until I noticed a paper fall from her bag. As I went to grab the paper and hand it to her I read it and it was a flier for a fundraiser through a community meal for the elementary school at Sandy Point Beach. I handed the flier back to her and we talked for a little bit and I found out how to participate in the event by raising money, and that's when I finally figured out what I'm gonna do before I leave for college.

The event is supposed to happen next month so my mom and I decided we want to show our culture through decorations, and delicious food. We decided to go to Home Depot for some wood and paint, because we were gonna do a Japanese/American inspired booth. The foods we were gonna make were different kinds of sushi, ramen, and takoyaki. We also were gonna make desserts like matcha swiss roll, and warabi mochi.

Finally the day came for the fundraiser and it was a beautiful day. I saw so many people setting up tables with food from so many different cultures, and there were so many different people of all generations and backgrounds. As we set up our booth we were having some problems with a little bit of wind, that's when we heard a voice coming towards us. It was the girl who I saw from the grocery store, and she was accompanied by another girl. She finally told me her name was Rosa and her friend's name was Sophie, who came all the way from El Salvador to hang out with her friend. The two girls helped us with our booth by getting food out and putting up decorations. By the time the booth had finally been put up, tons of people had arrived and donated money by buying food and items from all of the community members who decided to participate for the community.

In the end we ended up raising around $10,000, most of which was because my family and I participated in the fundraiser to help raise the money. We also decided to donate $5,000 to the fundraiser. After the event, the community decided to split the money to go to the high school and to the streets of the neighborhood and save a little to improve the local park.

Once fall came around it was time for me to leave my hometown and head off to California. As I am about to board my plane, I say goodbye to my family and they send me off with tears in their eyes. I am ready to start my new life at Berkeley and meet new people in a new environment.

People Coming Together
A Story of Identity and Community

Written by Ms. McNeill's GCC Class Spring 2023

By Aiden Alexander

It was a busy day walking through the streets of Annapolis. Not too much farther, Johnny and I were going to an old music venue with some friends, Mike, Joe, and Grant. The Three musketeers to my D'Artagnan. The four of us were headed there for a hardbass rave.

"Wait up," I heard a familiar voice shout from behind me. I turned around and found Mike, with Grant in tow. "Joe is waiting for us there, let's not wait for the delinquents to get him," he said.

"Fine, but you better not slow us down," I chimed back. Mike is a good man, a little blunt at times, but he means well, and besides, he's right. The venue I'm going to perform at is a joint notorious for its large punk scene. Ah well, leave them to be and they will pay you no mind. I only hope that Joe knows that, seeing as he just moved here from a farm out West.

We moved quickly to the building, a bar with a music venue inside of it. "What are we waiting for?" Grant asked. He's a bright kid, a little naive, but still, he's good company.

After making our way in, we found Joe. Sure enough, he was in trouble. Surprisingly, he avoided messing around with the delinquents, but found himself being hounded by some nationalists. No fool in his right mind would mess with someone who lived through the constitutional crisis and fought in Iraq. If only Bush lived up to his promises and left when it became clear we were not wanted. But still, such thoughts are

234

not for a music venue, and I still have to pay the bills. "Thanks for helping me out," Joe sheepishly said.

"No problem, just keep clear of those people," Grant retorted.

"Anytime to help our friend," Ivan said. Ivan was the youngest of us, and a total poser. He was decked out from head to toe in leather gear. He barely even knows what the symbols he shouts mean.

Enough reminiscing, my slot is almost here, and I better get ready to go. I bid my friends farewell and went to the booth. As I set up and got ready, I noticed just how sorry the state of us were. In our perpetual rat race, we who have been left behind are treated like dirt. I saw miscreants who served time for crimes of necessity, delinquents who have nothing better than to drink. Addicts looking for one more hit of Krokodil, not knowing or caring about how it is slowly and painfully killing them. And those who belong to no class or caste, castaways lost in a sea of shattered dreams and broken promises. We are all here searching for our escape, and I have been chosen to try and alleviate the pain, if only for a moment.

That's what I like about my instruments, they are synthetic, computer generated sounds. They have no concept of emotion or life. They have their task and I am their master. They obey my every command and fill an empty void with fast paced, loud music.

I think all this and more as I begin to play, the music filling up the room. As I fall into a routine I've practiced nearly

235

100 times, I look out into the crowd. I see stomps to the beat, shakas being thrown around, and people dancing to the music. They were loving every second of it. I was accomplishing my goal, I took these tired, disenfranchised masses, and I gave them their escape.

As I finished and the crowd before me began to dissipate, I found my musketeers. "Well done," applauded Grant.

"Bravo, give us an encore," joked Mike.

"Not bad, I could do better," Joe said sternly, "but seriously, you did well, much better than the rest of us."

We all got our laugh and set off to my place. I began to think about whether or not what I do is what's best for the people I come in contact with. At the end of the day, it matters not. I made my choice, and I can only hope that I helped those in need whenever I was able to, and that the music I perform helps with the suffering of those who come to see it. As we exit the building, I think back on how much the world has changed since I was growing up.

By Kendall Borden

Sometimes it's hard to see the world outside of ourselves. Most days it feels like your issues and feelings are the only ones, but everyone has a story to tell. That's why being involved in my community is so important to me. Stepping out of my own head made me realize that things weren't going too well for most people around me. People were dealing with a lot of loss and stress that was almost too much to handle. All of this started weighing on me and I needed to talk to someone. So I reached out to my friend Sara from freshman year. We'd grown apart over the summer but once we started talking it was like we never missed a beat. We spoke for hours about our lives and how things were different. As she talked I could tell everything was really weighing on her too.

We decided we needed a distraction that would also help the neighborhood. After thinking about it Sara and I came up with the idea of a community quilt. We'd make the patches and anyone could add anything they wanted to honor someone or give a message. The community center and a few local businesses were more than happy to help us, and we got started. With a few small loans we bought supplies and met after school a few days a week. We started out with about ninety patches that anyone could pick up at the community center and decorate. At first only a few people came by, so I started a social media page for the community center and advertised. By the next week the word had spread to more people than we could've imagined. It took forever to sew together the patches, but we had so many people volunteer to help us.

About two and a half months later the community's quilt was complete. The collaboration and effort from everyone ended in a celebration where we gathered to hang up the quilt at the community center. The fact that the idea that I had brought so many people together was the best feeling ever. And I could tell that Sara felt better too. Everyone was excited to point out their patch and look at the work of others. Our small neighborhood in Annapolis was able to come together and make something that was a little bit of all of us and that was the best part.

Sabrina

By Samyra Boykin

The fresh smell of extra moist soil, spray paint, and watermelon sour patch kids. That's my home, but these blank white chipping, brick buildings. They hold a smell of car petroleum, and cat pee. Why anyone would live here, I have no clue. All I know is that this will be a long week. The only supposed "friends" I have are my cousin Ivy, and Ms. Garcia. Ms. Garcia is a retired artist from the '70s. She was known for her street art and graffiti work. It's similar to my dad, they both made great pieces and some of my main influences. But sadly his influences don't stay enough to become an inspiration.

Today was my third day in Annapolis. And the lack of rain and gray skies is strange to me. But nonetheless, I shall preserve. I needed something to spend my time on and Ms. Garcia had given me the rest of her spray paint to use. I stand up from my crouching position, and take a few steps back. I soon analyzed all of my supplies. Three baby steps in front of me were a ten-foot ladder, a floor tarp, a smock to cover my clothes, and a variety of spray paint colors. They ranged in different shades and hues of the rainbow.

I placed my red beats over my ears and blast Childish Gambino. And I pick up a random color, which surprisingly is the same color as my headphones. I started to shake the can up to mix the paint and pressed hard on the nozzle. I have no plan in mind, except to get rid of the blank, sad, chipped, neglected wall. The small 16oz can molded itself to my hand, and I follow its guide.

239

For me when I paint, an hour can feel like ten minutes. If it were up to me, I would continue from sunrise to sunset. But as the orange and yellow sun mixes with the green earth to make chocolate brown, I have to end my daily break from humanity. Did I almost fall, and break my leg from the scare? Yes, but did it snap me out of my trance? Also yes. Was I mad at who moved the ladder? Triple yes, but I looked down to see Ivy with a smirk on her face. Why she was accomplished with her actions, I will never know.

As I reached the bottom step, I felt the major presence of eyeballs behind me. I saw my mum and Aunt Isla looking proud. But I also saw Ms. Garcia and a good twenty percent of the other tenants. How did they find me? No clue, but both the answers to my questions and the "added help" from the neighbors will have to wait til tomorrow.

The navy blue sky slowly lightened to hues of cotton candy pink, and lavender flowers with coral reef clouds. This might be the only thing I'll miss from here. But my day must start, as my art should. But as my short walk to my spring project ends. I saw a large crowd, and my newly-dried creation, being painted over.

The lines may not be neat, and everyone might be overusing the amount of paint, but everyone is working together. The piece looks alright, but I'll go back to add my own ideas back on the wall. Hopefully, I can improve this work. Especially since I gained new cans, and passed my original goal. But only time will tell.

Koryn Jenkins

I remember when it was my 10th birthday, I had a big party. My Abuelita made my favorite dish, her famous Empanadillas. It was filled with beef and potatoes. This was the best birthday party ever. My papa made me a special bracelet, it was pink and white. My two favorite colors. He said it stands for hope, never give up and always do what you desire. Now my papa is gone. The New York City Police Department took him away while we were partying. They destroyed the whole place. They pepper sprayed my tio and the decorations, beat my dad, tased him, and spit on him. All to deport him. My mom rushed me and little cousins in the house, into the closet. I will always remember that day they came and ruined the best birthday ever. Now I'm 16 years old living in Annapolis, Maryland. . Living with my mom, baby sister and cousin. Everyday I think about how the police treated my uncle and dad. I want to make a change because what they did was not fair or right. I talked to my mom and she said I should do a community speech. I thought about that long and hard, and wondered how I would get people to come out to listen to me. My mom told me she would gather some people to come join my speech, she posted it on her Instaflap and hung up posters. I was going to give a speech on May 16. It's May 9th, I'm preparing for my speech everyday after school, with the help of my mother and tia this should be a wonderful speech.

The day before the speech me and my best friend decided to go to Quiet Waters Park to start setting up. This is the most beautiful park in Annapolis, at least in my opinion. We start setting up the chairs, tables, and then the podium. My best friend Ana, collected flowers so we could decorate the podium. She brung Birds of Paradise, the most beautiful flower ever in Annapolis. Later on we went to MOD pizza, they have the best pizza in the city. I got pepperoni and Ana got a chicken caesar salad.

The day of the speech, I decided to wear ripped denim blue jeans with a hoodie my dad bought me. The hoodie was all pink with the back saying "You Matter" big and white. My mom wore a flowy spring dress, she looked beautiful. It is 12pm, and my mom and I head down to the park to get ready. My speech starts at 1pm, but I see people here already. I didn't think a lot of people would show up, but there were about 200 people here and I was super nervous.

"Hello everyone. My name is Bri Lopez and I am 16 years old and I came here today to tell you about my dads story. He grew up in a nice big family, who lived in Brooklyn, New York. He has two beautiful daughters and a wife, which is me, my little sister and my mom standing right there. He worked at a famous Puerto Rican restaurant, called La Isla. He was a very sweet, outgoing and determined man. He wouldn't hurt a fly. On my 10th birthday he threw a big surprise party for me, it was the best birthday ever. After a while the New York City Police Department came and destroyed the whole place. They beat my dad, spit on him, tased him and even pepper sprayed my familia. I was heartbroken. They did all of this to my family. My dad. To me. Just to take my dad back to Puerto Rico. Police Brutality is real, and we all need to step up and protest for our rights and not let the police think they can treat us any type of way because we are all human! I know someone here has to have had a family member, friend, significant other, peer, killed or deported by the police. Not even just killed or beat up by the police. Innocent people they target. And for once more there is no reason. Take a stance. You all know your worth. We are all the same community. We are all familia!"

Everyone praised me and clapped, my mother started crying. I felt great inside. I go back home and my mom sees all over her facebook page my speech, and how I inspired my whole community. Later on she gets another notification about a block party down the street, someone is throwing. A celebration for speaking up for police brutality. Ana, my mom and I go down to the block party. It's a different culture here, different foods, different games. Everyone looks genuinely happy. I go dancing and eat, I'm really enjoying myself but then I also thank everyone for coming out to my speech. I'm really glad I am making a change in my community. At least it's a start.

By John Meyer

When I was a kid my dad was in the Army. We moved a lot due to the Army. Family was everything because I didn't keep friends for long. As a family, we had to work hard together to corroborate each other. But we all stayed really close, collaboration was important to us. We all wanted to do things together as a family and help each other. When I joined the Air Force, we were forced to collaborate with people who you didn't get along with. I found this relatively easy due to my childhood. Coming out of the Air force academy, my first assignment was in Annapolis Maryland. The Naval Academy was in Annapolis. Since I was in the Air Force, I had been jokingly harassed in my town. When I moved into my neighborhood, I noticed a lot of diversity. When I was running one day, I noticed a garden that looked like it was doing well but needed more help. Every day I would run past the garden, seeing the same people. I wanted to help but didn't know how to garden. I met this big strong man named Curtis. He was great at gardening which was shocking. He taught me some basic skills and helped me plant peppers. I really enjoyed gardening. The garden was off of main street. It was close to Bates Middle School. Sometimes school kids would come to the garden and teach me better strategies about gardening.

I started to fall in love with the garden. As time went on, I felt like I needed to do something about the garden. I wanted to help but didn't know how to. Then I had a thought. Our neighborhood could run a party...a block party for the garden. This could attract people to the garden and get the government to recognize the project. But I would need full commitment and collaboration from everyone in the community. So, 1 by 1 I talked to people and everyone liked the idea. The community had a meeting and set a date for the fourth of july. The event would have a garden presentation and harvest, fireworks, and live music. Fourth of July came and we started setting up the event. So, the event started and it was going really well. The music was great, there were parades and the garden was getting a bunch of attention. Then, our mayor showed up. Which was exactly what we wanted. She was fascinated by the garden. By the end of the night the mayor asked if she could buy some of the vegetables from the garden.

Three weeks later I got an email from the mayor saying that she recognizes that I started the event and asked if she could help aid the garden. This was amazing. Right after I got the email, I went to everyone and told them the good news. We all agreed that a bigger area for the garden and for the garden to be recognized by the city as a public project. The next day, the dumpsters next to the garden were being loved and an empty lot was being dug up for another garden. Then a sign was planted next to the garden with the name: Seedfolks garden. Everything the people had fought for came true. I was just so happy to be able to help everyone out. All the community needed to do was to work together to get what they needed. Collaboration is key to being seen as crucial.

Timmey Jefferson
by Logan Holley

My name is Timmey Jefferson, I am 14 years old. Me and my dad live in a tiny 2 bedroom apartment in Annapolis MD. My mom died when I was 4 years old from a heart attack. I have a neighbor who has a 5 year old kid. This kid, Logan, has a condition called terminal cancer.

His doctor said he only had 50 days left to live. Even though he was sad he was like a pot of gold at the end of a rainbow. I say that because he was so bright and so joyful even when things were tough. Me and other neighbors had texted each other to talk about ways to cheer him up. Me and my neighbors decided we would make a blanket. We decided to call this plan, "Project Logan." We decided that we need a place to do this project.

We constructed it at this lady named Stacy's house. We talked about how much we wanted to pitch in. We also talked about how to get the cheapest products to make this happen. We talked about that because we live in a poor neighborhood. So we don't have that much money to make this.

So we all pitched in about 45 to 50 dollars. We decided that we would all make the blanket together. It took us only 2 days in total to make. We decided that we were gonna wrap it in wrapping paper. We decided to all write an inspirational quote on the back for him to read. We gave it to him 15 days before he died. He carried that blanket everywhere he went, to the store, to his bed, quite literally everywhere.

Just because you don't live in a wealthy area or you aren't financially stable doesn't mean you can't help. We all can play a significant role in someone's life no matter big or small. We chose to enlighten that boy's life. We chose to make his last days his best days.
Koryn Jenkins

I remember when it was my 10th birthday, I had a big party. My Abuelita made my favorite dish, her famous Empanadillas. It was filled with beef and potatoes. This was the best birthday party ever. My Papa made me a special bracelet, it was pink and white. My two favorite colors. He said it stands for hope, never give up and always do what you desire. Now my Papa is gone. The New York City Police Department took him away while we were partying. They destroyed the whole place. They pepper sprayed my tio and the decorations, beat my dad, tased him, and spit on him. All to deport him. My mom rushed me and little cousins in the house, into the closet. I will always remember that day they came and ruined the best birthday ever. Now I'm 16 years old living in Annapolis, Maryland. Living with my mom, baby sister and cousin. Everyday I think about how the police treated my uncle and dad. I want to make a change because what they did was not fair or right. I talked to my mom and she said I should do a community speech. I thought about that long and hard, and wondered how I would get people to come out to listen to me. My mom told me she would gather some people to come join my speech, she posted it on her instaflap and hung up posters. I was going to give a speech on May 16. It's May 9th, I'm preparing for my speech everyday after school, with the help of my mother and tia this should be a wonderful speech.

The day before the speech me and my best friend decided to go to Quiet Waters Park to start setting up. This is the most beautiful park in Annapolis, at least in my opinion. We start setting up the chairs, tables, and then the podium. My best friend Ana, collected flowers so we could decorate the podium. She brung Birds of Paradise, the most beautiful flower ever in Annapolis. Later on we went to MOD pizza, they have the best pizza in the city. I got pepperoni and Ana got a chicken caesar salad.

Jai

By Jailah Jennings

I walked downtown on Clay Street one Saturday morning in Annapolis, Maryland. I was looking for something to relieve my overwhelming thoughts, feelings, and emotions from these stupid arguments that continuously rise up between my divorced parents that can never seem to agree.

As I came down Clay St. I came across a dark alleyway, and in the alley was a blank brick wall along the sides. It was right down the street from Miss Shirley's cafe, which is my favorite. The wall was unmarked, no scratches, marks or anything almost as if it had a purpose. But on the ground beneath the wall there were a few spray cans just on the ground.

I began to sort through the cans and colors to use on that wall in hopes that they will then find some sort of relief of these feelings, thoughts and emotions that's hurting my heart. I shook up the red and the blue and started to create these lines and shapes that were supposed to represent everything I felt. The lines were sharp as my anger and droopy, because I was ashamed and when the red intertwined with the blue, there was purple. Purple was fear...fear that it truly might never end, but then came yellow thick bold lines and there was hope that someday it will.

In all this, I did not realize the time. It was getting dark soon and I had to go back home, in expectation to meet with that wall again the next Saturday, and many more Saturdays to come.

That next Saturday, I went down to that alley off of Clay St, and when she turned the corner, I saw someone else in the alley. There in the alley was a boy, his name was Nashawn, and his name was written on the wall with a crown above it.

I told him my name and though I saw it written, I asked him his name. We then began to create along the wall covered in brick, it seemed they both had something to say in one way or another.

By Thomas Meyer

When I was a kid my dad was in the Army. We moved a lot due to the Army. Family was everything because I didn't keep friends for long. As a family, we had to work hard together to corroborate each other. But we all stayed really close, collaboration was important to us. We all wanted to do things together as a family and help each other. When I joined the Air Force, we were forced to collaborate with people who you didn't get along with. I found this relatively easy due to my childhood. Coming out of the Air force academy, my first assignment was in Annapolis Maryland. The Naval Academy was in Annapolis. Since I was in the Air Force, I had been jokingly harassed in my town. When I moved into my neighborhood, I noticed a lot of diversity. When I was running one day, I noticed a garden that looked like it was doing well but needed more help. Every day I would run past the garden, seeing the same people. I wanted to help but didn't know how to garden. I met this big strong man named Curtis. He was great at gardening which was shocking. He taught me some basic skills and helped me plant peppers. I really enjoyed gardening. The garden was off of main street. It was close to Bates Middle School. Sometimes school kids would come to the garden and teach me better strategies about gardening.

I started to fall in love with the garden. As time went on, I felt like I needed to do something about the garden. I wanted to help but didn't know how to. Then I had a thought. Our neighborhood could run a party...a block party for the garden. This could attract people to the garden and get the government to recognize the project. But I would need full commitment and collaboration from everyone in the community. So, 1 by 1 I talked to people and everyone liked the idea. The community had a meeting and set a date for the fourth of july. The event would have a garden presentation and harvest, fireworks, and live music. Fourth of July came and we started setting up the event. So, the event started and it was going really well. The music was great, there were parades and the garden was getting a bunch of attention. Then, our mayor showed up. Which was exactly what we wanted. She was fascinated by the garden. By the end of the night the mayor asked if she could buy some of the vegetables from the garden.

Three weeks later I got an email from the mayor saying that she recognizes that I started the event and asked if she could help aid the garden. This was amazing. Right after I got the email, I went to everyone and told them the good news. We all agreed that a bigger area for the garden and for the garden to be recognized by the city as a public project. The next day, the dumpsters next to the garden were being loved and an empty lot was being dug up for another garden. Then a sign was planted next to the garden with the name: Seedfolks garden. Everything the people had fought for came true. I was just so happy to be able to help everyone out. All the community needed to do was to work together to get what they needed. Collaboration is key to being seen as crucial.

Aaliyah Savoy

I still remember the day I lost my love for cooking. It was May 26th, 2018. The day my mom died, everything changed. My favorite memories with her are all in the kitchen. My family was torn apart when she died and everyone just went their separate ways. After a few months, I finally got tired of everyone acting so weird, and I decided I was going to move out. I searched for apartments in Annapolis, Maryland. I just knew I couldn't grow if I stayed in Camden. About two weeks later it was moving day. I only said goodbye to my little sister and promised her I'd be back to visit soon. I put my body into my car and got on the road.

Two months later and I'm finally done furnishing my apartment. As I go downstairs to get to the dumpster I see a poster that reads "Community Dinner, Bring food from your culture, Everyone Welcome!" I've never been more inspired. I quickly dropped off my trash and planned on what I was going to cook. It was finally the day of the dinner and I even woke up early so that i could go to the store before it got busy. I decided that I would make tostones, fried chicken, baked mac n cheese and sancocho.

I started cooking as soon as I got home. I cleaned my chicken, boiled my noodles and cut up my vegetables. I looked at the time and realized that I only needed to pack everything up in their containers. I did that and went to get ready. I wore black and red and did my hair and makeup. I grabbed the containers and headed to the car.

I got to the venue where the dinner was being held and put down my food. I found a seat at a table where no one else was sitting, and waited for the dinner to start. After a while it started. I walked up to start trying everyone's food and accidentally bumped into someone. It started a conversation and I learned that she is also Black and Dominican. I tried some of the collard greens she brought and they were so good. We talked for a while longer and some other people from the neighborhood came and joined in. I met so many new people I didn't even know lived near me. I felt so much less lonely after this dinner especially knowing that there was also another person who was Black and Dominican.

After that dinner I contacted the person who hosted it and we decided as a community to host dinners every other week. A new person comes to the dinner almost every time we host one. I feel that these dinners have made a closer and more tight knit community especially since a lot of the people I've met also were getting away from their families or lost a family member, just like I have.

The Quiet Man Who Cares

By Benjamin Tolen

The still house that sits on the end of the street who many know around Annapolis. Many people, parents, and children pass by the house everyday morning and night to get to the park using a dirt path right next to the house. The path had to be cleared every other week so it did not become overgrown with vegetation.

The man who lived in this house was old and very much kept to himself all day. People would wave to him when he would walk to his mailbox, but his ignoring silence led them to build negative connotations associated with him. Parents stopped letting their kids wave to him or say hello which hurt the man though he understood. The man would watch as kids run up and down the path laughing and screaming in joy which he appreciated. One day just like any other people walked and ran by the house to get to the party, but there was an eerie silence that appeared looking at the house. A few days went by, nobody noticing any difference with the house, but people noticed the path starting to become overgrown.

Nobody knew who kept care of it because it was such a normal part of everyone in the neighborhood's life. People started to come to the conclusion that the old man had been keeping care of it and nobody thanked him for it. Many felt bad for how they acted towards him, but it was too late. The neighborhood came together to build a garden of flowers down the path to represent the old man.

The old man always loved watching kids play and being able to allow access to all his neighbors to the park always made him feel good. The old man would have been proud to see how his passing brought everyone together.

Max

By Abdullah Arshad

Max was tired of being bullied. He had been picked on since he started high school, and it was getting worse every day. He tried talking to his parents and teachers, but their was no one willing to help him. That's when he decided to take matters into his own hands

"I'm sick of being pushed around," Max said to himself as he scrolled through his phone. "I need to do something about this."

He searched the internet and found other students who had been bullied in his School. Annapolis High School was famous for always being on the news for repeated violence, the School was like a warzone, no one cared about the situation surrounding the community. Everyone shared similar stories of being picked on and harassed, "I feel like a punching bag, taking hit after hit" he read as he felt anxious recalling the moments where he had been bullied in front of everybody, with no one to turn to for help. That's when he got an idea.

"I could make an online platform where we can all come together and take a stance against bullies," Max said.
He talked to his friend, John, who was a tech whiz. He had met him In the computer lab where he saw him coding. Together, they created a website where bullied students could connect and share their stories. They wanted to create a safe space where students could support each other and take action against bullies.

As the word spread, more and more students joined the platform. They shared their stories and found comfort in knowing that they weren't alone. They started to organize and take action against bullies in their school.

Max and John became the leaders of the movement, and leaded the frontline for action. They organized meetings and rallies, and soon the school administration took notice.

"What's going on here?" the principal asked, as he walked into the gym where the students were gathered.

"We're taking a stand against bullying," Max said, as he stepped forward.

The principal listened to the students' stories and promised to take action. He set up a task force to address bullying in the school and encouraged the students to continue their efforts.

Max and John's platform became a model for other schools around the country. Gaining more popularity they were interviewed on national news programs and received praise for their efforts. The school gained national recognition for reforms done by such eloquent student's

"I never thought that we could make such a difference," Max said to John, as they sat in their bedroom, looking at their website.

"It's amazing what we can accomplish when we work together," John replied.

Max smiled. He knew that they had made a positive impact on the school and changed the lives of many students. And both were proud of what they have been part of.

Ava

By Sophia Canuel

As I walked my dog Pluto, I noticed all the commotion around the neighborhood. The street grew narrow with an abundance of kids running around begging their parents to play with their friends. Then I remembered today is the neighborhood block party, where every year our neighborhood does one big block party to raise money for the community. It celebrates the summer starting and Maryland crab season starting! Only this year Zola isn't here for it. I urged Pluto to pick up, because I need to help Nana make the cookies!

"Ava, what is taking you so long, go help Nana make the German Tea cookies" my mother announces.

I reply, "Sorry sorry, I'm going to in one second..."

I rush to my room and hide under the covers, this isn't how today was supposed to go. Zola was supposed to be here picking out our outfits and frantically getting ready. This is the first block party without her since she had to move back to her family in Australia. After many calls from my mom I pull myself together and go helpout Nana.

" Hi Ava I'm so excited to make cookies with you" Nana exclaims I forget about Zola as I need the dough and toss the balls in powdered sugar. Nana and I don't even need the recipe anymore, it's muscle memory from every holiday that we make these for. A smile drifts onto my face as Nana's comforting voice distracts me, telling stories about how she used to naked the German Tea Cookies with her Nana back in Germany.

"Someday I will take you to visit and you will see how beautiful Germany is, and then you will tell your grandchildren stories about when you went to Germany; while you share the recipe of our family's cookies." I long to leave and skip today as if it never happened, the block party won't be the same without Zola.

The aroma from the oven fills the house, " I know that smell coming on the cookies are done, let's go guys we are going to be late" Dad shouts We head out of the house and set up our families stand. Mom lets me leave and roam around, usually this is one of my favorite days; but not today because I have no one to walk around with. It feels without Zola, we were a pair always together 24-7. And whenever I see a neighbor they just ask where she is, if she's called, when she's coming back...I'm not in the mood to deal with that today. I pass all the familiar faces in the stands and make my way towards a new stand I haven't seen before.

"Well hello how are you doing today, would you like to try some of our very own stew?"Kim asks

"What do you mean our, who made it" I respond

"Well, I made it but everyone contributed. Samuel grew the beans, Linda made sure all the vegetables grew by picking weeds, and Olivia grew the tomatoes. If I named everyone that helped we would be out here for days! I call it the everywhere stew, each ingredient of the stew was grown by a different neighbor from recipes and parts of their own culture. Some use this day for profits but just look how we all worked together to make our lovely garden; and look what we made out of it" Kim said.

She does have a good point, originally the annual block party was to meet new neighbors and hear their stories, it seems somewhere along the line the meaning got lost. I told myself to try the stew as it really helped me realize the importance of today.

What was once a memorable day to look forward to having fun with my friend Zola and talking to the neighbors, isn't so upsetting that I don't have my friend for it anymore. Instead, I spent the rest of the block party walking around tasting everyone's food and asking about the recipes and how it connects to them. I found so many differences and similarities in each other's cultures, which helped me find the true meaning behind the food everyone makes.

Margot

By Madeline Davis

I woke up on the living couch from a nap on a Tuesday morning in Annapolis, Maryland. My favorite tunes were playing in the next room over. I slowly got up and walked into the melodic room. Beyonce's song, Halo was playing. I remember dancing to that song with my mom every Saturday when we used to go to Quiet Waters Park. It's been awhile since I went, but I remember all of the fun I used to share with my mom listening to Beyonce's voice singing in the background. The music came to an end, and I saw my mom start to get ready for some event later in the day. Then it hit me, I suddenly remembered I had a neighborhood block party that very same day!

I rushed from the kitchen to my bedroom on the second floor. I couldn't wait to see my friends! It's been forever. The last time I hung out with them, it was at the garden. We used to all show up in the outfits our parents had picked and get ready to hang around the growing atmosphere. Now I am picking out my own outfit... "Hm, maybe a yellow shirt with some jeans?" I shook my head. It didn't fit who I was. "Maybe a black skirt, with this blue top." I smiled, I felt like I was able to truly connect with myself, now being able to make my own decisions. I put on the outfit I chose to wear and headed back downstairs to have a talk with my mom.

This specific block party was special, each person is supposed to bring their favorite music along with them. My favorite music is pop. I've always enjoyed it and I know it's probably everyone else's favorite too! "Hey mom, don't forget to bring the speaker, we'll need it to play our music!" She nodded back with a grin expressed on her face. I couldn't wait to dance to all of the music, I can't wait to hear everyone's favorite tunes!

We started packing up the car, and everything managed to fit into the small compact car my mom bought in 2017. As we drove my mom suggested turning on the radio.

"Would you like to pick our first song?" My mom says with her eyes glancing over her right shoulder, towards me.

"That's alright! I'd love to hear what your favorite songs are!" I say joyfully eager to hear what my mom enjoys listening to. She starts to play songs by the famous country singer: Morgan Wallen. I was surprised to hear that her favorite song was something I never would've listened to without mention. As the song starts to end, we start pulling into the gravel parking space, in walking distance to the community beach. Me and my mom started walking towards the beach and past the place that overflowed parts of our community with joy. My feet touch the sand and suddenly I hear a familiar voice call out my name...

"Margot?!" Said a girl further down the beach.

"Teresa?" I said in a joyful manner. Is that you? Her hair was darker and straighter than the last time I saw her. Teresa and I grew up together, but ever since we started High School we haven't been in much contact. "It's been forever, how are you?" I said, trying to hold the smile back.

"I'm great! High School is rough for me at the moment, but I'm super happy to see you!"

"As am I!" I replied.

We ran down to the water to meet up with other familiar faces I hadn't seen in ages. Alex, Ben, Amelia, and Julia were all there standing in the water. I hadn't seen them since 2019, they all looked more mature, and different. I was beyond excited to reunite with the five of them.

We talked and talked for ages until it was finally time to share our musical interests! I decided to go first, playing my favorite song Halo, by Beyonce. I've liked this song since I was young and many people started to enjoy it. As the night went on it became Teresa's turn to share hers. She started to play this heavy rock song, by ACDC. I had no idea she liked this song. It turned out that everything I thought I knew about her was wrong! But I enjoyed this song, and so did everyone else! Throughout the block party everyone grew closer and closer figuring out everyone's favorite artists, and bands. For some reason the fact that we all had different tastes in music brought us all closer together!

Hanging out with my childhood friends was like dancing in a meadow. I enjoyed every minute with them and we were all able to Honor each other's differences and use it to make us even closer! We all promised to keep in touch until the next block party. And so that we did.

Lucia

By Aidyn DeMarinis

I looked outside hearing loud music and I saw people in the neighborhood laughing and eating together. "Dad," I called out to a dark room in the house, "what's going on outside?"

"They're holding a block party outside. You know, like food and drinks and other stuff. I think it's to celebrate the spring and the reopening of that garden thing that they did last year." My dad answers back as I hear the TV flick on.

"Block party?" I think. "Sounds like fun!" I rush to my kitchen and start digging through our fridge. That's when it hits me when I see the ricotta cheese, I'm going to make my mom's famous cannolis. I hurry off and make the cannolis as the aroma fills my house. I used to make cannolis with my mom all the time, but she passed two years ago and dad has never been the same. All he does is stay in that little room all day in the dark and watch TV. Once the cannolis are finished I take the plate outside and place it on one of the many tables lined along the street. As soon as I walk outside the sun hits me in my eyes and the smell of the Chesapeake Bay hits my nose. I look around to see kids playing and adults talking, I suddenly get very nervous as I feel so out of place. I started looking at the other dishes that people had prepared like crabs with Old Bay and nachos, plus other foods I'd never seen before. Then I feel a tap on my shoulder, I turn around and see an old woman. She has dark hair and is quite tall and is wearing a vibrant smile with even more vibrant clothes.

"Hello, what's your name sweetie, I don't think I've seen you around before." Says the woman, "my name is Florence."

"My name is Lucia. I made these cannolis...if you want one." I say moving aside to show her the plate.]

"Wow, these look lovely! You know, this reminds me of an older resident, cannolis, maybe you know her...Maria Pope. I remember watching her when she was a little girl playing with the other kids and always making those cannolis and other sweet treats for me. You guys look a lot alike actually if I wasn't wearing my glasses I'd probably call you Maria." She says while silently laughing to herself.

"Really?! She was my mom!" I say as a smile appears across my face. Me and Florence continue talking about my mom and her old childhood memories. The more I talk to Florence the more I feel comfortable in the neighborhood. We had other people come to us and talk to us and a lot of people told me how good my cannolis were. I really started to feel more embraced by the community and that's why I decided to convince my dad to come outside. "Hold that thought Florence." I say rushing to my house. I open more doors and run into my living room. My dad pauses the TV and looks at me.

"Luica, what are you doing here? I thought you were at the block party?" He says turning to me and standing up. "Is everything okay?"

"Dad!" I say out of breath. "You have to come to the block party!"

"I don't kn-"

I interrupt my dad and grab his arm and start pulling him to the door. "Dad please! Please!" He bulgrently gives in and allows me to pull him outside. We walked over to the table I was previously at with Florence and the others. "Florence, this is my father."

"Hello Florence-" my dad starts up but Florence interrupts him by bringing him into a hug. She steps back and he smiles. That's the first time I've seen my dad smile in 6 years.

"Oh Lucia! There's someone I want you to meet!" Florence says, turning her attention to me as my dad strikes up a conversation with one of the other dads nearby. A boy around my age appears with a ball in his hands. He has a toothy smile and dark brown hair. He sticks out his hand and we shake.

"Hi, my name is Henry. I'm Florence's grandson. Do you want to go play with me and my friends? My grandma won't stop talking about you." I look over his shoulder to see a group of kids beckoning me over. I look up at my dad and give a nod of approval and I quickly hug Florence and before I follow Henry to him and his friends. Best block party EVER!

James

by Andrew Duhon

My name James I have lived in this small town for most of my life, I have never been married I have no family just friends that live far away, I work at home and have a dog, Every weekday morning I wake up and drink my orange juice and go on a walk with my dog, During the dog walk my older neighbor Camron a vietnam vet stops me and others my water and my dog a treat Most of the time I ignore him, But today is different, I stop and say good morning. He invites me into his small house on the corner and we talk on the porch about my dog and his garden, he lives by himself in a small brick house on saint pauls street two blocks from the water,

Camron asked me 10 minutes into the conversation if I would like to host a dinner for members of the garden and family club. I responded with why should I say because you keep your lawn In such great care, I had never really thought of it like that. I really just cut the grass and spread the weeds. But of course I said yes, I Left after we discussed the detail such how many people would be attending but really had no idea what I was getting myself into,

When I got home after the walk I called my mother who lived in London who was always parting and especially social but that really never passed on to me. After my long conversation with her I made a plan on how to host the food I need the drinks and other friends of mine to invite.

Yo Soy Bad Bunny

By Hugo Garcia

Me llamo Bad Bunny y voy hacer un evento musical para poder comunicarme con las personas a través de la letra de mis canciones y los actos que contribuyen con los derechos de las mujeres. Este evento tengo planeado hacerlo para no solo para defender los derechos de las mujeres si no también ayudar a la comunidad gay haciéndoles saber que sus preferencias no los hace diferente y que todos tenemos derechos.

El evento será anunciado en mis redes sociales para hacerse viral y que todas esas personas que se sienten identificadas con la letra de mis canciones incitan a más gente a escuchar mi música.Yo estoy aportando a la comunidad no solo con palabras sino también con acciones de protesta que se hacen virales.

El día del evento me vestí con ropa de mujer y salí al escenario cantando una canción en donde hay ciertas partes que se refieren al maltrato de mujeres y como ellas no se tienen que dejar maltratar por un hombre.Al final del concierto la gente aclamaba mi nombre y eso me hizo sentir que hice bien mi trabajo.

Al día siguiente salí en las noticias como un héroe para toda esa gente que necesitaba abrir los ojos y darse cuenta que todos merecemos respeto y que todos somos iguales con los mismos derechos.

Valentina

by Kimora Gillis

I am Valentina (Val) Reyes. I am Afro-Latinia. I am fifteen years old and am a part of the LGBTQ+ community. Me and my parents just moved to a new neighborhood a couple of weeks ago in Annapolis Maryland because we needed a bigger house as me and my three brothers were growing out of the old one. I've become close with my neighbor because we attend the same school Annapolis High School. I consider her my best friend because I tell her everything including me being a part of the LGBTQ she is basically the only person I told because I know she doesn't judge me.

During the middle of the week my friend Mara told me about the new event at our school, the Beautifully Black Expo .She figured it would be a great way for me to get to know people since she knows I'm not much of a talker. I figured I would go because maybe there will be new information about our black historians which I love to learn. I thought maybe I'd meet people there who have the same thing in common.

The day came quicker than expected and there I was standing at the entrance of the auditorium as scared as a deer caught in headlights. There were a lot of people but all I could hear was talking, no speaker was in front of the crowd and there weren't many students like I thought there would be. I finally walked in after spotting Mara sitting with a group. She had a huge smile on her face as though she had just received the best news of her life, excited that I was actually here. I began walking over asking her why there was no speaker and she told me that students just use this as a way to get out of class, explaining why only a small amount of people are here and a big amount in the halls.

Looking around I found a place to sit by myself for a couple of minutes because I'm not really fond of Mara's friends . As I'm sitting there I kind of zoned out listening to a tune in my head not even noticing that I began humming the light tune out loud. Although I am zoned out I feel a presence in the seat beside me and as I look next to me the person looks at me and it's like all the noise faded away and we were the only people left in the auditorium.

She was beautiful, she had asked my name and I told her Valentina and in return she told me her name which was Neveah. She had asked me what tune I was humming and I told her the song which was called a song by the five heartbeats an oldie, which I love because I feel like old music just has more soul and meaning. I expected her to laugh but she didn't. She began singing some of the lyrics and I could only look at her with a silly smile, finally finding some joy in being at this event.

Next thing I know Neveah pulls me up and walks over to the front of the auditorium sitting me down. She grabbed the mic as I looked at her crazy wondering what she was doing, she had introduced the guest speaker playing the intro song which to no surprise was the song I was humming. As the guest speaker came Neveah and sat down beside me as the guest speaker looked at us and nodded in agreement of the song

273

choice being that he was going to talk about all things black history and culture including music dance etc.I turned with a smile on my face seeing Neveah smile at me as we both looked ahead and payed attention.

After the Expo Neveah stayed behind to help clean up and asked if I would stay behind also, I kinda just stared at her because I was scared people would think it was more than a friend thing. But eventually I gave her an answer letting go of any care of what people would think because honestly I wanted it to be more than friends. As we cleaned I noticed Mara smiling from the door then running away as I smiled back happily that I finally found somebody who was similar to me with the same gender orientation and interest of black culture. A few days after the expo was a monday and it seemed as though the day had brighted more than last monday as people are being more talkative and i am talking to others and surprisingly holding Neveahs hand in the hall not caring who sees or judges me for being me.

By Jordan Hauf

Hi, I'm Bob Shmimleton and I live in Annapolis. It is a generally nice place. But one day I was walking down the street when I saw a guy being made fun of for being gay. At the time I was in a hurry to get home to eat dinner so I wasn't paying much attention. The next morning I got up to go to school.I go to Annapolis high. On my way to school I saw the same person as the day before looking really sad. I was kind of confused why but then remembered what happened. I did not know if it was my place to say anything so I just kept moving on. And then I saw him again in the library a little later that day also looking sad. So this time I went over and asked why he looked so sad. He did not tell me at first but eventually he did. He told me that it was because of the incident yesterday. I told him I was sorry for not stepping in but I was in a hurry. He said it was alright and after that I bid him a good day and left. While we were talking though I noticed how upset it made him and how other people probably went through the same thing.

As I was thinking about our conversation that night when I went to bed I realized that something needed to be done about the bullying. So the next day in school I was brainstorming some ideas as to what I could do to help. I went through a couple ideas and then I thought about a gathering. A gathering where everyone who wanted to come could without worrying about anyone making fun of them for their differences. While I was thinking about this I was considering the costs and other things. Although I knew it would be expensive I also knew this was very important for the people who were being made fun of.

So the next day I asked my parents to help me put my plan into action. They said they would help as long as I had it planned. So for the next few days I made sure I had everything planned. All the things I wanted to do I could not do myself. So the next day at school I asked the principal if we could have a ceremony for anyone who wanted to come to the community gathering. Some people came and actually seemed interested. So at the end I asked everyone who was going to come to write their names down so we could have a meeting later on.

The next day we called everyone in and talked about what they wanted to do at this event. I told them the overall goal was to have a lot of fun activities we could do together. When we started the meeting everyone was really quiet and did not say anything. I knew they were uncomfortable so I just told them to write their ideas down for now. And they did with excited expressions on their faces. So when they were done I looked at their ideas and saw that they were pretty good. So I told them to go home and I would get everything ready and it would just be a couple days.

So for the next couple of days I spent my free time planning where everything would go and what to bring and stuff. Then the day came when the event would take place. I got in the car and my parents drove me to the park and when we got there some people were already there. I could tell they were excited. So I started setting things up and as I was more and more people started showing up. Even more people than I had planned because the people that I had planned on showing up told their friends about the event and they were interested as well. I eventually finished and everyone was there by the time I had. Then we finally started.

In the beginning all of the other kids that came were really quite and shy. But then I started getting really energetic and eventually some people joined me. Then a lot of people started joining until everyone had joined. I believe they started to realize that they were not going to be judged for their differences. Everyone looked like they were really enjoying themselves. After a good few hours of all of us playing and messing around we sat down and had some soda and snacks. Everyone thanked me for setting the event up and that they had a great time and did not feel like outsiders after that.

Over the next couple of months we had similar events like that. We had most of the people who had come to the first event as well as some familiar faces. Everyone who had come said they had a great time and appreciated it. As well as it made them feel like there was a place they belonged and there were people that were kind of the same as them that they could make friends with. Overall the community was improved in a way that made usually non social people feel welcomed somewhere and increased cooperation and communication between me and my new friends. The plan is to keep these events going and to make it so that everyone who feels left out no longer does and everyone who needs a friend has one.

Alejandra

by Diego Hernandez

My name is Alejandra Chavez. I am a 12 year old girl. I live in Annapolis Maryland.I've always loved painting. I used to paint with my older sister before she passed. Her passing was difficult not just for my family but my community.

She truly was the glue that held everyone together she could always make everyone smile. Since she's been gone everything fell apart, rolling knolls isn't the same community it once was. We became a broken community that doesn't talk to one another.

For the first time in months I saw Jessica, my old best friend. For some reason we fell apart, we used to be inseparable. I wanted to talk to her but my throat went dry like chalk, I was scared for some reason, Instead I went back home. On my way I saw Jessica's mom, Ms Raymundo, she just looked at me and kept walking. At that moment it hit me.

I can't continue like this. I won't continue like this. My community is broken. My sister would have never wanted something like this to happen. Before she passed she said "no matter how big the problem you can always solve it".

I told my mom about the situation and how I felt and she agreed she had similar feelings. She was hurt by how the community (neighborhood of rolling knolls) fell apart.

My mom told me about how when she first moved here they were all more than family, that lit something in me. I knew I had to do something to bring everyone back together. I had to take action to break the awkward silence.

Me and my mom came up with some ideas of what we could do. We thought of having a community meal everyone will collaborate in bringing one part of the community meal. Before anything though I needed to talk with my best friend. I went over to her house and we both broke out in tears. We talked about my sister and I realized she wasn't just my sister but also Jessicas.

She said " Ella era mi hermana tambien" I said " Ella era mi mundo " my sister meant the world to me. I knew she would hate the idea of how we're a broken community. I told Jessica about my idea of the community meal and she agreed it was a great idea. We told Ms. Raymundo she said she would be glad to bring the pupusas.

Me Jessica and my mom went around the community inviting everyone to the community meal. Everyone said they are glad to help and are excited. The meal is gonna be downtown by the bay. Jessica and I were in charge of planning and setting up the meal. We found a great spot.

We got to work first we cleaned up, then decorated, then we started setting up the food and activities. Downtown was a great place to bring everyone together. The beautiful view of the bay truly makes the afternoon one to remember. As everyone arrived I helped everyone settle down and prepare for the meal. I was happy, I was making a difference and bringing my community back together.

Everyone brought something to the community meal. I was so happy we were collaborating together to do something positive.

I made the horchata for the community meal, Everyone said it was delicious, Everything at the meal was delicious. It was a success! All of the neighbors were talking and having fun. Jessica brought some board games to play.

The community meal brought back together my broken community. My family was so proud of me. But more importantly I knew my sister was proud of what I did. The community of rolling knolls was back to normal. It's great how a simple meal made such a big impact on my home. It filled me with excitement to see everyone getting along again after a weird year. Me, Jessica, and the neighborhood kids went to go play on the hill then the sun started setting. The hill where you can see all of the neighborhood. After the long day I sat down and watched the sun set over the green grass.

By Savannah Holmes

Well todays the day. The start of Annapolis's biggest music festival of the year, and it's coming to our neighborhood. I mean most people would be afraid of singing in front of everyone in their town. Well me, I'm not. Most people think I'm not capable of much because I'm young and "dumb". But that's not true. I am going to make a difference in this place .

Truth is I am scared but not to sing. I'm scared of what will happen to me if I do. My momma told me "don't you do it Maliah! it ain't your place!" Over and over again she begs me not to sing my song. Now right now you might be wondering; "what is this kid talking about?" "Why would we care about her singing a song?" Well my song ain't just a song. It's a message. A Message for my part of town. You see my neighborhood ain't one of them neighborhoods with big pretty white houses and even green lawns, and clean perfect paved sidewalks and streets. My neighborhood is different. When you walk outside you see most people standing around drinking and yelling. You see old man Hector walking around with his beer bottle.

The one thing he has to his name. You see Ana through her bedroom window, people watching. Sometimes I wonder about her, she isn't like the rest of us. Only thing I know about her is that she helped with the community garden. Anisha, well she's always at someone's house. But that's because the last place she wants to be is her own. Her momma and her daddy fight a lot. One time they were up at 5 am screaming and cussing each other. The whole entire Annapolis could hear them. And there was Anisha sitting leaning on the pole of her porch, watching the stars. Or maybe asking God why she was given them parents.

Mama says that God gave everyone everything for a reason. She says that he makes you go through things to achieve greater things in life. That's the hard part about being a christian. Sometimes I ask God why he does these things. But pastor Cornell tells me that we don't understand his ways. Which clearly, I can see. Every now and again I ask God the same question. "Why did you take my daddy from me?" Momma doesn't like to talk about it much. She tells me "I don't understand it either baby, But it is what it is." I can tell she wonders the same things I do.

My daddy was shot in a shootout that happened in my neighborhood about 2 years ago. He was outside on his way home from going to buy some eggs for the next day's breakfast. Momma told him he shouldn't go late after dark, but he insisted. He did want to wake up early and get it in the morning. All I know is it was around 9:17 P..M and the first bullet was fired. Daddy had just told momma around 30 something minutes ago that he was on his way home. Many bullets bursted from each gun. Lasting around 5 minutes. Momma had pulled me to the ground and told me to stay there for a while. But all I could think about was if my daddy was alive or not.

After about 10 minutes the police came and many fire trucks were out there. Everyone had popped out of their homes and came to see the damages. I saw a couple bodies on the ground. Then I saw one in the middle of the street. Carrying a grocery bag. I ran, I ran as fast as I could. I didn't care if my momma was yelling or the police chasing me. I ran to the body and fell to my knees. It was my daddy laying there. Lifeless and empty. All I could do was cry. Nothing else. I had just lost my dad to a gun.

That's what my song is about. It's about gun violence in cleveland. This has got to stop. I am not the only person in this neighborhood to have lost a loved one to gun violence. Many people in Ohio feel my pain. And that's why we all have to come together. We have to unify as a community to stop this problem. All day I've been thinking about whether I should speak out against this. Am I really just "young and dumb?"

As I walked to the festival I saw a lot of people around. Most were from my neighborhood but some weren't. I smelled the potluck from a mile away. The food trucks and cotton candy machines. Kids were running around the place like a playground. I remember when I was that young. Seeing the community like this made me smile, seeing us united as one. aS I walked through the people I saw, the gangsters of the neighborhood. The ones that were involved with the shooting with my dad. As they walked past I looked them dead in their eyes. Not breaking any eye contact. Behind them I saw Kaleb. He saw me and walked over to me. He's the son of one of the gangsters in our town. He has dark curly hair that covers half of his eyes and forehead. He's pretty tall and has brown skin. Even though he's part of the gang, nothing about him scares me. Most gentle gangster you'll meet. "So I heard your singing today, Maliah." He said sternly. "Yep! What about it?" I snapped back at him. "Didn't know you could sing, read your name on the program." He said. He smiled at me and then he walked away. He would look so much better if he actually cared about the city's well-being.

As I walk up to the stage a small woman comes up to me. I recognized her.. It was sae-young. She was the lady who stayed in her house for like a long time. But then she started helping with that community garden. "I hear you are singing in the festival?" she says with a bright smile. "Yeah Ms.Young, I am!" I say brightly. She smiles and touches my arm. You know the way grownups say " I hope you do a good job" without saying they hope you do a good job. As she walks away I take a look at the stage. It's really big. I mean can I really do this? What if this causes more problems? As I take the stage a lot of things are going through my mind. It's like A tornado. But the one thing that's in the center is my dad. I want him to know that I won't give up. I will put an end to the gun violence in this community.

I looked at my mother's desperate look in the crowd. Sorry momma, but I have to do this. As I take the mic, I think to myself; "C'mon girl this is just the beginning." I speak out to the microphone: "Hello everyone, the song I will be singing is a solo written by me. My song is called; 'We are the change.'"

By Brianna Kauffman

I was moving out of my parents house. I was so excited about what university had to offer for me. Box by box my childhood room became more bare, then out of the corner of my eye I saw my old laptop. I went towards it and wiped it off, it was obvious that it was collecting dust, then I ravaged through the boxes trying to find its charger. The thought of being reunited with all of my old photos and games gave me such a rush of nostalgia. I soon found the cord and crawled into an empty corner. I plug it up and... it works.

Upon logging in, I find notifications, "what?" I mutter to myself in confusion. I dived deeper, the notifications were coming from an app I used to use, Chaos. When I first signed up for chaos I was 14, I newly moved to Annapolis from Montgomery, being young and queer was no joke there. The south wasn't really welcoming of anyone who wasn't straight and white for that matter. I was always seen as a tomboy and "not like other girls", I used to hate frilly dresses and heels and opt for large hoodies and dirty sneakers, and growing up all of my friends were guys. Being queer wasn't great in my family either. They were devoted Christians. As a kid, nobody took a second glance at me, that was until middle school. While all the girls were so comfortable with their growing bodies and peaks, I continued doing what I was comfortable with, wearing my large hoodies and dirty sneakers.

I covered my chest any chance I could and depised all of the other changes happening with my body. My voice, my curves, my menstrual. It became so bad to the point where I used bandages to bind*. I was so confused and so sick of myself, I turned to the internet for help. After a couple of google searches I found the term transgender. I felt like I finally found who I was. That same night I took shears and cut all of my hair off, shaping it to look more masculine. I still remember the euphoria I felt when I looked in the mirror, I was jumping off of the walls. I wrapped my hair in one of my moms fancy scarves and fell asleep, feeling as happy as ever.

I woke up to the scarf on the ground and my father standing and the foot of my bed. "...jessica?" his voice tumbled, he didnt sound mad, he sounded concerned. I jumped out and ran to the bathroom, silently sobbing on the way. I slam the door behind me and break down, I hear my moms footsteps and she knocks on the door, "please come out sweetie.". I was terrified, after half an hour I let my guard down and opened the door. I met with my mom with a disgusted expression.

"What's this?", she leans over to study my hair, "what did you do.". "I was just trying to switch it up." I've had long hair my whole life up until that moment. I was hoping that my parents would believe the lie but they could see right through it. They bought me a wig and signed me up for after school bible study. It was never discussed again.

I felt like I was trapped. I fell into a depression, then my depression turned into ignorance. I was so negative, I hated myself even more than I did before. That was until I found chaos.

Chaos was a community site, there's multiple groups and servers of like minded people. While creating my profile, I realized I had to think of a name ,"...j- joe- jodie? jodie.", I was thinking out loud. I registered then I was looking at the servers, then I stumbled across a familiar word, transgender. I was taken back, then I checked the server out. I was greeted with numerous pronouns, labels, and sexualities. I was so curious, I spent hours just scrolling through, I was invested. I officially joined the server and started on my introduction post. "Jodie - 14 - " I paused mid sentence, what were my pronouns? I erased and retyped countless times. I decided to scrap the post and continue browsing.

I found the vent channel, I was scrolling and reading a few, then I decided to create my own. I've been penting up so much since the hair incident, I just had to let it all out. I remember all of the supportive replies and love and appreciation. I felt like I truly found my people. Out of all of the likes and private dms one stuck out to me, roxy. Roxy was around my age, 15 or so, she was one of the sweetest girls I have ever met. She dmed me to tell me that she has been in the same situation as me and she is always there if I need to talk. I've never felt so seen and supported,I nearly cried.

I continued to talk to Roxy, through all of my ups and downs she was always there, words can't describe how I felt towards her. My heart skipped a beat everytime I saw her name. She found a way to surprise me everyday. Even though she's no longer in my life, I'll forever appreciate her. While looking through the messages, I felt that way all over again. I wish I had a person like Roxy in my life now. Roxy wasn't the only person I met in chaos, the whole community was close and we were all like best friends, but one at a time people left the platform. Eventually, me and roxy logged off, I haven't heard from her since. I still think of her from time to time.

I take a deeper dive into the messages, and I find a phone number. I don't have recollection of ever texting her off of chaos, but I decided to take my changes and see if that's still her number.

"Hi, is this Roxy?"

I felt stupid for texting the number, so I turned my phone off and continued packing. After packing everything up I realized I got a notification.

"This is Roxanne, yes, who's this?"

My stomach sank.

"This is Jodie"

I waited.

"From Chaos? How did you get this number?"

"Old messages, How have you been?"

We texted for hours. I felt so connected to somebody ever. I went to sleep in my new dorm with a huge smile on my face. People in the community like Roxy helped me find my confidence in my gender identity and helped shape the proud person I am again. And even though we don't talk anymore I will be forever thankful for them.

Thomas's Chapter

by Aidan Kirkpatrick

I found myself in a diverse neighborhood in Chicago, having recently moved from Germany to start anew. The community meal was held in a local community center, which was buzzing with activity as people from all walks of life gathered to share a meal. The tables were adorned with colorful tablecloths, and the air was filled with the aroma of various cuisines from around the world. The atmosphere was warm and welcoming, with people chatting and laughing, creating a sense of camaraderie.

As a newcomer to the neighborhood, I was eager to get involved and make connections. I wanted to be an active participant in the community and contribute in a meaningful way. The community meal presented an opportunity for me to share a taste of my culture and make connections with others who were also passionate about building a strong community. I hoped to not only contribute through my traditional German dish but also by actively engaging with the community members and learning about their stories and experiences.

Being passionate about cooking, I decided to prepare a batch of homemade schnitzel, a classic German dish, for the community meal. I spent hours in the kitchen, carefully pounding the meat, dipping it in flour, egg, and breadcrumbs, and frying it to golden perfection. I also made a tangy sauerkraut side dish to complement the schnitzel. It was a labor of love, and I poured all my culinary skills into the dish, hoping it would be well-received by the diverse group of people attending the event.

When I arrived at the community meal with my platter of schnitzel, I was met with curiosity and excitement. Many people were eager to try the dish, and I happily shared a taste of my culture with them. I explained the traditional German preparation and ingredients used in making schnitzel, and it sparked conversations about different culinary practices and cultural traditions among the community members. Seeing the joy and appreciation on their faces as they savored the schnitzel was immensely rewarding. It was a small but meaningful contribution to the community event, as it fostered cultural exchange and appreciation among the diverse group of attendees.

As I was serving the schnitzel, I struck up a conversation with a young woman who was attending the community meal with her family. She was curious about the German cuisine and had never tasted schnitzel before. We sat down together, and I shared stories about my homeland and the significance of schnitzel in German culture. She, in turn, shared stories about her family's culinary traditions and how food brought her own community together. We found common ground in our shared love for food and cultural exchange, and our conversation flowed effortlessly. It was a heartwarming interaction that deepened my connection with the community and made me feel welcomed and accepted.

As the community meal came to an end, I felt a sense of fulfillment and gratitude. The event had been a wonderful experience, and I had made new connections, learned about different cultures, and contributed through my cooking. I left with a heart full of warmth and a sense of belonging in my new community. In the days that followed, I continued to participate in other community events, building on the connections I had made and becoming an active member of the neighborhood. The community meal had been a stepping stone for me to integrate into the community and establish meaningful relationships with my neighbors. It has also reaffirmed my belief in the power of food to bring people together and bridge cultural differences. I was grateful for the opportunity to contribute to the community and create a positive impact, and I looked forward to many more experiences that would further strengthen the bond among the diverse group of individuals in my new community.

Leon Nees

I've lived in Michigan for all my life. I was born and raised here, I met and lost my wife here, and I raised and since six months ago lost my only daughter too. My daughter and her husband passed away and left their only child, my granddaughter, Irene, behind. Since I was the only family she had left, she moved in with me. She moved in with me but she isn't really here. Irene and I aren't very close at all, as much as I'd like to be. When she was little her and her parents would visit me often, but as she got older I started seeing her less and less, until they'd only come by once or twice a year. The physical distance between me and Irene isn't the only problem. Irene and I are very different. Irene comes from a different world than I do. My parents immigrated here from Ireland when my mother was still pregnant with me. I grew up in a catholic household, with many other siblings. Irene is Afro Irish, her dad was African American, and she's gay. Now neither of these things matter to me, but Irene thinks they do, and even though I've tried to show her these differences don't matter to me, I've never been very good at conveying my emotions, it isn't my strong suit. So since Irene's sixteenth birthday is almost here, her first birthday since she lost her parents, I've decided to do something special for her.

I'm sitting at my desk on my computer sending an email to Nora when Irene walks in, I hastily hit send and power down the old computer as she says "What are you doing?".

Thinking up an excuse on the fly I say "Emailing an old colleague of mine, he just retired".

She stands there awkwardly for a moment before she says "Well I'm heading out now, I'll see you later". I smile at her and wish her a good day at school and wait until I hear the sound of the front door closing. I wait another five minutes or so until I'm absolutely sure she's gone, and then I start off for the garden.

When I get there I see Curtis, Nora, and Mr Miles waiting for me. They all have bags and look ready to start. Curtis hands me a bag and says "Took ya long enough".

We chat for a few minutes and then start decorating, the hours go by quickly, and slowly more and more members of the garden come bringing food, or to help set up. Everyone knows why Irene came to live with me and they all empathize with our situation, so when I asked them to do this for me they were all very eager. Everyone wanted to pitch in to give Irene a party for her birthday, everyone wanted to help welcome her into the little community that we've built for ourselves here and for that I am very grateful.

As I'm hanging up the last of the streamers and thinking about what I'm going to say to Irene I glance down at my watch and realize the time. By this time Irene will be almost home from school! I hastily pin up the last streamer, climb down from my stool, and announce "I'm off to get Irene!".

I rush out of the garden and start on my way home as quickly as I can manage, I want to beat Irene home from school. I round the corner into the street of our townhouse and I hurry up the driveway and through the door. I look down and see Irene's shoes and backpack still aren't here. Good, I beat her home. I walk into the kitchen and get myself a glass of water, then take a much needed moment to catch my breath. I sit down at the counter and let myself breathe, I'm not used to moving so quickly. As I'm feeling my heartbeat slow and my breathing get less heavy, I hear the door click. Irene is home. I put my glass down and get up, starting towards the door.

She sets her backpack on the ground and goes to start untying her shoes. "Wait!" I say a little louder than I meant to, she looks at my quizzically so I continue "I need to take you somewhere".

She looks at me, confused, and says "Now?", and I nod. She looks at me for a second before opening the door again and waiting for me to lead her out. I walk down the steps and to the bottom of the driveway, turning around to make sure she's following me. I see she is so we continue walking back to the garden at a relaxed pace, not rushed like earlier since we could take our time. We walk in silence occasionally glancing at each other until we are infront of the garden. We walk through the gate and she looks around. She takes in everything, slowly and carefully. She looks at the streamers we hung, the cake someone brought, and the balloons we blew up, until her eyes land on me. I open my mouth to speak but it now feels like my head is empty, all the things I planned to tell her are gone. I put my hand in my pocket and take out a folded piece of paper. I unfold it to reveal an old photo from when Irene was just a baby. Her mom and her dad are sitting next to me and I have Irene in my arms. She's looking up at me with her big eyes and a smile on her face trying to take my glasses. I'm looking back at her smiling, this was her mom's favorite photo. She would say I was looking at her with all the love in the world. I stare at it for a few seconds and then reach my hand out to Irene, handing her the photo. She stares at it for what feels like hours and then I realize tears are falling from her eyes, wetting the paper. She looks up at me and starts crying even harder. This is the first time she's cried in front of me since she's been here. Up until now she's been hurting alone.

I take the few steps over to her and she falls into my arms. I hug her tight, and we stay like that until she's done crying. She wipes the tears from her face and looks up at me. For the first time in a while I know what to say to her so I look at Irene and say "I love you Irene, no matter what. You are my granddaughter and I love you no matter what".

Charlotte Sapienza

I watch as Mom, Dad, Elena and Miriam clean off the tables under the market's plain, boring, dark wood. The signs sway in the wind, and I find myself swaying too. Mom's in the fruit section, Dad's in dairy, Elena's in the veggies and Miriam is in the meat and fish section. That's all of them. There's not anything I could do, no use for me being here. I wonder why they even make me go if Dad always tells me to sit and wait? The market opens at 10, but the sun hasn't even fully risen yet.

I'll just be standing here, swaying and drawing, forever. I place down my sketchbook and walk off.

There are some nice houses near the market, but it takes a little bit of walking. I step over broken glass and litter, and walk past a building with a pretty, green, garden in front of it, but then I see the house with the beautiful, glowing, yellow door, and it draws me in. I walk up to the bright blue speckled fence, and see an old woman with shoes that match the door. They have white and blue flowers that look as if they could pop out and sing to me. I've seen this lady before, and usually she brings out canvases and paints the most compelling things I've ever seen. Dogs, cats, fruit, veggies, flowers, and much much more. She normally has these little paint tubes that she brings, ones with tiny cursive letters stretching across the front of them and color splattered on the white caps, but today she carries big buckets of paint. There's tons of colors, but there's no paint splattered on them. Has she never used them? I look up from the paints, to her face. The woman chuckles,

"Hi sweetie! What are you doing over there?"

I keep staring, before coming to the realization that she spoke.

"O-oh! I'm sorry, um, I was just looking at your paint!...What are those things out here for?" I say, nervously.
She explains that she is getting rid of them, and she suggests I take them. They're outdoor paints, so it's not like I could paint in my sketchbook with these. But.. I could paint other things? A door, a fence, what else? I look up at her, and she smiles at

me. She has this kind expression on her face, one that I don't see often, and it almost feels warm. It must have spread to me, because I suddenly start smiling so much that my face hurts. As she is handing the paints to me over the fence, I grab them, and yell,

"Thank you!," as I run down the street back to the market.

My family is still working in the market, just like before I went down the street. My sketchbook is in the same place along with my pencils. I put down the paint buckets, and I notice how sad the market looks. Of course it's filled with tons more color once all the food gets here, but the building and tables themselves are plain and basically screaming for help.

"Mom, Dad!" I yell, "Come here!"

They rush over, with worried looks plastered on their faces, but they fall when they see me smiling. Mom sighs.

"Maisy, don't get us all worried like this! What's up with you?"

Her eyes scan everything around me, and she looks at the paint, then up at me. I smile, in a pleading way.

"For what." She frowns.

"I can paint stuff outside with this! There's so much I could do, you know how boring the market looks, I can fix that! And if we go back, there's even more colors for me!"

While my mom stands there, looking confused, my dad smiles back at me. "That's a great idea Maisy! The wood's been looking pretty sad recently, it needs some renovation."

"Where did you even get this? Don't tell me you took it," Mom says.

"Down the street! The lady said she'd be happy for me to take more!"

Mom sighs, but she gives in eventually, even though Dad and I had to do some persuading. We went back and got the rest, and I learned the woman's name was Mrs. Layla. She told me I could come to her house whenever I wanted and paint with her!

As soon as we got back, I got to work. I painted on all of the signs, the fruit sign had fruit, the meat and fish sign had meat and fish, and so on! I added colorful patterns to the empty spots on the wood, I got a ladder and climbed to the areas I couldn't reach. I painted tables, benches, anything I could. At some point, people started flooding in. Sellers, buyers, all sorts of people came up to me and complimented my painting, it was great!

On Sunday, we had double the vendors we normally would, and people even had to share tables! There were tons of different types of people, all being friendly and kind. Elena found out that lots of these people were from the garden down the street, and Mrs. Layla had told her friend Nora all about me and Nora told people from that garden! Mom told me all this success and growth with the market was because of me and my painting, and that it brought the place to life. I finally had something to be useful for my family, and I could help out a bunch. Mom was proud of me, Dad was proud of me, and my sisters too! Usually Elena has a scowl on her face, but that all changed after today! Before we left for home, I painted one last thing. It was my family, all together. Everyone was smiling, in the same way that Mrs. Layla smiled at me.

Sophia Smith

My father and mother are artists. My father is a painter, he sells and teaches people about painting. And my mother is a writer. People commission her to write anything, sometimes even books. And they have taught me a lot like how to not let people get to you and that the opinions of people that really matter are the people that care about you and other stuff like that. But sometimes it's hard to not care what people say about me so I use my art to show the different people of my community what I'm feeling and hope that other people feel the same way.

But recently a new student has joined my school. His name is Carlos and for a few days he's been following me because he thinks I'm an interesting person. So I've been getting to know Carlos a lot more mainly because he doesn't know anyone and I was the first person that talked to him. Then I felt like spray painting, then I realized that Carlos lives pretty close to me and then I showed him some of my spray paintings and he loved them. He shared that he's a writer and he likes to write about people, places, and how his life is going.

But a few months later I went downstairs for breakfast and my mom turned on the tv. And then I heard screaming coming from the tv. I turned to face the TV and then I saw a police officer slam a kid that goes to my school on the ground and then shoot him in the arm. The boy's name is Jason and the news says that the boy is in the hospital but his arm is not ok. I went to school and I saw Carlos in 1st period and asked him if he saw what happened on the news. He said that he didn't. I told him what happened and said that it was crazy. Like you know it happens but you never think that it'll happen to you or someone you know.

During a brief period Carlos and I thought we should do something. We came up with a lot of ideas but he thought that we should do something that would really stand out to our community. So he convinced me to use my art to make more of an impact so the people know that someone cares for the guy. So I sketched out a few designs and got my spray paint and I went to work.

Juan

by Abner Aguilar

I am Juan, a Salvadoran immigrant who recently moved to the US. I was walking home after a day of work. I had just moved to this new building about a week ago. I saw a man taking care of some eggplants planted next to the building with many other little lots next to it. The eggplants were big; they looked like purple footballs growing on a tree! I asked him in very broken English what he was doing "Taking care of my eggplants" he said. I told him my name was Juan and that I was new to the building.

The man introduced himself as Amir and welcomed me. But the lack of my English made it difficult for me to communicate well with the man. I told the man in Spanish we say "berenjena" and asked him if I could plant maiz (in English corn). I asked Amir if I could plant the corn in the lot next to him. "That's okay," he said. The next day after work I passed by the store to get some corn seeds. It was raining and few people were out. It looked like a ghost town. I went to plant my corn as the rain stopped. I see Amir I say "Hola" he says "Hello". I finished and by that time everyone had gone inside, I went inside and went to sleep thinking of ways to learn English and meet my neighbors.

After a couple of weeks my corn started to grow, I saw the community become more open towards me it was difficult for me at first not speaking the same language as others very well but over time i started to learn at first with the names of crops my neighbors grew, one man Curtis - who was built like a linebacker- grew tomatoes I told him in Spanish we say "tomate" he was a very nice man contrary to what many might assume if they saw him. I had bought a Spanish-English dictionary to help me communicate with Amir, Curtis and others at the garden. I started to form weekly meetings with Amir and Curtis where we could exchange crops and recipes that each of us used our crops for. I talked about making corn flour like I did in El Salvador. Curtis made tomato sauce while Amir said he just cuts his eggplants and roast them.

Through these meeting's I, Curtis and Amir were able to learn more about each other and our languages, we grew by accepting new languages and cultures. It seemed as if every week our meeting's grew, the meeting's also added diversity and acceptance. We started to use Spanglish between Me, Curtis and Amir. Others made the effort in joining us to learn Spanish and English. The community as a whole was no longer frightened by the idea of somebody not speaking English; we were thrilled to see new people join the Garden. On the best days the Garden looked like a colony of ants, everybody working and helping one another. Step by step I was focused on helping others who were new (like I had once been) be welcomed into our community garden.

Maria

by Harlie Edwards

I grew up in Venezuela and always loved the arts. As I grew older I wanted to move away and see new places with a new job and new life.

Atlanta Georgia was a hot city where I would be able to find new groups of people and new interests. I had been walking around all day trying to find the apartment building I had gotten a place at. It was mid summer, June. I was tired, sweaty, and getting reasonably frustrated. I couldn't ask for help because even if I could pick up a decent amount of English I still had a hard time with responding in english.

I found the building number finally and when I went in it was easy enough to get my keys and find my room, I didn't have too many bags other than a backpack, and two suitcases. So after a day I really just wanted to throw them on the floor and lay down.

I woke up in the morning and felt a lot more refreshed than I was when I had laid down the night priar. I got up and went through my bags until I found a pair of knee length shorts, a striped t-shirt and some sneakers I have probably had for years. It was going to be a long day because I had to look for an extra job to help support myself as I tried to keep up my art hobby. I enjoyed painting a lot but it also costs a bit of money. I remembered passing by a cafe right before arriving at the apartment building.

With my bag, wallet and keys I left the building looking for the cafe. I walk down the bright early noon streets looking for a familiar building. I was about to pass it when I saw a lit sign that said, "Sanderson's Cafe" and I remembered it being the same one from before.

I saw a crowd building on the side of the building and felt curious so I decided to take a look before going into the cafe. As I passed the corner, the wall people were grouping in front of became visible and I can see why people were standing there. The wall was a massive mural of different paintings of all different styles and focal points. The people were talking about all sorts of things, but I heard one thing a few times, people were wanting something memorable, something that they hadn't seen before. I looked back at the wall when I heard a young woman's voice directed at me, "Are you going to add something?" I turned around and saw a woman slightly shorter than me with a long black braid, she was holding out a few paint markers and paint brushes. I immediately had an idea and forgot the reason I was at the cafe in the first place. I smiled at her and reached out for a paint marker.

I started to paint, sometimes switching between the colors. I was going to paint an orchid Cattleya mossiae, it was the national flower of Venezuela. It meant a lot to me because of how hard it was to leave to come to a place I can barely communicate. The same woman from before spoke up, "Is that an orchid? You are really talented!" I quietly thanked her the best I could while painting. "Y'know? I think it looks a lot more complete now with that!" I smiled once again at her and looked back at the painting, I would now be able to see a piece of my home every time I saw the cafe.

By Alexa Lim

I've always wondered why my mom kept her background story, I always wonder why she kept it to herself. My mom, Marry, immigrated to the U.S. with her family when she was just 8 years old because of the Vietnam war they had to go through. They escaped the ruins that lay in their country to give my mom a better life and settle in a much safer place with better opportunities than in their homeland. My mom has always loved music. Her father was a guitar player back in Vietnam and also a singer yet he could not use these skills he had to make a living because it wasn't a good source of income. My mom was in a better palace but not in better circumstances because her family was not able to make enough money for her to pursue her dream of playing an instrument. She was only able to finish elementary school because she had to help her family make a living. I felt grateful for what I have accomplished and the conditions I am in when I learned of this.

Marry always felt nonchalant whenever I tried to talk to her about anything related to my music things, I felt neglected that she never seemed Interested. My mom has told me her dreams and why she acted this way because she wanted to keep me away from anything that might ruin me. All this time I thought she hated me for what I was, but she was just trying to protect me. I noticed gradually how my mom worsened with her sickness, her eyesight has gotten worse and so has her body. As I am a part of the Orchestra in my school and play the violin and piano, I've always been interested in music. I wanted to make my mom feel what she has always been dreaming of all her life. Since my mom can barely walk I decided to put the whole show in front of her, inside our house. A whole orchestra inside with violin, cello, viola, bass, saxophone, etc.. As we started to play in front of her she heard the pleasing sound she had always longed for. Marry, my mom bursts into tears with happiness. I have never felt appreciated for all the experiences and for all the times I played with my group. After this, I tried to teach my mom how to play the piano and violin and the basics of music theory. I would always play with her myself, hoping that I could somehow heal her with my playing. I taught her how to play, nonetheless, she is not able to physically play it because she's not capable of moving at full capacity.

I love my mom. Despite her age, she was still able to be part of the community I'm in. Our relationship strengthened because we were able to bond through music and because we share the same interest we can understand each other more than anyone could. We both healed because of music. I felt loved by my mom and my mom was able to accomplish the dream she has always wanted since she was a kid.

By Ada Rosenblatt

A new year means a new house in a new state, new people in a new school. Dad being in the army means we never get to stay in one place longer than a year or so. I think the hardest part about it is meeting new people-I always have to make new friends, and at this point, my best friend is my guitar. We finished unpacking everything so I decided to take a little tour of the neighborhood. I was sitting against a brick wall making songs up as I went along, when these two teenagers that looked around my age came over. We introduced ourselves and they asked to take turns playing on my guitar-it actually sounded really good. They were both 16 as well, and their names were Tristan and Cammy. We stayed there-just the three of us for the rest of the day until it started getting dark and we had to go home for dinner. For the next couple weeks we would meet up at that wall, just doing the same thing over and over and talking about what's happening in our lives. We became really close and quickly became inseparable-just by making music together.

After about a month of hanging out with each other, we began to realize one guitar wouldn't be enough for the three of us. Cammy said she knew of a music store a few blocks down so I walked over there and went inside. There were so many guitars.. My jaw dropped. The owner of the store was really nice, he and I talked for a while, and I found out that since there weren't very many customers anymore that he wasn't making enough money to keep the shop open. I wanted to help so I got

Tristan and Cammy to come over and they bought themselves guitars. We also made some posters advertising the store, and hung them up around town. Quickly more people started filling up his store, and our trio started playing songs outside to draw attention. I realized how much making music was connecting us, and wondered how many others in our area could connect with each other by music. I told the owner of the music store about my thoughts and we came up with the idea of having a community music party/event and inviting as many people as we could. He said my trio could host it outside his store, and to feel free to borrow as many of his guitars as we needed, in thanks to getting him so many customers. Right away, we started planning the details out and telling everyone we saw about it. We sent invitations out, and hung up signs.

About an hour before the time we told people to show up at, we began setting everything up and decorating. Before we knew it tons of people were arriving-and I mean tons of people. We handed guitars out, and the owner was giving lessons to some people. It felt as loud as a real concert. Everyone was talking to each other-even people they had never met before! It made me so happy to see that our goal was working out. People were forming into groups to play together, and at the end of the night, each group took turns playing something for everybody. I kept having people come up to me as they were leaving, thanking us and asking when the next event would be. It was amazing seeing everyone collaborating and really enjoying it! The four of us decided to make this a recurring event, and have one every other Saturday night. Thanks to the donations we got as well, the music shop began to thrive!! We also decided to give pretty cheap guitar lessons to anyone who wanted them. I began to notice more and more people coming, and saw people switching up their groups and talking to new people. Our community became very connected, so connected to the point where I could go up to anyone comfortably and just talk to them, and others felt the same way. I think everyone became much less shy and introverted, all thanks to the music events twice a month.

Benson

by Valentine Schiller

When you get older, you start to lose time for things you used to enjoy. As a kid, my family always had the latest technology and games. Granted, we always found time to get outdoors, and technology wasn't really that good back then, but we always enjoyed what we were given. However, things changed as I got older.

All of a sudden, I had a house to upkeep, a job to manage, and meals to prepare. I never had time to buy all the latest games and game systems, or even computer games when they came out. I was always busy with my job. I'm 87 now, and I finally got some free time after I retired from my job, and I heard everybody in town talking about this game called "Minecraft," and how they could all play together from different places. I looked it up, and it turns out I could get it on my computer. I had some money to spare, so I bought it to see what was so good about the game.

I got into the server, and I tried talking to people, and a young man named Marcus helped me learn the controls. He was nice, and basically taught me all I needed to know to be good at the game. I happened to see him walking down the street one time, since everyone in our server lives in this town, and we became pretty good friends. Soon enough, I got pretty good, and I was starting to be a helping hand to the community, building houses, landmasses, and everything in between.

At first people told me I was too old to play, or that my jokes weren't good. But they just kept getting used to it, until I was on regularly (except when I took breaks to go on walks.) They even started laughing at my jokes. And the kids started being nicer to everyone else on the server. They all obeyed the rules, and no one broke anyone else's things. It was so amazing, and from afar, you couldn't even tell it was a game. The hills and valleys stretched out for miles, the green against the sun shone like a light against a window.

The town we built was small, but it kept getting bigger. Every right click was a beautiful symphony of sounds and creation as we built up, down, and all around. And eventually, we finished. It was perfect. Our community was perfect. My back might not have been forgiving when I went out to see our real community, but it sure forgave our hard work on our little digital community. One that had no boundaries of where in town people were. As long as they were in town, they were invited. And that is how community should be.

About the Class - Sobre la clase

The Global Community Citizenship (GCC) course is a graduation requirement for students in Anne Arundel County Public Schools. The course was developed to help students see themselves as change-agents in their schools and communities. By building awareness, while understanding perspective, students begin to appreciate differences while recognizing and valuing the things they have in common.

Leading tenets of GCC are inclusion, empathy, and acceptance with the goal of developing students as thoughtful citizens and changemakers.

While this course is focused on "community," it also fosters the growth of a community of learners because students in schools with a strong sense of community are more likely to be informed decision-makers, ethically engaged, socially and emotionally competent, and academically successful.

El curso Ciudadanía Comunitaria Global (GCC) es un requisito de graduación para los estudiantes de las Escuelas Públicas del Condado de Anne Arundel. El curso fue desarrollado para ayudar a los estudiantes a verse a sí mismos como agentes de cambio en sus escuelas y comunidades. Al desarrollar la conciencia, mientras comprenden la perspectiva, los estudiantes comienzan a apreciar las diferencias mientras reconocen y valoran las cosas que tienen en común.

Los principios principales de GCC son la inclusión, la empatía y la aceptación con el objetivo de desarrollar a los estudiantes como ciudadanos reflexivos y agentes de cambio.

Mientras este curso se enfoca en la "comunidad", también fomenta el crecimiento de una comunidad de estudiantes porque es más probable que los estudiantes en escuelas con un fuerte sentido de comunidad sean tomadores de decisiones informados, éticamente comprometidos, social y emocionalmente competentes y académicamente exitosos.

Made in the USA
Middletown, DE
31 May 2023